East Coast
Eventide

THOMAS KORON

PAGE PUBLISHING, INC.
Conneaut Lake, PA

First originally published by Page Publishing 2021

ISBN 978-1-6624-1342-1 (pbk)
ISBN 978-1-6624-1343-8 (digital)

Printed in the United States of America

AUTHOR'S NOTE

This is a work of fiction. The characters and many of the places that are contained within this story are a product of the author's own imagination. Any resemblance to certain locations and/or actual people, alive or dead, is purely coincidental.

CAST OF CHARACTERS

Members and Associates of the Hoboken Gang

Frank "Frankie" Moniarti—an Italian mobster who also deals in office supplies.
Megan "Meg" Moniarti—Frank's wife of twenty-seven years.
James "Jimmy" Moniarti—Frank and Megan's son.
Annabelle Carter—longtime girlfriend of James Moniarti.
Teddy Pazzelli—Frank Moniarti's closest associate.
Silvia Pazzelli—Teddy Pazzelli's wife.
Charley Bennetti—Frank Moniarti's bookkeeper.
Sandy Granger—a prostitute who used to work under Silvia Pazzelli and has known Charley Bennetti since childhood.

Members and Associates of the Newark Gang

Nicholas "Nicky" Malone—an Irish mobster who is also a World War II veteran and runs a chain of men's clothing stores.
Angela "Angie" Malone—Nicholas Malone's wife.
Ronny Steiner—a fellow World War II veteran who is loyal to Malone but also occasionally does side work for other people. He also operates the Lucky Nine's Pool Hall.
Roger Bradshaw—the head of security at Nicholas Malone's underground casino.

Leroy "Sly" Robinson—a car thief and auto mechanic from Detroit who does occasional side jobs for Nicholas Malone.

Doyle Reynolds—a car thief from Detroit who serves as Leroy Robinson's partner.

Members and Associates of the Atlantic City Gang

Vincent "Vinnie" Plemagoya—a Puerto Rican mobster from New York, who has caused problems for members of the Hoboken and Newark Gangs.

Pedro Navilla—Vincent Plemagoya's closest associate.

Natty Rosebrook—Vincent Plemagoya's gambling partner who is also the owner of Rosebrook's Used Cars.

Tony "Bank Shot" Tyler—an amateur pool hustler who also serves as an associate to Vincent Plemagoya.

Members and Associates of Fossgate's Fine Jewelry

Marvin Fossgate—the owner of Fossgate's Fine Jewelry in Atlantic City.

Donald Rothstein—a longtime salesman at Fossgate's Fine Jewelry.

Members and Associates of The Golden Sandbox

Scotty McCormack—the owner of The Golden Sandbox.

Randy Wyman—a security guard at The Golden Sandbox.

Melanie Ann Hillsdale—a showgirl at The Golden Sandbox.

Conrad Hillsdale—Melanie Hillsdale's overprotective father.

Members and Associates of the Atlantic City Police Department

George Antill—mayor of Atlantic City.

Marty Albertson—the chief of police in the Atlantic City Police Department.

Benjamin Jordy—an agent with the Atlantic City Police Department's Internal Affairs Division.

Captain David Van Bulkem—supervisor to the detectives in the Atlantic City Homicide Division.

Detective Jacob Farmers—a fifteen-year veteran in the Atlantic City Homicide Division.

Detective Stanley Morris—partner to Jacob Farmers and three-year veteran in the Atlantic City Homicide Division.

Patrolman Billy Walker—a young police officer and late friend of Stanley Morris.

Betsy Walker—Billy Walker's widow.

PROLOGUE

Welcome to areas of the world where the air oftentimes feels thick from the heavily congested rows of buildings, nonstop traffic, and a dense population of people. It's a place where the wind can often feel harsh and brisk when it blows inland from the shoreline. Occasionally, tourists may hear a crumpling noise from a loose leaf of newspaper caught blowing in the wind, or the sound of distant sirens, or even the far-off meowing of an alley cat. And unfortunately, for many of the local citizens and tourists in these areas, crime has become a regular part of their lives here. Some people commit crimes for the sake of forwarding their own prosperity, and others do it just in order to stay alive and hope to somehow create a better future for themselves. Depending on whether you win or lose, you may walk away keeping your rewards, and then again, you might not. But one thing's for certain, there's no other places in the world quite like them. This is life on the East Coast.

PART 1

Friday, October 12 to Sunday, October 14, 1962

CHAPTER 1

Friday, October 12, 1962
Into the Storm

It was a darkly overcast and unseasonably warm day in Atlantic City for being this late into the year. James Moniarti looked down at his watch as he waited under an awning in front of a coffee shop to shield himself from the rain. He had just left a meeting with a real estate client; and he had been working overtime to wrap up a deal for an upcoming department store on Pacific Avenue. A taxi pulled up to the curb, and James quickly walked up to the rear door and got in.

"Where can I take ya?" the taxi driver asked, as he positioned the rearview mirror to meet with Moniarti's eyes.

"Can you run me over to Fossgate's Fine Jewelry really quickly? They close in about a half hour." James reached up to wipe the dripping rain off his forehead with his right sleeve and then exhaled deeply as he leaned back in the seat of the taxi.

"I can sure as hell try!" the taxi driver said with a nod. "I know some pretty good shortcuts around here. We should be able to getcha there in time."

James smiled with relief. "Good. They have a sale on engagement rings, and it ends today!"

The taxi driver's eyes grew wide in the rearview mirror. "Engagement rings? Wow! Congratulations, pal! Ain't that somethin'?"

James turned his head sideways to look out the window. "Thanks. She doesn't really know yet. I plan to surprise her over Thanksgiving."

The taxi driver lifted up his eyebrows. "Hey, best of luck to ya, pal! I been married for over twenty-five years already! Come back and talk to me once you've reached your tenth anniversary!" The taxi driver laughed, as he pulled away from the curb and out into traffic.

As the taxi drove on through the rain, James looked down at the jewelry store catalog in his lap and found the page that he had bookmarked that morning. He had been involved with Annabelle Carter for just over seven years now, and they had shared the same apartment together for almost three years. He looked up from the catalog as the taxi pulled to a stop right in front of Fossgate's Fine Jewelry. James got out of the back seat of the taxicab, holding the catalog over his head to shield himself from the pouring rain. He handed the amount of the fare over to the taxi driver, plus an additional five dollars for arriving at the destination on time.

"Hey, thanks, kid!" The taxi driver enthusiastically shook his hand as he took the money. "And I wish ya the best of luck on your future adventures!"

James smiled thinly and then nodded at the driver as he leaned back out of the passenger-side window of the taxi. He turned around to look at the business hours that were posted on the front door of the shop and then glanced down at his watch. He still had fifteen minutes left before they closed.

It had turned out to be a rather busy time of the day to try to catch the end of a sale at Fossgate's Fine Jewelry. There were businessmen and ladies of fashion alike wandering around the sales floor of the store. James shook his head as he looked at the line of people inside.

"Here goes nothing," he said to himself under his breath, as he opened the glass door to the front of the jewelry store.

The counter that held the engagement rings was positioned toward the far end of the showcase room; and James looked around at the other customers to make sure that there was nobody he knew in the store. The last thing that he wanted to deal with was somebody letting the cat out of the bag to Annabelle that he had been spotted looking at engagement rings before his proposal could take place.

James Moniarti had been raised to be a man of class; and his mother and father had taught him well in the ways of table manners, social etiquette, and proper treatment of a lady. If he could just manage to find the ring from the catalog somewhere behind the glass jewelry counter, he would have an increased sense of hope that he might be able to exit the store more quickly than some of the other jewelry shoppers. His next task would be to find a proper hiding place to keep the ring for the next month and a half; until they took their trip over to Cleveland to spend Thanksgiving with Annabelle's parents. His plan was to take a surprise detour into Mill Creek Falls along the way and propose to her near the waterfall, while surrounded by the colorful autumn leaves. They had met during their sophomore year in high school and decided to move into an apartment together shortly after graduation. James had selected the seventh year of their relationship for his proposal out of superstition; he figured that choosing a lucky number would hopefully lead them into a better future.

As James approached the jewelry counter that contained the engagement rings, he saw that the man behind the counter was standing near the far end, waiting on an older couple who had probably gone out jewelry shopping for their anniversary. He managed to reach the glass counter and then gently slid in between the people who were crowded around it. He suddenly felt a lump grow in his throat as he looked down and saw the very same engagement ring from the catalog glistening behind the glass. He raised his finger to try and get the salesman's attention, but the jeweler kept his eyes pointing down at the counter; and James could hear the older couple requesting to see another ring from behind the display case. He looked nervously down at his watch and saw that there were now only twelve minutes left until closing time. *I had better make this fast!* he thought to himself. *Then make it out of here during rush hour traffic and home to hide this before Annabelle gets back. Where can I put it where she won't find it?* His hands suddenly began to tremble as the salesman finally looked up and made eye contact with him.

Suddenly, James could hear the bell from the front door sounding as several footsteps hastily made their way across the carpeted entryway into the jewelry store. There was the sound of muffled voices quickly speaking to each other, as five masked men entered the showroom. The masked man who stood at the front of the group rapidly fired three shots from an automatic pistol towards a tile in the ceiling and then shouted, "Everybody better stop and get your hands up in the air! This is a robbery!"

There was a moment of screaming as the shoppers panicked, and then James watched as an elderly woman collapsed into the arms of a nearby jewelry shopper, and the five masked men also looked over as the man who caught her had begun leaning backward under the unexpected addition of her weight.

"All right, they've got the right idea! Everybody get down on the floor!" the masked leader of the group shouted.

James Moniarti seized the opportunity of the distraction and quickly crept behind the jewelry case. He remained low and spotted an entryway into a back room, where the employees of the store must have entered in from the rear parking lot. He slid low on his stomach across the floor, hoping that none of the buttons on his dress shirt would snag into the fibers of the red carpeting. His vision suddenly became blurry, and dizziness swept over him, as his forehead began dripping with sweat, and he could feel his heart thumping against the concrete that was beneath the carpeting. *This can't be happening!* he thought to himself. *This honestly can't be happening right now!* He slid further away from the jewelry case and used his hands to slide his body across the floor as his legs remained motionless. He moved rapidly and was afraid to look back at the terror that was still unfolding on the salesfloor. He grasped the doorframe to the back room, and he could feel the sweat from the back of his body dripping across his ribs. He silently prayed that he would remain unnoticed and that he might be able make it just a few feet further.

Once he pulled himself onto the tile floor of the back room, he rolled over onto his back to keep the buttons on his shirt from loudly scratching against it. He continued to slide against the tile floor, which felt cold against the sweat on his back. His blurry vision had begun to subside, but the dizziness continued. As he got to his feet, he carefully braced himself against the wall. He began squinting before his eyes grew wide, and he saw that there was a telephone on the back counter by the coffee supplies. He then removed his dress shoes, scooped them up into his arms, and silently walked on his socks toward the back counter in the room. Moniarti grabbed the phone in his trembling hand and then quickly dialed the number for the operator. His throat felt tight and dry, but his voice remained clear and soft as he timidly spoke into the receiver, "Hello…Operator… There's a robbery at Fossgate's… Send the poli—"

And then the phone line suddenly went dead.

CHAPTER 2

Eye of the Tornado

The early evening sky was fading into a dark gray color behind the overcast clouds, and the rain had momentarily subsided. A sapphire-blue 1956 Oldsmobile Super 88 pulled up to a sawhorse that was positioned alongside a marked police car to block the road. The brakes of the Oldsmobile let out a faint squeak as the vehicle came to a stop. Detective Jacob Farmers put the car into park, and then he and his partner pulled out their badges to show to a pair of uniformed officers through the windshield. The officers both nodded and then moved the sawhorse out of the street. Jacob Farmers put the car back into drive and then slowly proceeded down the street. He waved at the two uniformed police officers and then squinted his eyes as he looked down the street towards Fossgate's Fine Jewelry. The musty smell of his aftershave clung onto the humid air, which had caused his partner to keep the window down a crack during their ride over from the police station. He reached over into the glove compartment and grabbed the case that contained his glasses and his notebook.

He then looked over into the eyes of his partner, Detective Stanley Morris. "It's just like the talk that I gave ya during our first assignment together. This ain't the same as workin' in small-town Missouri where you come from. This is Atlantic City! And here, the crimes have a habit of getting a lot messier than anything that you might have been used to back there."

Farmers let out a weak snicker, and Stanley Morris lowered his head down as his sharp blue eyes formed a stern look of indignation. Jacob Farmers looked forward as he placed his glasses over his eyes and peered off into the distance. "I've got fifteen years with this police force, and you've only got three. That means that I will be askin' all the questions, and you're gonna be takin' down whatever anybody says to us."

Farmers then extended his notebook over to Morris with a condescending smirk, and Morris took it from his hand without breaking his fixed look upon his partner. He could smell the stale coffee and cigarette smoke on his partner's breath during the usual haughty lecture that he had gotten whenever Farmers felt like he had the upper hand.

Morris took the notebook and then reached his other hand into the pocket of his overcoat and pulled out a roll of breath mints. "Yeah, well, you might want to freshen up a bit before you try questioning any of the witnesses."

Farmers reached over to open the door and shook his head at his partner's offer. "Smart-ass," he said under his breath and then took a mint from the roll before opening the car door.

Stanley Morris tucked the notebook along with the breath mints back into the inside pocket of his overcoat, and then he stepped out from the passenger side of the Oldsmobile onto the sidewalk. He looked up at the sky, which had grown increasingly dark over the last few minutes, and then exhaled slowly and deeply. *I don't know if I will ever get used to this,* he silently thought to himself. *And I don't know if I can ever really get used to him. A city as dignified as this one deserves so much better.*

He looked back down, and Farmers was staring at him curiously. "This is hardly the time or the place for bird-watching, Stan. We've got a crime to solve. Let's get on with it. Let's go straight into the eye of the tornado."

Morris narrowly shook his head, and then they began slowly making their way down the sidewalk toward the jewelry store.

"Maybe I was taking a moment out to pray that we actually solve this one, Jake. Did you ever stop and think about that? We have a city that we are responsible for keeping safe, above all. Not to mention, my professional integrity and your job promotion are on the line here. I mean, what guarantee do we have that there isn't going to be another mess like this a week from now, if we aren't able to quickly solve what's already happened?"

Farmers shrugged with his hands in his pockets as he kept his head down from the wind. "This is life in the city, kid. We can't control what's gonna happen here or what other people are gonna do. All we can do is try to clean up the mess whenever things go wrong like this."

Morris looked down the sidewalk towards the jewelry store. "It's been awhile since things have gone wrong like this! Three robbers, one cop, and one store clerk are all dead now! Granted, the robbers should've known better, but I just wish that I could've been here to try to stop it from happening in the first place! Billy Walker was a good cop and a good man with a family."

Farmers looked over at Morris and lowered his eyebrows. "I only got the chance to meet Billy Walker a few times. Never really got the chance to know him quite like you did. But I can fully understand why you'd be so upset."

There was a small group of uniformed police officers that were gathered around in a circle on the sidewalk in front of the jewelry store. There was a bright flash, as one of the officers took a picture of the ground, where one of the robbers was still lying facedown.

Jacob Farmers looked at the bullet holes in what had remained of the glass door. "There were five robbers. If we can account for three of them, then finding the other two should be possible if we keep doing our homework."

He pulled a maroon handkerchief out from his pocket and slowly pulled open the front door to the jewelry store. As they walked down the carpeted corridor that led into the showroom, Farmers leaned back over his shoulder toward Morris. "Walker was the first one in here," he whispered. "He never really stood a chance. He was outmanned, outgunned, and fresh outta luck."

Morris followed Farmers into the showroom and looked down to see that there were three more bodies sprawled out in a triangular formation around the floor.

Farmers began pointing his finger around the showroom. "Looks like he got one of them on his way in, and then they got each other with the second one."

Morris took a pen and the notebook from the inside pocket of his overcoat and began drawing a diagram of the positions of the bodies. "Yeah, for being *fresh outta luck*, as you would say, he had some pretty quick reflexes for being under that kind of duress."

Jacob Farmers looked around the room past all the uniformed officers that were gathered around the area taking pictures. "You said that there were five people killed. So far, I've counted three robbers and one police officer," Farmers said. "So where was the jewelry store clerk?"

Morris moved ahead of Farmers and motioned him forward with his finger as they walked across the showroom to the jewelry counter. The two detectives walked around the jewelry counter and looked down to see where the jewelry store clerk had been forced to lie facedown into a thin layer of broken glass. "Right down here," Morris said. "They shot him while he was in a submissive position, no less."

Morris shook his head at Farmers. "Isn't it strange how you were lecturing me in the car about how you've been doing this job for twelve years longer than I have, and yet I have to show you how to look for clues at the scene of a crime?"

Jacob Farmers reached into his overcoat pocket and pulled out a plastic bag and a pair of rubber gloves. "Put a lid on it, Stan. I was just testing you. You'll never be able to outsmart your mentor no matter how hard you try."

Farmers leaned down and pulled a ruby bracelet out of the thin pile of bloodstained broken glass and placed it inside of the plastic bag. "I was blessed with a keen eye for detail. More than likely, the robbers were wearing gloves to cover up their fingerprints, but as you know, there is only one way for us to tell that for sure."

He then stood up to meet face-to-face with Stanley Morris, who still had his eyes firmly fixed on the ruby bracelet in the plastic bag. "He was just trying to work for a living," Morris said. "Why didn't they just take the money and then let him go on back home to his wife?"

His eyes then moved up to meet with his partner's. "Because this is a city where, if people don't choose to press their luck, then it's considered to be an opportunity lost," Farmers replied. "That's why. Some people grow a bit impatient in a situation like this, Stan."

Farmers gently placed the bag with the ruby bracelet inside of the pocket of his overcoat and took off his rubber gloves. He then pointed his finger over his partner's shoulder. "Let's go into that other room. I hear voices coming from back there."

Jacob Farmers and Stanley Morris entered into the back room of the jewelry store, and they saw three uniformed police officers standing around a tall, thin man in a black suit with silver hair surrounding the sides of his bald head.

His voice was loud, fast, and edgy. "It all seemed to have happened so fast! I heard the men come in, and then next thing that I knew, one of our shoppers had fainted into my arms! There was nobody there that could help either one of us!"

One of the uniformed officers placed his hand on the man's shoulder. "It's okay, Mr. Rothstein. Just take your time. You have been through quite a tremendous ordeal. We'd like for you to meet Detectives Farmers and Morris. They are here to help you and to try to piece together everything that happened here."

Donald Rothstein nodded with a series of rapid jerking motions. "But I just…I couldn't stop them from shooting that clerk! I couldn't even help that woman who had fainted! They forced us all to lie facedown on the floor, and the next thing that I knew, I heard one of the robbers shouting, and then a gun went off! We all felt so helpless!" Rothstein slowly began to shake his lowered head and started sobbing.

Morris bit down hard in anger towards his suffering before opening his mouth to speak, "But you are not helpless now, Mr. Rothstein. You are a witness to a very ruthless crime, and you are working with us for the safety of your community. And that aspect alone, makes you a hero."

Donald Rothstein broke off from his sobbing and lifted his eyes to look at Morris and then at Farmers. "Just promise me that you'll catch these guys before anybody else gets hurt. I have never been so scared in my whole life." His reddened, watery eyes squinted, and then he shook his head rapidly with his eyes shut, attempting to block the memory of the violence.

One of the uniformed police officers closed his notebook and tucked it away with his pen into his breast pocket. "Can we ask you to come with us down to the station to look at pictures of some possible suspects?" the officer asked. "Even though the men were wearing masks, we want you to look closely at their eyes and mouths and see if any of them might match anything that you can remember about the robbers."

Rothstein nodded and then turned around to exit through the back door with two uniformed officers.

"We'll be down at the station after we finish up here and gather up everything that we've got on this so far," Jacob Farmers said, as he waved at the three men, and one of the uniformed officers nodded at the detectives.

Approximately twenty minutes later, a short elderly man in a long fur overcoat entered in through the back door, escorted by two other uniformed officers. It was Marvin Fossgate, the owner of the jewelry store. He walked in with his head down and immediately approached a table in the center of the room. He pulled a tissue from a box towards the closest edge of the table. The business owner was visibly shaken and held a tissue under his nose as his eyes flowed with tears.

"I can handle this one," Farmers said, and Morris nodded as he held his pen over the open notebook.

A uniformed officer looked over his shoulder toward the two detectives. "Marvin Fossgate, these are Detectives Jacob Farmers and Stanley Morris from the homicide division, and they'd like to ask you just a few questions, if you wouldn't mind."

Fossgate slowly nodded and then loudly blew his nose. His hands were still rapidly trembling, and his eyes were red and puffy underneath his tan leather Italian flatcap. He took another tissue from the box on the table and began to clean the lenses of his bifocals before placing them back on his face.

"I'm sorry about what happened here, Mr. Fossgate," Farmers said with a sympathetic tone.

"Why would somebody ever want do something like this?" Fossgate asked, as he spun his arms around the room, with his eyes firmly fixed on the detective.

"We really wish that we had a logical answer for you, Mr. Fossgate," Morris said, as he stepped up next to Farmers.

"I never even saw any of this coming! Forty-five years in business, and this is the first time that something like this has ever happened!" Marvin Fossgate held his shaking fist up in the air. "And I'm going to see to it that it's the last! I'm closing these doors for good!"

Stanley Morris nodded and said, "We can certainly respect your decision, Mr. Fossgate." The two uniformed officers that had escorted the jewelry store owner in through the back door then exited the room to assist the other officers with their investigation of the showroom.

Farmers looked over at his partner before returning his view to Fossgate. "Now, about the robbery. Do you recall owing any uncollected money to anybody?" Farmers asked.

Marvin Fossgate's eyes grew wide with fury. "Of course not! What sort of a business did you think I was running here?" Fossgate shouted. He held his hand up to Farmers. "I won't even waste my time answering that question! Just get out there and find the guys who did this! Can you at least do that for me?" Fossgate asked.

Farmers let out a deep sigh and then said, "We're workin' on it. What can you tell me about what happened here?"

Marvin Fossgate looked over at Detective Morris and then said, "I wasn't even here when it happened! All I know is what the other officers have told me. Five guys walked in through the front, and only two of them made it out the back!" He quickly raised his arm and pointed towards the back door leading into the alleyway before he continued, "The same door that I just came in from! And the clerk that they killed, he worked for me for twelve years! Just keep that in mind while you piece the rest of this thing together!"

Stanley Morris placed his hand on his partner's shoulder. "Okay, I think that's enough. The rest is up to us now." He folded the notebook shut and placed it back into his pocket. Fossgate scowled at Farmers as he heard Morris click his pen closed, and then the two detectives followed the last remaining uniformed police officer out the back door into the alleyway.

"They even cut the phone line," the uniformed officer said, as he pointed at a severed wire that hung against the back wall of the building, and then turned back to look at Farmers.

"That was my understanding," Farmers said to the uniformed officer. "But what do you suppose happened to the guy who phoned in the robbery?"

The uniformed officer just shrugged and then shook his head. "Your guess is as good as mine."

CHAPTER 3

Campaign Promises

It had been a busy time at city hall, with election season coming up once again. The four-story brick building sat at the corner of Tennessee and Atlantic Avenues, with a central clock tower rising high above the Romanesque Revival structure. Mayor George Antill was pacing around his office with his head down and his hands clasped behind his back. He briefly stopped to look up at Marty Albertson, the chief of the Atlantic City Police Department.

"There must be something further that can be done to lower the crime rate in this city," Antill said. He was dressed in a white suit and had a round, aging face with a receding hairline. His lips were pursed in frustration as he spoke, "My chance at reelection is coming up, and my professional reputation is at stake here, and I really don't want a few unruly punks to think that they can get the best of me."

Marty Albertson sat in a leather chair near the mayor's desk with a thick manila folder resting flat on his lap. "Your Honor, if you don't mind me saying, some of what has recently happened here might turn out to be a fluke occurrence," Albertson said and shrugged. "I mean, if you look at how much crime is on the rise in some of the larger cities, I'd say that we're doing a pretty decent job of keeping things under control here." Albertson straightened his navy-blue striped tie and cleared his throat. "I don't know if there is anybody out there who can do a better job of making the locals and tourists feel more welcome around here than you. You've got more experience with this job, and you're a lot more down-to-earth than any of the other candidates are. You should have no problems once Election Day gets here."

Mayor Antill quickly pointed towards Albertson and raised his voice. "Those are usually the famous last words! All that I can keep thinking about are the headlines back in November of 1948, when I was still a lawyer practicing in Chicago." Antill raised his hands up to spell out the headlines. "*Dewey Defeats Truman!* I swear that I have been having nightmares about that lately! So if you tell me that I should have no problems come the night of the election, I'm holding you to it!"

Antill sat down behind his desk and spun around in his chair. "After all, we rely on luck around here in Atlantic City, don't we?"

Marty Albertson raised the corner of his mouth in a nervous smile and then said, "Yes, sir, we do! Which is why I wanted you to look at these figures and see that up until recently, the crime rates had been dropping so far this year." He placed the manila folder on the mayor's desk and then reached for a handful of candies that were in a crystal dish toward the edge of the desk.

"Hey! Don't do that! My grandkids live off those things when they come here to see me!" Antill said and then smiled and winked at Albertson before getting up from behind his desk to pat him on the shoulder.

"I'm sorry, Your Honor. I guess I should have asked you first." Albertson grinned as he shook his head.

George Antill walked over toward the second-floor window of his office and blankly stared out into the distance. "I will look those figures over tomorrow with my morning coffee and hope that you're right about some of these recent events being a fluke occurrence." The mayor turned around to face Albertson and raised his eyebrow as he said, "But if I end up losing this next election, there could be other people who might also soon be out of a job. If you catch my drift?"

Marty Albertson tensed up in his chair before saying, "No need to worry about that, sir. Consider yourself covered when it comes down to Election Day." Albertson then began slowly shaking his lowered head. He looked at the mayor pensively. "However, sir, there are people out there who are putting a whole lot more on the line than their public image and their professional integrity. Some people are out there risking their lives." Mayor Antill's eyes widened, as Albertson's look began to soften. "We lost Patrolman Billy Walker during that robbery that you've been so concerned about. He had a wife and two small children," Albertson said. "The funeral has been scheduled for Sunday evening at St. Nicholas of Tolentine Church over on Pacific Avenue."

Antill's face became somber. "Give me his widow's address, and I'll send along a letter of condolence. In fact, we can do even better than that. If I send her a letter and the department sends along some flowers, then we can both plan on attending the memorial service on Sunday. Does that sound like a deal?"

Albertson nodded and then said, "Of course, Your Honor. I think that we should all continue doing everything humanly possible to help her, especially at a difficult moment like the one that she is faced with right now."

Mayor Antill's somber look broke away into a thin smile, and then he said, "All right then, we've got a plan! Now, get yourself outta here! We've both got a lot of work to do between now and then!"

Marty Albertson got up from his seat and placed his gray Stetson hat on top of his bald head before saying, "If you want to start drafting the letter up tonight, the widow's name is Betsy. The letter is going to Betsy Walker, and I'll telephone you tomorrow morning with her home address."

The smile quickly ran away from the mayor's face. "I noticed how you didn't say *their* home address," the mayor somberly replied. "It's always such a shame when an officer goes down in the line of duty."

Albertson slowly turned away from the mayor and began walking toward the door to his office. "Yes, sir, it is," Albertson said.

"And it's a lot more personal when you are forced to see it from our perspective."

The mayor held the door open and looked blankly over Marty Albertson's shoulder and out into the vacant hallway of the second floor. "I will make sure that I wear my best suit to the funeral, and I promise that I won't be late," Antill said softly.

"I figured that you would, Your Honor. Just remember that there has got to be enough protection around this city for there to be any voters left to show up at the booths on Election Day," Albertson said, as he walked out into the hallway without looking back.

"Duly noted," Mayor Antill said with a nod and then slowly closed the door to his office.

CHAPTER 4

Meant to Last

Across the New York Harbor, three men in their early twenties had just left from a late-night Brooklyn barbershop, getting haircuts and a clean shave. They walked without speaking a word to each other and gathered into a silver 1954 Ford Crestline, with two of them entering in the front and one getting into the back seat.

"So where we goin' from here?" Tony Tyler asked from the back seat of the car.

"To go drink up all our fills until things start to calm down back where we were," Vincent Plemagoya said, as he leaned back in the passenger seat to make eye contact with Tony Tyler through the side mirror, and then continued, "I can hear Manhattan callin' my name. There's so much that we could do there."

Pedro Navilla nodded as he started up the engine and began heading towards the Brooklyn Bridge, and Tony folded his arms up in the back seat, before nervously asking, "Any way we could get some music on the radio to help me settle my nerves?"

Plemagoya laughed and then turned the radio up high, as they drove across the bridge that stood high over the East River. There was the sound of smooth jazz music, and then there was a voice on the radio that began reciting a commercial. *Are you tired of looking around town for the best in the latest of men's formal clothing? Then look no further! And stop on in to Malone's Menswear! Where our customers are treated with the courtesy that they deserve, at a price that they can afford! We carry the finest lines of formal menswear out of any clothing chain found on the East Coast! It's clothing that's meant to last! With locations throughout New York City, Rochester, Ithaca, Camden, Hoboken, Newark, and the newest location in Atlantic City...*

Tony Tyler quickly leaped up in the back seat of the car and yelled, "All right! Turn it off! Let's go someplace where we can actually hear some music!" The Crestline then continued on across the Brooklyn Bridge before exiting off into the Two Bridges district of Manhattan.

"We got a good night ahead of us," Plemagoya said, as he folded his arms behind his head and then reclined in the passenger seat of the Crestline. "Should be smooth sailin' from here on out."

* * *

The grandfather clock in Frank Moniarti's living room had just rung the stroke of seven o'clock when the phone in his den began to ring. He was seated at his chess table next to a bright lamp, gluing the top back onto one of the pawns, after his wife had accidently tried to suck it up with the vacuum cleaner. The phone in the other room sounded out its third ring, as Frank arose from the cushioned hardwood chair. The pawn began wobbling as he set it back down onto the chess table. The chess piece then rolled over onto the table, and the round head became detached from the pawn once again, as it rolled down off the table onto the green shag carpeting below.

"Shit!" Frank yelled out, as he walked hastily into the den.

He was still wiping the glue off his hands with a handkerchief just before he answered the call, "Hello?" He suddenly heard the voice of his son on the other end, speaking rapidly and frantically into the receiver. "Whoa! Hey! Jimmy, slow down!" Frank said, "I'm having a hard time understanding you. Just tell me everything that happened from the beginning, and then we'll figure out what to do about it." Frank looked out of the window of his den and into the dim sunset that was fading behind the tree line in his backyard. "No, your mother isn't home right now. She took the dogs out for a walk. It's just you and me here right now for the time being." Frank let out a sigh of frustration but tried to stay calm. In a situation like this, his son needed his help; and in order to gather up information, he had to find a way to remain levelheaded at a time like now. "Whatever's happened, just promise me that you're safe," Frank said. "Where are you now?" The voice on the other end of the line now became calmer and more coherent, and Moniarti began to loosen up his grip on the receiver. "Okay, you're near the car park off Interstate 95?" he asked. "Good, I mean, just as long as you're safe now. I'm on my way!" Frank hung up the receiver and looked over at the family portrait that was hanging on the wall of his den. He began to feel an overwhelming surge of anger well up over his body at the thought of his son having his life threatened. His hands now began to shake, as they balled up into fists of rage; and he suddenly heard the sound of distant thunder. He slowly looked back towards the chess table; and he could still hear the faint buzz from the radio that he had left on in the game room: *Malone's Menswear! It's clothing that's meant to last!*

CHAPTER 5

Keeping Appointments

Nicholas Malone wearily unfolded a newspaper in his lap in the back seat of a taxi. Underneath the heading of *The East Coast Herald*, he began reading the cover story that said, "Five People Killed in Standoff with Police Following Robbery," along with a black-and-white picture of several police cars parked up and down both sides of the street in front of a jewelry store. *Jesus,* he thought to himself. *Don't these people realize that there is a much more honest way of making a living in this city?* The rain seemed to be coming down from the sky in buckets as it splashed across the windshield of the taxi, providing an intricate rhythm to the hypnotic sound of the wipers moving back and forth.

The taxi driver suddenly interrupted Malone's focus on the newspaper. "You said to drop you off at the next block, right?"

Malone folded the newspaper back up and set it on the seat next to him. "Yeah. Just pull up to the curb at the next corner. I know my way around this area."

The taxi stopped at the next corner, and Malone was slow getting out of the back. He was a tall man, with broad shoulders and a muscular build. His physical posture always appeared to reflect a man of enduring strength. There was one reminder that Malone still carried around with him from one of his earlier experiences near a coastline. It had been over eighteen years since a bullet had shattered his left hip on the day that he had landed on the beach at Normandy. Since he had returned home from the war, he usually walked with a cane. His left foot had pointed slightly outward since that injury, but he had always thought that it had beaten the alternative of being paralyzed, or even worse. If the gunman had been a better shot, he wouldn't have survived to have asked for a stronger dose of morphine after the medics had removed the bullet from his body.

"Hey, you need a hand there, mister?" the driver asked, as he looked down at the cane. The handle was in the shape of a silver wolf head, and it glistened radiantly against a streetlight in the humid rain.

"No, thanks, that's rather thoughtful of you. But I've gotten used to traveling around this way at my age." After he got out of the taxi with his newspaper under his arm, he gave the driver a five-dollar bill and said in a low voice, "You can keep it." He then pulled a pack of Lucky Strikes out of his jacket pocket. "It looks like I might be working overtime tonight, so don't wait up for me," Malone said to the taxi driver as he lit a cigarette underneath his black Stetson hat and then threw the extinguished match down onto the wet sidewalk.

As he stepped onto the curb, he looked up at the old wooden sign that read Lucky Nine's Pool Hall. He opened up the door, stepped inside, and then reached up with a silk handkerchief to brush away the rain and any loose ashes off from his black suit. The loose ashes very well might not have shown up against the white pinstripes on his suit, but Nicholas Malone was a businessman above all, and a genuine businessman had to look professional at all times. Malone took a look across the smoke-filled room over toward the bar and saw the familiar yet aging face of Ronny Steiner standing behind it, drying a whiskey glass. He saw the white towel swirling around gracefully in the reflection of Ronny's thick glasses. Both men had served in the military during World War II and had maintained a close friendship since then.

"Hey, Ronny, could you get me double shot of scotch and a beer?" Malone asked, as he crushed out his cigarette in the ashtray.

"You plan on stayin' for a little while tonight, Nicky?" Ronny asked, as he placed the drinks on top of the bar.

"I'm thinkin' so. I'm a pretty patient man, Ronny. I know that I will find who I'm looking for, if I just wait here for a moment or two." Only a short while later, a blond-haired man in a gray suit entered in through the back door. *And now my patience pays off,* Malone thought to himself as he swallowed back what remained of his beer. He grabbed his glass of scotch off the bar and slowly got up from his barstool.

While he was slowly approaching the man in the gray suit from across the room, Malone heard a voice shrilly cursing the fact that the cue ball had just gone down into an adjacent pocket from the eight ball. *Scratching on the kill shot,* he thought to himself. *This kid could stand to learn a lesson or two tonight. Even the greatest pool players have to start off as amateurs.* Malone thought back to some of his younger days, prior to the war, and all the lessons that Ronny had taught him before he finally had enough courage to play a game of pool for any sort of real money.

The kid who had just lost the game, and probably the shirt off his back, approached his opponent and said, "Play ya again? Double or nothin'?"

Malone lowered his head so that his hat concealed his eyes as he slowly walked past their pool table. *You gotta learn when to quit, kid,* he thought to himself. *You're nothing more than a naïve little sacrificial lamb in a place like this.* The two men agreed to play each other again. Malone then turned his attention away from their next game, finished the rest of his scotch, and then set his empty glass on one of the tables in the back before intensely focusing his eyes on the tall man in the gray suit.

Malone met the man in the gray suit back in the darkened hallway towards the restrooms and near the dimly lit back door from which the man had entered. It was Frank Moniarti.

"Hey, Nicky! I'm glad that I was able to find you here tonight! I'd been hearin' lately that you were…on vacation." Moniarti then made an uneasy smile as he extended his hand over to Malone.

"Never mind what you've been hearin' about me lately," Malone said in a low voice. "This isn't about me. It's about you." Nicholas Malone then shook Frank Moniarti's hand. "I don't know about you, but I could use some fresh air," Malone said, as he smiled thinly and then continued with, "The smoke in here seems to be getting to me." Malone winked and then put his hand on Moniarti's shoulder as he led him out the back door.

CHAPTER 6

A Business Proposal

The night outside had become thick and balmy, as it often was after a hard rain. As they stepped out into the back alleyway, the two men finally made solid eye contact.

"Okay, regardless of what you may have been hearin' about me lately, I understand that we're in the process of makin' ourselves a deal," Malone said. "You're interested in doin' business with me, and I needed to find a way to keep the heat off."

Moniarti gave Malone a steady, piercing glance and said, "Could that possibly be one of the reasons why I'd been hearin' earlier that you were unavailable?"

Nick let out a small chuckle under his breath. "Word travels fast in this city, and everyone around here knows that I'm the one that they discreetly come to whenever there's a problem. And it takes people like you, in your given situation, to help keep some of my people in business."

Malone reached into his jacket pocket and pulled out another Lucky Strike. When he extinguished the match, the smoke seemed to linger in the humid air as he exhaled the first puff out through his nostrils. "So do you still need a solution for your problem, or what?"

Malone said with a squint in his eyes. His hip usually hurt him after a hard rain.

Frank Moniarti appeared somewhat uneasy as he reached up to rub the back of his neck. "Yeah, but we still gotta figure out a plan for where and when. After I heard that you were unavailable earlier, I started to think about relocating, ya know? Just to consider some other options."

Malone patted Moniarti on the shoulder. "You can just leave it all up to me. If you're still interested in buyin' a car, I'm still interested in sellin' one." Nick smiled at Moniarti through a thin haze of cigarette smoke. "Here, Frankie, let me show you a little magic trick that I learned while I was overseas."

Malone flung his cigarette down the alleyway, and Moniarti watched it bounce off from a board on a picket fence and then disintegrate into a burst of orange-and-red embers. Nick reached back into his coat pocket and pulled out two nonfiltered cigarettes.

"Have you ever drawn straws before, Frankie?" Malone asked, as he twirled one of the cigarettes between his fingers.

"Sure," Frank said. "Who hasn't? Besides, I hear that it's pretty popular whenever important decisions need to be made quickly."

Malone's smile widened. "Good. Well, these are evenly matched odds in a game of chance," he said, as he snapped one of the cigarettes over his right-hand middle finger. He then held them up near the dim streetlight with his right hand covering all but the final inch of each cigarette. "If you should happen to choose the unbroken one, your new ride will go over to that old metal factory you've got over in your neck of the woods, on the docks up in Hoboken, and you'll get to choose when that happens," Malone said. "Now, if you should happen to grab the broken cigarette, this handy little new machine is gonna end up goin' over to my storage warehouse down in Ocean City, and I get to tell you when pickup's gonna be. Sound fair enough?"

Frank kept his eyes on the cigarettes in Malone's hand. "Yeah, as long as we can be civilized about this, Nicky," Moniarti said. "I have people in this industry that I trust, and then there's quite a few people around here that I don't really trust. But time is of the essence right now, and if there's one thing that I've learned around here, it's that making any kind of a mistake in business this risky can become *very* costly."

Nick gave Moniarti a sharp, irritated glance. "Look, we're both professionals here. I've heard about all the problems that you've been having lately. Whether it's in the newspapers or I happen to find out about it otherwise. And that's why you came to me. Trust can only come from experience, Frankie. And you're just gonna have to learn to trust me on this one," Malone said in a calm voice.

Moniarti reached for the cigarette that was furthest away from Malone's palm and chose the one closest to his fingertips. His eyes grew wide as he saw that he had chosen the broken one.

"You lose," Malone said and shrugged. "I guess that luck just ain't on your side, Frankie. I would avoid playin' at any of the tables tonight if I were you. But I hope that this makes you feel just a little bit better. We'll meet one week from tonight, over at my storage warehouse in Ocean City, and your automobile will be of the finest quality. If you really know what's best in this given situation, you won't question my judgment. Now, do we have a deal?" He gave Moniarti an inquisitive look before lighting up the unbroken cigarette.

"Of course. Yes, we have a deal," Moniarti said. "And I never back out of a promise. I can assure you of that. I'll be there."

Malone gave Frank a friendly smile and said, "All right then, let's get back in there. We'll put all our other business aside for now, and above all, let's not forget why we're here. To make the most out of a Friday night." They both looked at each other, nodding in agreement.

The time had come to take action. Vincent Plemagoya was making quite a name for himself lately along the New Jersey Shoreline, and he had also been stepping on a lot of people's toes along the way. Malone had recruited his best connections from Detroit for this given job, Doyle Reynolds and Leroy Robinson. The automobile that Moniarti had requested to purchase had to be equipped with certain options that he had specifically requested to be installed. Malone's men already were aware of every feature that the car was supposed to come equipped with, which was going to require his men to make a special trip over in Tobyhanna, Pennsylvania, along the way, and that was going to end up costing Moniarti considerably more during his time of purchase.

He allowed Frank to go back into the pool hall first. It was only customary to give one of his customers some additional time to get approved, and this aspect of an inside consultation didn't involve a credit check; it involved getting additional service men lined up on their end, just in case anything with the vehicle turned out to be defective. That was what Frank Moniarti had Teddy Pazzelli for. He wasn't only Moniarti's driver, but he was also a top-notch auto mechanic. People oftentimes tended to rely more on other people who they had asked certain favors from before, and Malone never really took that aspect of the business too personally. They were businessmen after all, and in this business, who you trusted and who you chose not to trust could change by the day or even by the hour. Malone dropped a lit cigarette on the cement and extinguished it with the thick sole of his newly shined wing tip shoe. He wondered how that young kid who had scratched on his final shot was fairing in his next game. He let out a deep breath and opened up the door to go back inside of the pool hall.

CHAPTER 7

A Game of Chance

The number of people inside of the pool hall had grown considerably since Malone had gone out into the back alleyway to speak with Moniarti. This was, however, a Friday night, and the best way to prevent any potential suspicion regarding recent activities outside was to walk in and out of the men's room, and then from the shadowy hallway, back into the pool hall. It would make it a bit less noticeable that he had come back in from the alleyway. Malone walked from the dark hallway up to the bar and watched Frank Moniarti standing at the pool table across the room, talking things over with his associates. He watched as they all gathered close together to hear each other more clearly over the music playing from the jukebox. Two hundred and fifty thousand dollars was a lot of money, even for a man in Frank Moniarti's position. But Malone was going to make absolutely certain that the final product was well worth the price. Everything was going to be crafted to meet all the required specifications, and every additional feature was going to be tested well in advance. If something went wrong with this job at any given point in time, it was going to be their fault and their fault alone.

Nicholas Malone sat patiently at the bar while Moniarti discussed the business proposition over with the men at his table. "Do you want me to set you up with another double scotch, Nicky?" Ronny asked.

Malone looked up at Ronny and then beyond him, into the mirror behind the bar. He ran his fingers over the short stubble that had begun to collect on his jaw since yesterday morning. "Sure, Ronny," Malone said. "I don't think that I have to be anywhere else just yet."

He turned around and glanced back at the two young men who he had passed by on his way to meet up with Frank Moniarti. "That kid's a real sharpshooter," Ronny said, as he set the newly filled glass on the bar.

"Yeah, looks like his opponent's takin' quite a beating. So tell me, has he been comin' in here for long?" Nick asked, as he turned around to face Ronny.

"For just the past couple of months, and kind of sporadically. That might explain why you haven't seen him here before, Nicky," Ronny said. "He goes by the name Tony 'Bank Shot' Tyler." Malone slowly nodded and then paid Ronny for his drink.

He looked over at the table where Frank Moniarti and his men had been talking. He saw a young kid in his early twenties, with glasses and thick black hair, wearing a maroon suit, walking over toward him. Malone kept steady eye contact with the young kid as he walked up closer to the bar.

"Mr. Moniarti wants me to tell you that you have yourself a deal," the kid said. "But uh, we're gonna supply our own test-driver to make sure that all the added features are workin' properly." The kid put his elbows on the bar as he sat down next to Malone.

"All right," Nick said. "Everything that he asked for will already be tested by then, but I can certainly understand if he wants to see how everything works with his own two eyes. And it isn't exactly like I can give him an instruction manual for this thing. My guys over in Detroit know exactly what genuine quality means, and as the old saying goes, you get what you pay for." Malone reached into his jacket pocket and pulled another Lucky Strike out of the pack. "Frankie and I go way back," Malone said as he shook out the match. "He's heard how I do business. If a customer ain't happy, then I ain't happy. That sorta thing just ain't really a very good business practice." He winked at the kid as he tilted his hat. "I guess that I'll be seeing all you guys at the warehouse next week. Frankie will know where to go."

The kid in the maroon suit let out a nasally sounding chuckle as he got up from his barstool. "All right. We'll be there." He gave Malone a thin smile over his shoulder and said, "Oh, by the way, my name is Charley Bennetti. And I'm Moniarti's bookkeeper, just in case you were wondering." Then he walked down the front of the bar and out the front door.

Malone extinguished his cigarette in the ashtray on the bar and took a long pull off his drink. He could feel the sweat collecting behind the brim of his hat, as he reached into his pocket for a handkerchief. He lifted the hat off his head and then slowly ran the handkerchief across his hairline. *It's just another relentlessly humid night here in Atlantic City,* Malone thought to himself, as he checked the mirror once again to make sure that his hair was still straight and orderly. Behind his reflection, he could see the young man who had scratched on his final shot only moments ago.

The kid, who had just lost yet another game, threw his hands up in agitation and looked up at the ceiling as he hurled his pool stick towards a bench directly behind him. The kid dropped a bundle of twenties on the green felt of the pool table and said, "That's it, Tony! I quit! That's eight in a row now!"

Malone shook his head. *Eight in a row? I wonder if that kid's even old enough to shave,* he thought to himself, as he pulled his eyes away from the mirror.

The kid picked up his leather jacket from the bench near the table and walked over to the bar next to Malone. "What do you need, kid?" Ronny asked, as he turned around from the sink.

"Just gimme a glass of water," he said, breathing heavily. "Hell, I ain't got nothin' left. Bank Shot beat me cold!" The kid's face was flushed red with a mixture of anger and embarrassment. "Eight games in a row, and now I'm gonna be walkin' home because he just won all the money that I had saved up for a taxicab."

Ronny gave the kid a sympathetic look and said, "You gotta ask yourself sometimes what it is that you're learnin' from this, kid. I've seen him clear some people out for a hell of a lot more than he just got you for."

The young man looked down at the floor and just shook his head. "Those stories ain't gonna be of too much use to me now," the young man said. "But thanks anyway, Ronny. I'll know to watch out for Tony Tyler from now on. That boy ain't nothin' but trouble."

Ronny set a glass of water on the bar. "That would be pretty smart, kid," Ronny said. "Sometimes, it ain't whether you win or lose. It's a matter of knowin' when to quit."

The kid nodded at Ronny and then chugged down his glass of water. "I ain't never takin' another beatin' like that again," the young man said. "I know that's for sure."

Malone raised his eyebrows as he looked away from the kid. *Never say never*, he thought to himself as the kid starting walking towards the front door.

"You need a refill, Nicky?" Ronny asked, as his eyes followed the kid walking out the front door of the pool hall.

"Sure, Ronny. That kid's got a lot to learn about life," Malone said and then let out a small laugh. "What I wouldn't give to be that age again."

Ronny let out a hard laugh and said, "Yeah, tell me about it. The crowd in here just keeps lookin' younger and younger to me year after year."

Nick looked past Ronny and could see Tony Tyler's silhouette standing anxiously about three feet behind him. Malone turned around slowly and looked right into Tony's eyes. "Can I help you with somethin'?" Malone asked.

Tony was shifting his pool stick between his hands in a methodically rhythmic motion and said, "Hey, mister, I'm Tony Tyler, but everybody around here just calls me Bank Shot. I was wonderin' if maybe you might wanna shoot a game or two against me?" His voice sounded proud but thin.

"That depends," Malone said in a low, casual voice. "I don't usually play against anybody for pocket change. And besides, aren't you out a bit past your bedtime? You should probably run on home now before your mother starts to worry."

Tony's eyebrows lowered from the insult, and then he blurted out, "Fifty bucks a game!"

Nick gave the young man a gentle smile and said, "How about best out of five? Winner takes all."

Tony's eyes quickly grew wide with excitement, and he said, "You mean play for 250 bucks? Sheesh! You're on, mister! I'll be gentle with you!"

Tony walked back quickly to the table to set up a game of nineball, and Nick got up to select his pool stick. Malone knew from experience that the best sticks were almost always located along the back wall where all the billiard tables were. The back rack of pool sticks rarely got used, except on Wednesday nights when the Vietnamese billiard players would come in. He chose to spin each one of the sticks around in their plastic holders to see which ones might be bowed or warped. The first one looked relatively decent until he saw the tip of the stick wobble at the top as he spun it. He went on to the next one and saw that it was loosely connected at the center because the two pieces didn't quite match up. That was even worse than trying to shoot pool with a stick that was bent. The next one that he saw looked almost brand-new. The stick had no visible dents or scratches in it, and it spun around in the plastic holder effortlessly, as if it were still fresh from the factory. He took it down and rolled it across the billiard table just to make sure that his eyes weren't deceiving him. *Yeah,* Malone thought to himself, *this is gonna be my weapon of choice. I'll try to go easy on this kid tonight. He may think that he's got it all for now. But he's about to learn the same harsh lesson that he was out to try and teach that other kid who was here tonight.* Malone smiled at Tony from across the pool hall as he picked up his pool stick and walked over to their table.

Malone looked up at Tony from under the dim light above the pool table and then said, "Okay, kid, let's play."

CHAPTER 8

Saturday, October 13, 1962
Another Sleepless Night

It was just after midnight by the time that Frank Moniarti had stepped out from the back door and into the alleyway behind Lucky Nine's Pool Hall. And the rain had started back up again. He looked up and saw a bright pair of headlights slowly approaching him. It was a dark blue 1955 Buick Riviera, and as the passenger-side window rolled down, Frank recognized Teddy Pazzelli through the thin mist of car exhaust that floated up through the rain.

"Get in, boss. We've gotta talk," Teddy said, as he opened the door.

Moniarti got into the car and looked over at Teddy as he took off his hat and then set it on the dashboard. "Yeah, we do! I take it that you've heard about what happened at the jewelry store?" Frank asked, with a glare of agitation in his eyes.

"Yeah, Frankie, I heard about that," Teddy replied. "The person who organized that job, if we can even call it that, was just plain sloppy."

Frank rolled the window up tight. The pouring rain was starting to add to his already increasing level of agitation. Teddy knew that the longer he drove, the calmer Frank would become. They had worked together long enough at this point to where Teddy knew the sort of mood that Frank was in, and he also knew that Frank Moniarti was a man of action. This was the time for them to start putting together a plan.

"Foolish and sloppy are just the start of it!" Frank barked. "No respectable businessman around here orders his men to storm into a jewelry store and go wavin' their guns around in fronta people like that! That just ain't right! It takes a certain level of brains, muscle, and experience to get you further ahead, not fear!" Moniarti shouted. "And, once you start gainin' respect around here, and you have the brains to make smarter decisions than that, then you are able to gain your credibility without the use of fear! Especially, that type of fear!" Teddy lifted the right side of his face in a half smile to let Frank know he approved of his speech, so far. It was going to be another long night.

Teddy looked over at Frank briefly as he drove along the expressway entrance ramp. "Let me guess, Plemagoya?" Teddy asked.

Frank began shaking his head back and forth before he could even answer the question. "Yeah, you guessed it!" Frank replied, "Who else woulda been that careless? I mean, he sends a group of guys into the place. They're so inexperienced that three of 'em got rubbed out by the cops, but in the process, they ended up takin' a rookie police officer and some poor salesman along with 'em. Men with families who just happened to have made the mistake of showin' up for work that day! Not to mention all the other people who got traumatized from those morons shootin' up the ceiling like that! I never even heard a gun go off until I was fresh outta high school! Well, anyway, so this botched robbery happens, and next thing I know, I got my son on the phone all shook up and askin' me for help!"

Teddy rolled his eyes as he drove on and said, "Life can be full of all sorts of unpleasant surprises sometimes."

Frank fixed his gaze in on the headlights as they glowed over the passing strips in the road. "Now, the city's all shook up, and now, in their eyes, somebody's gotta pay!"

Frank looked over at Teddy and saw him shrug. "Yeah, it seems like Vinnie's been a real problem since he got here. He's made a few friends around town but even more enemies," Teddy said. "He shoulda done his homework a little more thoroughly regarding proper business practices around here! I mean, am I right, Frankie? This kid gets run outta Brooklyn because he burned a few too many bridges, and now he's tryin' to make some of his old bad habits some of our future problems? I mean, I agree with you! That just ain't right, and somethin' needs to be done about it."

Frank let out a sigh of anger and frustration as he thought about just how quickly that Vincent Plemagoya had become this arrogant. "Listen, I'm kinda hungry," Moniarti said. "You getting hungry? I skipped supper at home tonight. I mean, if I can't recognize what Meg's got cookin' on the stove, I ain't puttin' that garbage nowhere near my stomach. Ya know what I'm sayin'?"

Teddy let out a hearty laugh of relief as he felt Moniarti's tension level finally starting to settle down. "That's good, Frankie. Yeah, I hear ya," Teddy replied. "Silvia's been tryin' real hard to get me to eat a few vegetables more often. And that's not workin' out too well." Teddy put his blinker on as their car reached the next expressway exit.

Frank reached into his pocket and pulled out a handkerchief to wipe the sweat off the back of his neck and said, "I'm kinda cravin' some steak and eggs. What do you say?"

Teddy looked both ways as he turned right from the stop sign at the end of the expressway exit. "Sounds good to me. I'm more in the mood for some coffee myself," Teddy said. "There's this all-night place that we can go to that'll have your steak and eggs and plenty of black coffee, and they got some pretty good Danishes there, too. Besides, I have also been studyin' some of our friend's behavioral patterns as of late. Guaranteed, we'll get a close glimpse of him tonight."

Moniarti raised an eyebrow and said, "You better not be jokin' with me, Teddy! It's been a really long night already as it is!"

Teddy took one hand off from the steering wheel and patted Frank on the shoulder with it. "No, I'm not jokin' with you," Teddy said. "I've got some reliable sources that have been watchin' over him since before that sorry joke of a robbery ever even happened."

The two men pulled into the parking lot of a roadside diner. As Teddy put the car into park, he gave his boss a moment to finish some of his final thoughts before they went out into public. Frank knew that, in this kind of weather, if someone should happen to pass by, their conversation would be drowned out by the sound of the rain falling against the roof of their car. And even if it wasn't, in this sort of heavy rain, their conversation would probably be the least of any passersby's worries. Frank looked over at Teddy as he folded his arms together.

"That was why I chose to go to Nicky," Frank said. "We may not have always seen eye to eye over the years, but when it comes down to handlin' a problem like this one, he's about the best you're gonna get. Besides, he already knows that my son was one of the people inside of that jewelry store. He made it out all right, but once I asked Nicky for a favor, I knew that he'd come through for me. He'd heard all about the problem before I even called him, so I know that he understands! Besides, it's gotten to the point where Plemagoya is becoming a threat to both of us."

Teddy nodded in agreement as he opened the car door to go out into the pouring rain. He looked over at Frank and said, "If Nicky's got the situation under control, I'll just have to take your word for it. Now, we've just gotta figure out a way to tie everything up on our end. But in the meantime, let's eat."

Once they were inside of the diner, the waitress seated them in a booth next to the window and brought out two cups of black coffee. "Thanks, princess," Frank said to the waitress, and then he let out a long yawn and rubbed his eyes. "I've been losin' a lotta sleep lately, Teddy. And over what?" Frank said, "Because some punk kid finally moves in and tries to shake things up for us? My father raised me to always be better than that. After we eat, I'm kinda interested to see what you know about our friend's behavioral patterns. If I don't make it home at all tonight, Meg will just have to accept the fact that I was workin' late and eatin' better food than what she was tryin' to serve me at home. Anyways, Teddy, thanks for all the work that you told me that these other guys have been doing lately. You're gonna end up savin' me a whole lotta time poppin' antacids. Now then, if we've got all night, let's talk about the past instead of the future. Do you remember that game we went and saw a few years back? The one where the Yankees stomped the livin' crap outta the Indians?"

Teddy raised his eyebrows behind his coffee mug and then said, "Yeah, I remember that game. That was pretty brutal."

Frank lit a cigarette as he looked out the window from their table at the diner, seemingly in a trance. "*Brutal* ain't even the word for it. I'm tellin' ya, those were the days."

CHAPTER 9

Ace in the Hole

The pool hall had slowly begun to clear out after Ronny had announced the last call for drinks. Taxicabs began to park in a single file against the curb and all along the sidewalk. *Another long day has finally drawn to a close,* Ronny thought to himself, as he made his way around the pool hall to collect the last of the empty bar glasses. After he had placed the rest of them on the counter, he saw Tony Tyler waving at him in the mirror from behind the bar. Ronny walked over to the pool table with a visible expression of annoyance on his face.

Tony gave him an arrogant smile that revealed a silver tooth on the right side of his mouth, as he said, "Hey, old man, you mind rackin' 'em up for us? I'm about to teach this old-timer a lesson, and I don't really wanna have the responsibility of rackin' the balls mess up my concentration."

Ronny flipped the small towel that he had been using to clean the tables off with over his left shoulder. "I guess," Ronny said. "But just remember that I am doin' this more as a favor to him than to you!" Ronny gave Malone an approving nod, as he pulled the rack out from underneath the table.

Ronny set up a game of nine-ball, carefully examining the tightness of the rack as a doctor might examine a sedated patient just before surgery. He leaned over the table and pressed his thumbs firmly against the lower part of the diamond shape in which the balls were arranged, and then he slid them toward the center of the table. "All right, let the games begin, but I don't want no trouble in here tonight! You got that? I've worked hard enough as it is for one day," Ronny said and then pulled the towel off from his shoulder and resumed cleaning off the tables that were surrounding the two men. "Oh, and uh, whatever happens in here tonight, I never saw it," Ronny said. "Business hours are over with now, and you two are here on your own accord. Understand?"

Tony looked up to see Ronny's silhouette behind the glaring light over the pool table. "Yeah, sure, I gotcha," Tony replied. "I'll call ya back once it's time to rack 'em back up again. This shouldn't take too terribly long." Tony Tyler gave Malone an extended gaze. "Whose break is it?" Tony asked as he grabbed the chalk off the pool table.

"I tell you what, kid. This was all your idea, so you can go first. The winner gets to break at the start of the next game," Malone said and then lit another Lucky Strike.

"Yeah, okay. Wow, mister, you sure are a good sport," Tony said, as he leaned over the pool table to break.

Malone exhaled smoke out from his nose as he watched the balls scatter across the pool table. *There goes the five, the two, and the seven,* Malone thought to himself as he took inventory of the balls that were left on the table. "Way to push 'em out, kid!" Malone said to Tony with a hollow grin.

"Thanks! Just gettin' warmed up. You sure that you don't wanna forfeit, mister?" Tony said and then arrogantly chuckled. "You still got plenty of baggage to clean up here. Besides, I'm not the type that gives up very easily." Tony leaned over the table, extending his pool stick back and forth, and then said, "Six in the corner!" He hit the cue ball, and it grazed the side of the six ball, which landed exactly where he had called it. "Four in the side!" Tony aimed and hit the four ball, but it wobbled around the pocket and then came back out again. "You're up!" Tony said, as he tossed the chalk over the pool table to Malone.

Nicholas Malone surveyed the table as he rubbed the chalk against his pool stick. "Good job, kid. You've mastered one of the first rules of the game," Malone said. "If you can't take a shot, don't leave one." Malone grabbed the bridge from underneath the table. The condition of his bad left hip didn't allow him the privilege of leaning too far over the table. "Okay, youngster, look alive," Malone said, as he bent down to take his first shot. "Like you said, four in the side." He sent the cue ball rolling down the entire length of the table. It hit the back wall and grazed the four ball upon its return, sending it straight into the designated pocket. "Three in the corner," Malone said, as he pointed the pool stick at the far left corner of the table. He shot, and the cue ball hit the three, and then stopped. The three ball went rolling slowly back into the left corner pocket. "What was that you were askin' me about forfeiting?" Malone asked and raised one of his eyebrows. He set the bridge against the table once again and then said, "Keep your eyes on the golden goose, kid!" Malone gave this shot an intentional degree of added force, hoping to help the kid feel better about himself. The cue ball struck the one ball, and both of them disappeared into the adjacent rear corner pockets.

Tony looked around the table, and only the eight and the nine balls were left remaining. He felt a sudden surge of unexpected confidence running through his body. Two hundred and fifty dollars could help to buy a lot of things, including that new motorcycle that he had recently had his eye on. He tried to steady his shaking hands as he leaned over the table with his pool stick. "Eight in the side!" he said, as he lunged forward into the shot. The eight ball landed right where he called it. "Hey, old man, what was that you were sayin' about watchin' the golden goose?" Tony gave Malone an arrogant smile and said, "Nine in the corner." He was pointing his pool stick toward the far right corner of the table. Tony gave the cue ball a gentle tap, and it rolled into the nine, sending it into the far right corner. Tony's face lit up with tremendous excitement, and then he said, "Ha! I win!"

Malone looked up from the pool table and into Tony's eyes. "That was only the first game, kid," Malone said. "Four more to go.

I hope that you ain't gettin' sleepy." Ronny came over to the table to set up the rack for their next game.

"All right, it's your break again. Try to make this one count even more than the last one did," Malone said and then took a seat on the long wooden bench next to the pool table. *If I give him just one more win, then he'll start gettin' sloppy,* Malone thought to himself. *This kid's got experience, sure, but it's only a matter of time before his youthful arrogance gets the best of him.* Malone's brief moment of introspection came to an end when he heard the abrupt sound of Tony breaking. The balls quickly scattered across the pool table, but nothing fell. "So let me guess, I'm expected to clean up after you now?" Malone asked, looking at Tony from under the brim of his hat. He got up, and slowly walked over to the pool table. "Six in the side, and three in the corner," he said, as he extended the bridge over the pool table to help correct his balance. Malone sent the cue ball halfway down the pool table where it connected with the six and then, in its deflection, hit the three, sending both balls into their designated pockets. "You were right, kid," Malone said. "I am a good sport, and I recognize a worthy opponent when I see one."

All through the night, the men played on, and Malone always made sure that the score remained as even as possible in order to make sure that the kid didn't suspect anything out of the ordinary, just good old-fashioned professional sportsmanship. Malone even tried to let Tony feel like he could have won in the third game and expressed a moment of sympathy when Tony scratched at the end of it. Tony had made the mistake of trying to sink the nine ball with an inaccurate massé shot. Malone had to refrain from audibly laughing. *How could someone who claims to be a professional pool player make such a ridiculous mistake?* Malone thought to himself as he watched the end of their third game. He decided that it was another lesson that Tony could only learn through experience. At last, they had reached their fifth and final game. Both men looked at each other with a determined sense of anticipation. They each had two wins and two losses, making this game the deciding factor as to who was going to walk away the ultimate winner.

CHAPTER 10

A Promising Lead

Frank Moniarti was growing increasingly weary of dealing with his insomnia. He had decided to try several different medications and some home remedies that his wife had read about, but nothing seemed to be working against it. His eyes had continued to grow increasingly bloodshot with every passing day. By the time that he and Teddy had left the roadside diner, the rain had subsided. They got back into the Buick Riviera, and Frank popped an antacid into his mouth to help settle his stomach. *Too much coffee lately,* Frank thought to himself. *Meg is gonna have my hide over this.* She had frequently been on his case about that lately. Especially, since the doctor had warned him about his high blood pressure. She had always been the type of woman who firmly believed in taking safety precautions toward the health of her loved ones.

He could still remember the exact time and place that he had first met Megan Marie Hollister. They both grew up in the Castle Point District of Hoboken and had both attended the same high school together. They had first met at Sybil's Cave with a group of mutual friends on Halloween night back in 1925. It was one of the most popular attractions in town for meeting on Halloween back then. The neighborhood kids would all gather together and tell each other ghost stories by candlelight and wait for the return of a ghost that some of the townspeople still firmly believed had haunted the grounds of that area.

It had happened during Frank's sophomore year, and Megan was only a freshman back then. That was the night that they had truly gotten to know each other. After the group's candles had all burned out, they were the last two people left inside of the cave. And neither of them had dared to walk outside of it out of fear they might end up getting attacked by an angry evil spirit on their way home. So they waited in the cave together until daybreak. Since their wedding day, over twenty-five years ago, the ongoing joke between them on their anniversary was that nothing could bond true love together quite as strongly as sheer terror.

Megan had given birth to their first son, James Michael Moniarti, on the morning of June 27, 1940. They had chosen to remain in Hoboken but had decided to move into a much larger house two years after the birth of their son, in the hopes of building a more comfortable future for their growing family. Megan had then given birth to their daughter the first winter after they had settled into their new home, and currently, Melissa Addison Moniarti was in the start of her second year at Pennsylvania State University. *My God, where does the time go?* Frank thought to himself as he looked dreamily out from the fogged-up windshield. The distant sound of a car horn brought him back from his reflections upon days passed.

Moniarti reached up and rubbed his eyes. They itched and burned as he rubbed them. "This plan's gotta pay off," he told Teddy. "I don't see much room for a second chance with this one. So what's all this information that you've been hidin' from me?"

Teddy reached down and started the engine. "He goes out gambling at least once every weekend," Teddy replied. "He plays poker against Natty Rosebrook. You remember him? The guy who runs that used car lot?" Teddy looked over at Frank.

"Oh yeah, I remember him," Frank said, as he rolled down the window a crack. The moisture from the rain was causing the windows to fog up. "He has a bad habit of sellin' people lemons. His reputation as a businessman ain't really the greatest," Moniarti said.

"I even heard that he got roughed up a couple of times by some of his angry customers. I guess some people don't take too kindly to payin' through the nose for a car that breaks down on 'em two weeks later."

Teddy let out a dimly audible chuckle, as he got back onto the expressway heading east. "Well, anyways, whenever he wins, he usually likes to live it up a bit afterwards," Teddy said. "You know, liquor, cigars, dames, the whole shebang. You familiar with The Golden Sandbox, Frankie?"

Moniarti's eyes grew big with surprise. "Yeah! Ain't that the showgirls' place that's owned by Scotty McCormack?" Frank asked.

Teddy looked over at Frank with a bright grin on his face. "Why, yes, it is!" Teddy replied. "Which means that we might just end up gettin' an eyeful while we're huntin' down Plemagoya tonight! So tell me, whatcha gotta say about that?"

Frank gave Teddy a playfully irritated look. "Get outta here!" Frank said, "You mean to tell me that it's gonna be a luck of the draw if we're gonna catch him there tonight?"

Teddy nodded slowly and then said, "Well, either way, we know that we can follow him around after he leaves the car dealership. He goes down to Rosebrook's garage every Saturday, like he's goin' to church or somethin'. I mean, the kid's got a real appetite for gambling, and I think that it's time that we upped the ante on him! Don't you, Frankie?"

Moniarti lit a cigarette and threw the match out the window. "Yeah, I'd say it's time for that puny little bastard's luck to run out! Period!" Moniarti said, "But let's be patient about this! Ain't no sense in bein' fast and sloppy about this! That's what his guys were like when they knocked over that jewelry store! I'd say that it's about time that we show him how professionals like us take care of business around here."

Teddy put his blinker on and then pulled over onto the ramp for the next expressway exit.

CHAPTER 11

A Night on the Town

Five blocks away from the expressway exit, Vincent Plemagoya was running a comb under the faucet in the bathroom at Rosebrook's Used Cars. Natty, the owner of the dealership, was not in the best of spirits tonight. Vincent had just beaten him at poker to the sum of about $150, which was nearly a quarter of a day's sales. Another night like this could land Natty in the poor house, or even worse yet, it might eventually end up running him right out of business. There was suddenly a hard knock against the bathroom door.

"Come on, kid! Whataya doin' in there? Lookin' for the lost island of Atlantis?" Natty shouted. "We're closed! I wanna go home now!"

Vincent viewed himself in the mirror admiringly. "Hey! Can it, old man! I gotta look sharp for the ladies tonight! That's somethin' that you mighta been doin', if luck had been on your side instead!" Plemagoya said and then snickered, as he slicked his thick black hair down almost against his scalp. The droplets of warm water were making small dark spots along the shoulders of his ivory-colored suit. "Say, how's business been comin' along for ya lately, Natty? I heard that some kid test drove a car of yours right into a fire hydrant the other day. Your luck's just kept gettin' worse and worse lately, hasn't it, pal?" Vincent said and then let out a loud, obnoxious laugh.

Natty was in no mood to deal with these sorts of antics tonight. Especially after having lost such a large sum of money. "That's it, you little punk!" Natty said, "You have until the count of three to come outta there or I'm gonna break the door down, and then you're really gonna be one sorry little—"

Plemagoya slowly opened the bathroom door and then said, "Hey, Natty, relax. Hasn't your doctor ever told you that gettin' that upset can be kinda bad for your health?"

Natty Rosebrook gave Plemagoya a piercingly infuriated look. "Get the hell outta here, Vinnie! Just because I choose to play poker with you, that don't mean that I like you," Natty said. "You're usin' up all your favors with a whole lotta people around here. This is the wrong town to be stayin' in if you ain't got any friends left."

Vincent suddenly pinned Natty up against the wall and then spoke sternly through gritted teeth, "What? Are you threatenin' me, old man?"

Natty casually brushed Plemagoya's hands away, and then gave him an indifferent look of sleepiness and boredom. "I ain't got the time to become any sort of threat to you, kid. You're already enough of a threat to yourself," Natty said. "One of these days, you're gonna end up realizin' that."

Vincent raised the left corner of his mouth in a faintly devilish smirk. "Cheer up, old man. You ain't gotta see me or deal with me again for another whole week. And then I'll come back around to brighten your day again. And just maybe next time you'll be the one to get lucky, and we can go back to being friends," Plemagoya said. "What do ya say about that, Natty? No hard feelings, huh?"

Natty rolled his eyes and then said, "Just get the hell outta here, kid. I've had more than enough of you for one night."

Vincent Plemagoya walked out to the dirt parking lot located behind the garage and saw a silver 1954 Ford Crestline waiting for him with its motor running. He walked up to the driver-side window and shouted, "Hey, Pedro! What's the story for tonight?" He then reached in and ruffled the driver's hair and walked around the back side of the car to the passenger-side door.

Pedro was already getting quite irritated with Vinnie, and he could already clearly see what sort of a direction that the night was heading in. "I've told you before, Vinnie! Don't mess my hair up!" Pedro shouted. "You know I hate it when you do that!"

Vinnie lowered his head to look Pedro in the eyes and then said, "Relax, lover boy, we're goin' some place nice tonight. My treat." Plemagoya opened the car door, and Pedro shook his head out of annoyance from dealing with Vinnie during the first few seconds of their encounter.

"All right, muchacho, but that's about the only thing that's gonna get me to like you again right about now!" Pedro said, "Especially after you just ruffled my hair all up! It took me a long time to get it to look like this!"

Vincent doubled over laughing as the Crestline turned in a circle to exit through the back lot of the garage. Pedro hit the gas hard, and gravel spit up violently as he pulled out of Rosebrook's Used Cars. He figured that if he couldn't annoy Vinnie right now, he could certainly get under Natty's skin. They had recently made a tradition out of turfing up Natty's lot whenever he had suffered from a losing night at poker.

Pedro looked over at Vinnie as he rolled up the window. "So where we goin' tonight, hombre?" Pedro asked. "The Golden Sandbox?"

Vinnie pulled a pint of tequila out from his jacket pocket and took a long pull off it. "Sí, mi amigo," Plemagoya replied.

Pedro watched Vinnie as he twisted the cap back onto the bottle. "All right, but you'd better not get us thrown out again this time!" Pedro demanded, as he built up speed along the on-ramp to the expressway. Plemagoya rested his head against the seat of the car and rolled over on his side. Pedro knew that Vinnie had probably been drinking for several hours by now and that he was more than likely going to be carrying him out of the club towards the end of the night.

"Hey, Pedro, let's stop by a liquor store along the way," Plemagoya said.

Pedro sighed, shaking his head, and then said, "All right."

Neither one of them seemed to take notice of the dark blue 1955 Buick Riviera that was riding along at a comfortable fifty feet behind them.

CHAPTER 12

Taking Risks

Frank Moniarti rubbed his eyes and then tried to look through the thick layer of condensation that had collected on the windshield of their car. "I can't quite make out the license plate number," he told Teddy, as he wearily looked over at him "But let's stay where we are. Don't start gainin' on him or nothin' because we might end up with one hell of a mess on our hands."

Teddy nodded slowly as he followed the silver Ford Crestline along the expressway entrance ramp. "Even if they end up stoppin' someplace else, we know where they're gonna eventually end up," Teddy said, as he pressed down on the acceleration pedal to keep up with the flow of traffic.

"I say that no matter what happens along the way, we just go straight there and wait for them to show up, however long that takes," Moniarti said.

"We probably know Vinnie's personal habits even better than he does by now," Teddy said with a faint smile, as he quickly turned his head over his shoulder to change lanes.

* * *

Pedro pulled into the dimly lit parking lot of the liquor store and parked behind the building. "You sure that you're still gonna make it through the night?" Pedro asked Vinnie, as he faintly heard him snoring over the quiet sound of the car engine humming.

Pedro nudged him, and Vinnie said, "Hey, yeah, I'm awake." He turned his head to the side and looked over at Pedro.

"So what're we drinkin' tonight?" Pedro asked Vinnie as he extended his hand for some money to cover the purchase.

Vinnie reached up to wipe the drool off the corner of his mouth and then said, "Hey, Pedro, if I start on tequila, I gotta end on tequila. And that's all there is to it. Those have always been the rules." Vinnie gave Pedro a twenty-dollar bill and said, "Don't come back with nothin' but the best!" Pedro let out a nervous laugh as he closed the driver-side door.

* * *

Twenty minutes later, Frank and Teddy still sat waiting in the parking lot of The Golden Sandbox. Frank looked at his watch impatiently and then said, "So where in the hell are they, Teddy? You told me the source that you got this information from was reliable."

Teddy looked over at Frank and handed him a book of matches to light his cigarette with. "Don't you worry, Frankie," Teddy said. "They'll show up. Trust me on this."

Moniarti lit a match and took a deep pull from his cigarette. "And so what if they don't show up here? Then where does that leave us?" Moniarti asked.

Just then, they saw the silver 1954 Ford Crestline that they had been following earlier pull up into the parking lot. "With all due respect to you, Frankie. I will kindly disregard that last comment," Teddy said with a growing smile.

The two men watched patiently as the car pulled into a parking space. Their faces lit up red in their dark car from the brake lights of the Crestline coming to a stop. As soon as the brake lights went off, Moniarti saw the passenger-side door swing open, and a man leaned his head out from the car, vomiting with tremendous force.

Frank covered his mouth to restrain a burst of hysterical laughter. "Yeah, that's him, all right," he whispered to Teddy. "Like I said, he's sloppy, *very* sloppy."

They saw the driver of the car get out and rush over to help his visibly intoxicated passenger. "That's Pedro," Teddy whispered to Frank. "That's who usually babysits him after he wins at his card games."

Frank shook his head and then said, "That poor bastard. If he does that again while the car is movin', he ain't never gonna get that smell outta there." Frank reached into his coat pocket and pulled out a notepad. Once the two men were out of their sight, Frank wrote down the Crestline's license plate number. He would make sure that it was given to the proper contacts tomorrow in order to carry out next weekend's assignment.

CHAPTER 13

Flirting with Disaster

As Vincent Plemagoya entered The Golden Sandbox with Pedro, they looked around the smoke-filled room to see if there were any familiar faces in there that might potentially cause their night to come to an early end. After all, Vinnie was making more enemies in this town than friends. It looked as though the coast might actually be clear tonight. At least, for now.

"Come on, Pedro! Let's sit down towards the front! You always seem to get the best kind of attention that way!" Vinnie shouted, and he grabbed Pedro by the shoulder to lead him towards the front of the club. There was a live band that usually performed there on the weekends, and they had become a local favorite with many of the regular patrons at The Golden Sandbox.

Once the two men reached a table that was close enough to the front stage, they sat down, and Vinnie's head was beginning to swivel around on his shoulders, as though he was feeling the aftermath of some of his earlier extracurricular activities of the night. Pedro silently hoped that Vinnie wouldn't end up losing consciousness inside of the bar. He absolutely hated it when that happened, even more than he hated it when Vinnie ruffled his hair. When the server arrived at their table, Pedro ordered a club soda, and Plemagoya ordered a double shot of tequila with a twist of lemon. There was a loud series of claps and whistles coming from the audience as a dancer left the stage.

The band began to play the next song after the applause had begun quieting down. The singer had made an announcement just before starting the song, "This next one goes out to all the lovely ladies in the house tonight." And his statement was followed by several loud whistles and catcalls from the men in the audience. The band then began playing, as the next dancer walked up to the stage. The dancer had certainly captured Pedro's undivided attention, but Vincent Plemagoya's eyes continued to circle around the club as if he might somehow spot somebody that he knew, watching him from a distance, or worse yet, start some kind of trouble involving somebody that he'd never even met before.

Plemagoya saw a woman with long, curly blond hair walking towards their table. She was wearing a white sequined dress and a pair of white high heels. Once the dancer got closer to their table, Plemagoya wrapped his arm around her hips, making eye contact with her from his seat, which was now pushed out away from the table.

"Hey, honey! What will you do for me for twenty bucks?" he asked her with a slurred speech, as his head continued to wobble back and forth.

The woman then leaned down closer to him, until she could smell the bitter stench of alcohol on his breath. Her blue eyes sparkled as she gave him a flirting smile. "Well, you might want to hang onto your money, dear," she said. "Do you see that man over there by the door?" Vincent unsteadily turned his head around sideways and saw a large and muscular man in a black shirt patiently standing in the corner with his arms folded. The same person who they had paid their cover charge to after they had entered in through the front door. "If you don't take your arm off me right now, you are probably going to need that money to help cover all your hospital bills," she said with a smirk and then gently brushed Vinnie's arm away from her hips.

After the dancer had walked away from his eyesight, Plemagoya then turned his attention over toward Pedro, and the music continued to play, as the sound of the band filled the nightclub.

Pedro rolled his eyes in irritation. "Vinnie, I think that maybe you've had enough fun for one night," Pedro said, as he watched Plemagoya guzzling down the last of his drink.

Just then, the large man from near the front door approached their table. "Hey, I think you guys need to go now," he said in a low voice. His stern look caused his eyebrows to lower into a menacing scowl.

"Hey, we don't want no trouble here tonight," Pedro said to the man, and then he put his hand down on Vinnie's shoulder. "Don't worry. I got him."

The large man gave Pedro a quick, sharp nod. "Sorry, Vinnie, we gotta go," Pedro said, and he scooped Vinnie up off from his chair, loosely placing his hat back onto his head.

"Now, you fellas be safe out there tonight," the large man said as he led them over toward the front door of the club.

The dancer that Vinnie had been harassing earlier now climbed the staircase that led up onto the stage. "Good riddance," she said under her breath and watched the two men disappear behind the closing front door.

CHAPTER 14

Playing for Keeps

Nicholas Malone was growing tired, and he felt as though he had already let this kid have enough moments to fuel his own ego. Malone reached down and grabbed the chalk off from the pool table. *Honestly,* he thought to himself, *this kid's got plenty of potential, but it's getting late now, and this masquerade has eventually gotta come to an end.* Tony nervously lit another cigarette and quickly shook the match out with several rapid jerking motions.

"So this is it," Ronny said, as he arranged the balls in the rack for the final time. "After this, it's time to call it a night, fellas."

Tony looked over at Ronny through a cloud of smoke. "And what if I don't feel like goin' nowhere just yet?" Tony asked, as he chalked up his pool stick.

"Then I'll throw you out into the alleyway like the filthy piece of garbage that you are!" Ronny said, as he emptied their ashtray into a tin bucket and wiped off their table.

Tony gave Ronny a devilish smile and then said, "Lighten up, old man. I was just givin' ya a hard time, that's all."

Ronny flipped the towel over his shoulder, as he looked Tony directly in the eyes. "Yeah, I understand that, kid. But I've been on my feet for the past twelve hours now," Ronny said. "So if some young punk tries to give me a hard time in my own place, I only see it fit to give him a hard time right on back."

Tony rolled his eyes and chuckled. "It's your break, mister," he said to Malone, making room for him to approach the pool table.

Malone grabbed the bridge from under the table and extended his left leg slightly into the air in order to support his body for the shot. "Don't scratch, old man!" Tony said and then arrogantly laughed.

Nicholas Malone looked up at Tony Tyler through the thin haze of smoke that was covering his face. He felt like he'd definitely had enough of this kid's arrogance, at least for one night. "You haven't really learned the proper sportsmanship of this game yet, have you, kid?" Malone said and now gave Tony a piercing glance of annoyance. "When you see that another player's about to break, figure out when to speak and when to shut up!" Malone said and then stood up straight as he began approaching Tony. "Now, I think that it's time for you to learn one of the most important lessons of all!" Malone said, as he lifted up his finger.

Tony turned around to put his cigarette out in the ashtray and then asked, "Yeah? And what's that?"

Malone took off his hat, set it on the bench, and then said, "To respect your elders, of course. You see, it's okay for us to call you *kid* because you haven't experienced life quite the way that we have yet." Malone nodded over at Ronny before continuing. "And for you to call either one of us an *old man* is just a tad bit disrespectful. Don't you think? We both have names. You can call him Ronny or even Mr. Steiner, if you choose to. After all, he was kind enough to rack up all our games for us tonight and allow us to play for money in his establishment. As for me, you can call me *mister*. I'm okay with that. I mean, anything's better than *old man*. If it hadn't been for an *old man* like me or for Mr. Steiner over there, you very well might not even be speaking English right now!"

Tony gave Malone a curious look and then said, "What are you talkin' about, mister? You're soundin' crazy!"

Nick gave Tony a controlled smile and said, "You really don't get it, do you? I'm talking about the war, kid. Until you watch some of your best friends get blown up before your very eyes and spend the better part of a year learnin' how to walk again once you get back home, if you were even fortunate enough to survive, then you really haven't paid enough dues yet to get away with calling me an *old man*. Until you do go through all those things, just like I have, you can still keep on calling me *mister*. Got it, kid?" At this point, Malone was less than three inches away from Tony's nose, staring directly into his eyes.

Tony's arrogant smile ran away from his face. "Yeah, sure, I got it," Tony said. "I didn't mean to ruffle your feathers or nothin', mister. I guess that I just never really looked at it that way before."

Malone broke away from his intense fix on Tony's eyes, and his stern face gave away into a gentle smile. "It's okay, kid," Malone said. "People can change. But it takes experience in order for that to happen, whether it's for the better or even if it's for the worse. Everybody has got the opportunity to change."

Malone went back to the front of the table to concentrate on his break and said, "Now, where were we? Ah, yes, you were just tryin' to tell me not to scratch." Malone gently placed his pool stick back into the bridge, and it seemed to take the leverage of the shot off from his bad hip. He concentrated his shot on the right side of the one ball at the front of the diamond shape, and he hit the cue ball with enough force to send it slamming into the rack with a loud crack that almost sounded like a gunshot. Three of the balls went down immediately on the break. The one ball landed in the left-side corner pocket with a violent thud. The seven landed gracefully in the left-rear corner pocket. And lastly, the nine ball went spinning down the table and disappeared with a yellow flash into the right-rear corner pocket of the pool table. Malone looked up at Tony's face, which was frozen with a balanced mixture of awe, terror, and disbelief. "Well, kid, thanks for the advice," Malone said, as he stood back upright after the shot. He then walked over to Tony and gave him a nod, patting him on the shoulder. "I figured it was possible that I just might end up learnin' somethin' from you tonight, after all," Malone said.

Tony rubbed the back of his neck, and his eyebrows began fidgeting. "What if I ain't got the whole $250 bucks on me right now?"

Tony asked. Malone had anticipated that this kid had probably been placing bets that he hadn't planned on being in any sort of a position to have to pay for. "I only got $150 on me from beatin' that chump that you saw in here earlier. I don't suppose that maybe you'd settle for a partial payment?" Tony Tyler said and then slowly took a couple of steps back from the pool table.

Malone raised his eyebrows up from under the brim of his hat and said, "Well, the answer to that is quite simple. Just ask Ronny. I'm a very patient man." Suddenly, Ronny came around the table and grabbed Tony by his arms, pinning them behind his back. Malone swung the thick end of his pool stick hard into Tony's ribcage and heard the wind rush out of him as his head flopped forward. He also heard the faint jingling of metal when he hit him with the pool stick. Nick reached inside of Tony's leather jacket and pulled out a set of car keys. Malone leaned in closer to Tony and said, "You got five days to pay me the whole amount, kid, plus interest! I will give you one day for each game that we played. That means that you have until next Thursday night to come up with all the money. Because it's technically Saturday morning, and I'm feelin' lenient. So I figured that I'd give ya a grace period. But I'm takin' the $150 for now, even if it's only for collateral. And if you don't have the rest of the cash by Thursday, your car's gonna become the newest decoration on the floor of the Atlantic Ocean! You got that? And then I just might have another special little surprise in store for you, too! Ronny, do you know which car is his?" Ronny Steiner nodded from behind Tony's shoulder. Tony Tyler then began to fight back hard, trying to break away from the tight hold that Ronny had around his arms, but it was of no use. Over the years, Ronny Steiner had gotten used to ejecting drunk patrons from his establishment that were nearly twice Tony's size whenever they had refused to accept that they had been cut off from the bar. Ronny had spent many years doing push-ups and bench presses in order to deal with any sort of potentially unruly customers.

Malone looked up at Ronny and smiled and then said, "What was that you were sayin' earlier about takin' the garbage out into the back alleyway?" Tony's eyes grew big, and he was still breathing heavily, as sweat began dripping down his reddened face.

"You guys can't do this to me!" Tony yelled loudly. He was half hoping that someone outside might hear him. But there was no point in that now. It had started raining again, and anyone who could be passing by on foot at this hour probably wouldn't be too interested in what might be going on inside of a dimly lit building at almost three o'clock in the morning.

Malone swung at Tony Tyler hard with his right elbow, while his left hand still supported the weight of his body with his cane. The side of his elbow connected directly with the arch on the left side of Tony's jaw. He grunted from the force of the impact and continued to struggle against the strength of Ronny's grip on his arms. They had begun to make their way toward the back exit to the alleyway, and during their struggle, Tony noticed why Malone had never removed his jacket despite all the humidity that had filled the air in the pool hall throughout the night. He saw the glimmering of a silver pistol handle under Malone's left arm, which dimly reflected some of the lighting from above the pool tables. Ronny pushed the back door open with his left foot, never loosening the tight grip that he had on Tony's arms. Malone reached into his jacket and quickly pulled out the pearl-handled silver Colt .45 pistol. He ran his finger across the side of the gun to make sure that the safety was still on. He rapidly turned the gun sideways and then forcefully struck Tony Tyler in the mouth with the bottom side of the handle. Tony spit blood out against the adjacent brick wall, and then Malone quickly hit him once again. This time, the bottom of the pistol connected with Tony's right temple, and the force of the blow caused Ronny to release his tight grip on his arms. Tony was now bent over in the alleyway, and his vision had become blurry from the force of getting hit. Malone raised the pistol one final time and hit Tony Tyler right in the back of his head, just at the base of his spine. He collapsed to the ground, unconscious, and his cheek splashed down into a puddle, as his face made contact with the hard, rain-covered asphalt.

CHAPTER 15

Don't Wait Up

Frank Moniarti rolled down the passenger-side window of the dark blue 1955 Buick Riviera to breathe in some fresh late-night air. Teddy Pazzelli wearily looked over at Moniarti, as the car traveled hypnotically down the expressway.

"Aren't you glad to know now that keeping an eye on Plemagoya has actually paid off?" Teddy asked.

Moniarti kept his eyes forward as the white stripes on the expressway kept dreamily disappearing under the hood of the car. "Yeah, I would've had us pop that little bastard right then and there, if I hadn't been worried about any witnesses comin' around the corner at the wrong time," Moniarti said. "At least, we've got some ideas as to where we might be able to find him now. I will see to it that Detective Farmers gets the license plate number from their car sometime tomorrow. Hopefully, that'll ensure that this little weasel doesn't travel too far away from us in the meantime." Moniarti stifled a yawn and hunched his shoulders in a stretching motion and then said, "I gotta get some sleep. I'm dyin' over here. I don't think that I've actually slept properly in a few days now, and my last words to Meg before I left the house were 'Don't wait up.' And you know how she is. She just gave me a mean look and then shook her head at me."

Teddy Pazzelli began to laugh quietly to himself and then said, "Yeah, I do know how she is. I can actually picture it already."

The early morning air had now become considerably less humid than it had been only a couple of hours ago. Moniarti looked down at his watch as he began to roll his window up. It was now nearly four o'clock in the morning. Frank lit a cigarette with a match and exhaled the smoke out through his nose before he rolled the window back down and threw the extinguished match out onto the expressway. "I'm just glad that we've found him and that we know his basic routine now," Moniarti said, staring out of the side window of the car.

"And once Nicky Malone gets us our new set of wheels, Plemagoya is going to be runnin' in circles around this area like a scared little rodent," Teddy said, as he looked over at Moniarti through the darkness. "We've got this one in the bag, Frankie. I told you that there'd be nothin' to worry about," Teddy Pazzelli said, and his teeth seemed to glow as he smiled in the dark.

Both men then looked ahead at the expressway through the foggy windshield. Teddy put his blinker on to take the next exit, and then he said, "That sure was nice of ya to tell Meg not to wait up. After I drop you off, I gotta go pick Silvia up and take her out to breakfast, and then we gotta go drop some numbers off to Charley. I should be able to get some rest after we get done doin' that."

Moniarti yawned and then rubbed his eyes with the back of his left hand before he quickly flicked the ash off from his cigarette out the window with his other hand. "Don't go runnin' yourself too hard now, Teddy. Otherwise, you could end up turnin' out like me," Frank said, and then he put his chin down against his chest, "old and grumpy!"

Teddy began laughing and then he said, "Yeah, that's good, Frankie! I'll try not to! Now, go ahead and get some sleep. I'll wake ya once we get there. All right?"

Moniarti threw his cigarette out of the car and then rolled the window back up. "Yeah, all right. Sounds good to me," he said, and then he pulled the brim of his hat down over his eyes and moved the car seat back into a more comfortable position.

CHAPTER 16

A Sore Loser

Tony Tyler awoke facedown in the alleyway behind Lucky Nine's Pool Hall. It had stopped raining, and he rubbed the side of his head, as he braced himself up against the wooden fence, trying to rise to his feet. He made it partway up, pushing hard on the ball of each foot, before collapsing back down onto his hands and knees. His jaw ached with a combination of numbness and a shooting pain that went back from his chin over toward the hinge. He began to swivel his head around on his shoulders, and his teeth clicked as he began to open and close his mouth. His jaw didn't seem to be broken, but his mouth and temple were swollen from the blunt force of getting hit with the pistol. He closed his eyes hard, as a spell of dizziness overtook him. The pressure on his arms from supporting the weight of his body revealed a sharp pain in his ribs, and his breathing became increasingly rapid and shallow. He reached up again, attempting to support the weight of his body against the wooden fence, and felt his knees shaking as he slowly began rising to his feet. He stumbled clumsily across the alleyway and braced his body against the brick wall of the building with his shoulder. He reached up with his hand and felt where the narrow part of the magazine on the pistol had split his lip open. He reached into the pocket of his coat and pulled out a white handkerchief and moistened it against the raindrops that had collected against the surface of his leather jacket. Once a small corner of the handkerchief had collected enough moisture, he pulled it away from his shoulder and held it against his mouth. After he pulled the dampened corner of the handkerchief away from his face, it was a bright red color, with rust-colored flakes of dried blood collecting into the fabric of the cloth. *How long have I been out?* he wondered to himself. *I don't even know where the hell I am.* He then began to slowly stumble down the alleyway towards the closest opening into the city.

He reached into the inside pocket of his leather jacket for his car keys, and his hand reached down to the bottom of an empty pocket. He then began feeling around at all the pockets on his leather jacket and down at the front and rear pockets of his blue jeans. "My car keys! My switchblade! My wallet! They're all gone!" he shouted out loud, as he reached the end of the alleyway. He quickly turned around and recalled being dragged out of the back door of the pool hall. He then suddenly remembered the smell of expensive cologne and the gleaming from the handle of a pistol as he closed his eyes, seeing only a flash, before darkness had become his only memory from that point on. He wondered how long he had been lying there in the alleyway and how far the people who had stolen his keys might have gotten from here with his car. He walked two blocks down the street and found the lot where he had parked his light blue 1961 Chevrolet Impala Bubble Top earlier on in the night. First, he saw the same old, white pickup truck that he had remembered parking to the right of, and then there was an empty space where his car had once been, with the pavement having been darkened by the force of spinning tires.

Tony Tyler pulled the handkerchief away from his swollen lip and then stiffly moved his head from side to side.

"Son of a bitch!" he shouted. "My car!" The sound of his voice sharply echoed in the night as he looked up into the starlit sky and gradually lowered his head back down to look into the parking space where his car had once been. He saw something on the pavement faintly glimmering in the humid air. As he walked closer, he found a quarter dollar right in the center of the parking space where his car used to be. He squinted as he picked the coin up off from the ground. *Great, I've just lost my car, and my wallet, and all that I have to show for a long night of pool playing is this lousy quarter? I had 150 bucks in my wallet before those guys took it from me,* Tony thought to himself. However, the twenty-five cents that he had now could potentially do a lot of good for him. It was nowhere near enough to cover the debt that he now owed, but it was enough to call someone to come and pick him up. He put the coin and the bloodied handkerchief into the pocket of his jeans and looked around for any sign of light glimmering through the darkness. *There has to be a phone booth somewhere around here where I can call a cab and then somehow find a way to get a hold of Vinnie to tell him what's just happened,* Tony thought to himself. *Maybe he can get me some money to get my car back.* His shoes began loudly sifting through the gravel. *I just have to figure out where it went to first.* He quickly walked across the dark parking lot and had gone a total of three blocks on foot before he found a phone booth outside of a gas station that had closed down for the night.

He was breathing heavily from the distance of the walk as he closed the door to the phone booth. *I need to get out of here,* he thought to himself. *But how can I do that without any money?* He looked up at the empty street and slowly tried to catch his breath. *Luckily, I found that quarter, so now I can at least call someone. But how am I gonna be able to afford to pay for a taxi? I got nothin' left at this point. Not even my pride.* He grabbed the phonebook and reached down into the pocket of his jeans to pull out the quarter before placing it into the slot of the pay phone.

"There goes a dime's worth," Tony said under his breath and dialed the number for a taxi. After the call was placed, Tony hung the pay phone up with a sweaty hand and heard his change fall into the coin return. He pulled the nickel and dime out and placed them into his pocket. *Twenty minutes until my ride gets here, and only fifteen cents to pay for it with? That's not gonna be nearly enough,* Tony thought to himself. He opened the door to the phone booth and then slowly walked out over toward the road. He sat down on the curb and reached into the side pocket of his leather jacket to light a cigarette.

"At least those bastards didn't steal these things away from me," Tony said to himself, as he lowered his head and extinguished the match under the sole of his shoe.

Several moments later, the fog in the road lit up with the glow of approaching headlights. Tony rose to his feet, shifted his shoulders, and straightened the collar of his jacket. *About time you finally got here,* Tony thought to himself. *Thankfully, it ain't wintertime yet.* He quickly walked over onto the sidewalk and waited impatiently for the approaching taxi to make its way up to where he was standing.

Once the cab pulled up, the driver reached over and rolled down the passenger-side window. "Are you the one that called for a cab?" the driver said in a deep voice.

Tony nodded and stepped closer to the open window. "Where can I take ya at this hour of the night?" the driver said, as he raised his eyebrows inquisitively.

"I need you to give me a lift up to the Skyline Hotel over on Illinois Avenue and Boardwalk," Tony said to the cabdriver, "But I've only got fifteen cents on me. Somebody stole my wallet. I'll have to find a way to pay you the rest of the fare once we get there."

The cabdriver began slowly nodding. "All right, kid," the cabdriver said. "But uh, once we get there, I'm gonna have ya leave that coat in my cab as collateral until you come back with the rest of the fare. Is that a deal?"

Tony looked down at his coat and then back at the cabdriver. He then began nodding before saying, "Yeah, sure, it's a deal. I'm not in too much of a position to argue with you right now. But I have a few friends at that hotel, and trust me, I'm good for every penny that I might end up owin' ya."

The cabdriver tilted his head over to the side and shrugged before looking back forward at the dark street. Tony reached up for the handle to the rear door of the taxi. As he pulled on the latch, he found that the door to the back of the cab was still locked.

The cabdriver began snickering and then said, "All right, but you're gonna end up owin' me even more for this service, too, kid." The driver turned around and unlocked the rear door.

As Tony got into the taxi, he ran his hand up through his hair in frustration. "Owe you for this, too? Like what? Do you want me to give you one of my kidneys or somethin'?" Tony asked.

The cabdriver laughed loudly as the car began slowly traveling down the dark, vacant street. "Just tryin' to loosen you up a bit, kid. There ain't no sense sweatin' nothin' at this hour of the night. I can safely tell ya that much," the cabdriver said, as he slowly looked Tony over in the rearview mirror, and then he looked back forward again, as he turned on the wipers to remove the steam that had collected on the surface of the taxi's windshield.

CHAPTER 17

The Porcelain Blues

Pedro Navilla sat alongside Vincent Plemagoya in the stall of an otherwise empty truck stop restroom. Vincent let out a loud grunt and then forcefully vomited into the toilet. Once his head came back forward, his breathing was heavy and sweat rolled down his face. Pedro handed him over a paper towel to clean himself up with. Vincent wiped his face off and caught his breath. He looked across the stall at Pedro with a sense of violent agitation in his eyes.

"I don't think that you understand, man!" Plemagoya shouted, "I'm gonna own this city one day! All I need to do is to get the cops on my side, and then I got it made!"

Pedro shook his head in annoyance and then replied, "Shut up, man! Just shut up! Can't you see that you've already caused more than enough trouble?"

Vincent leaned back up against the closed door of the bathroom stall. His facial expression suddenly lightened, and his head began to loosely swivel from side to side on his shoulders. "I didn't cause no trouble tonight," he said with a smirk. "I didn't do nothin' wrong at all. It was that guy who threw us out of that place. He must've been in a bad mood or somthin'."

Pedro lowered his eyebrows into a scowl and said, "I ain't talkin' about that stuff! I'm talkin' about that botched job at the jewelry store that you tried to get us to pull off!"

Plemagoya reached up and wiped off the corner of his mouth with his sleeve and then said, "Oh, right, that. Well, at least we're alive and kickin'! Aye, muchacho?" Pedro shook his head, climbed over Vincent, and then exited the bathroom stall.

As Pedro looked himself over in the mirror, he saw that his eyes looked tired and their lids appeared heavy, and his forehead had grown damp with sweat. He reached next to the sink and grabbed a handful of paper towels to wipe off his forehead. Pedro then looked back at the closed door of the bathroom stall.

"I knew that it was a bad idea to go into that place to begin with!" Pedro shouted. He could hear Plemagoya wobbling his shoulders back and forth against the door of the stall.

"You didn't go in nowhere! All you were there for was to take care of the phone lines and to make sure that some of us had a ride across the bridge back into New York!" Plemagoya yelled back.

"Shut up, Vinnie!" Pedro replied, "I shouldn't even be here taking care of you right now! I should still be back relaxin' at that other place we were just at!" Pedro turned the faucet on to splash cold water onto his face. He could hear Plemagoya fumbling around with the handle to the stall door.

"Yeah, well," Vincent said and then stumbled out of the bathroom stall, "like I told you, I'm gonna own this city someday. That place included."

Pedro made eye contact with Plemagoya in the mirror. He lowered his eyebrows and said, "You know those are some mighty big words comin' out of a guy that just got done singin' the porcelain blues! If only the dancin' ladies and that gorilla who threw us out of that joint could see you now! They'd be laughin' too hard to tell you to pour yourself another one!"

Plemagoya's forehead lowered in a fury, as he continued staggering toward Pedro. "They wouldn't be laughin' too hard after I got done with 'em!" Plemagoya said, "You know me well enough to know that there is a time for jokes and a time for respect! That's what's wrong with this city. Nobody here's learned to have any sorta respect for me just yet!"

Vincent Plemagoya came up from behind Pedro and met him face-to-face and then said, "And what about you, Pedro? Have you learned to respect me?"

Pedro allowed his face to form into a loose smile and then said, "Most of the time. But not really at a time like now. You gotta learn to put some kinda limits on yourself. That's what always seems to get you into so much trouble."

Vincent Plemagoya slowly looked down at the floor as he continued to stagger. He looked back up and said, "Limits don't bring any sorta respect for nobody when it really comes down to it, and that's all I ever really wanted from anybody, was just some kinda respect."

Pedro rolled his eyes before looking up at the bathroom ceiling. "Well, good luck with that!" Pedro said, "Nobody really seemed to respect you very much back in New York, either! Don't you remember even half the reasons why we were forced to leave that place?"

Plemagoya turned his head away and then said, "I really don't wanna go into all that right now."

Pedro lowered his eyes away from the bathroom ceiling and said, "Okay, well, if you're feeling better now, I don't know about you, but I could sure use some sleep." He pointed into the bathroom stall and said, "Your hat should still be in there. Do you want me to grab it for you?" Vincent turned back around and slowly nodded as he braced himself up against the sink.

Pedro walked back over into the bathroom stall and took Plemagoya's hat off from the back of the toilet. He placed the hat on top of Vincent's head and began smothering it back and forth, ruffling his hair, and saying, "There. How does that feel, *muchacho*?"

Plemagoya angrily pushed Pedro's hands away and said, "If you ever touch my head like that again, you're dead meat! Got it?"

Pedro snickered as he lowered his hands and said, "This isn't too much fun for you now, is it?"

Plemagoya lowered his forehead, and his pupils began to narrow into an enraged stare. "All right, I ain't got time to fight with you right now. Just get me outta this place," Plemagoya said.

Pedro placed his hands on Vincent's shoulders and quickly spun him around toward the bathroom door. "I was hopin' you'd say that," Pedro said.

As they walked back out into the parking lot of the truck stop, the cool evening air helped to wake Pedro up. Vincent kept his arm around Pedro's shoulder to help keep his body steadied. "I hope that next Saturday night turns out to be this much of a party," Plemagoya said, lifting his head up enough to make eye contact with Pedro.

"Come on, we're parked over this way," Pedro said, and Vincent quickly lifted his arm off from Pedro's shoulder.

"No! You come on! I gave you all this fun tonight at my expense, and you never even thanked me!" Plemagoya said and then pushed his arms down at his sides with agitated fists.

"You're an absolute mess tonight, Vinnie!" Pedro said, "I'm takin' you on back to The Skyline so that you can sleep it off. Otherwise, I'm just gonna have Natty take care of you every Saturday night from now on, and I will be able to enjoy myself without any of these kinds of responsibilities!" Pedro pulled open the passenger-side door to the silver Crestline and said, "All right, now get your ass in there before I change my mind!" He forcefully guided Plemagoya into the car and rolled the window down before closing the door again. "We're riding back with the window down tonight, and that's all there is to it!" Pedro said, and then he started the car up, he threw it into drive, and the tires loudly screeched against the pavement as the car went into motion. He quickly looked over his shoulder and then merged back onto the expressway.

CHAPTER 18

Lights Out

Teddy Pazzelli pulled the dark blue 1955 Buick Riviera up into Frank Moniarti's driveway and began driving up the steady hill that led up to the house. Teddy watched the headlights of the car cutting through the thick fog, and he could hear Frank's snoring becoming unsteady as he pulled up the hill of the driveway. The headlights of the car shone into the lower level of Moniarti's estate; and if Meg was asleep, she should remain that way, as all the windows in the master bedroom overlooked the backyard of the property. Teddy Pazzelli turned around the curve in the driveway and parked the car next to the fountain located in front of Moniarti's house before turning off the engine.

"Frankie?" Teddy said, as he began nudging his snoring passenger, "Frankie, wake up! We're back now!" Moniarti turned over onto his other side, facing toward the window. Teddy rolled his eyes, exhaled a breath of frustration, and said, "Frankie, if you don't wake up, I'm going to be forced to honk the horn, and that could wake your nervous wife up. You wouldn't want that, would you?"

Moniarti rolled back over to face Teddy, and his hat fell off from his head and landed in the back seat of the car. Frank Moniarti quickly snapped awake and leaned forward in his seat. "How the hell did we make it all the way back to Hoboken this quickly?" Moniarti asked wearily.

Teddy Pazzelli shrugged and then said, "Perhaps I'm just kinda sneaky that way. You trust me to drive you around all over the place without ever getting lost. Maybe I have mastered a few shortcuts that you've never noticed before." Teddy reached over into the back seat, retrieved Moniarti's hat, and then asked, "Do you think that you can make it up to the door, all right?"

Frank let out a long yawn, reclined back in the seat of the car, and said, "Yeah, I should be fine. I'm tellin' ya, Teddy. It's nights like these that remind me that I ain't so young anymore."

Teddy Pazzelli let out a soft chuckle and then said, "That's nonsense, Frankie. We're parked right next to the fountain of youth!" He raised his left arm up and extended his thumb over his shoulder toward the fountain located in front of Moniarti's house.

"That's real cute, Teddy," Frank said, as he sat up and placed his hat back on top of his head. "Remind me of that the next time that I throw my back out, would ya?" Teddy Pazzelli grabbed his sides in laughter, as Moniarti opened the passenger-side door of the car. "We both need to get some sleep," Frank said as he stepped out into his driveway. "Billy Walker's funeral is scheduled for later on Sunday. Jimmy said that he should be over here by three in the afternoon that day. Would you mind pickin' us up sometime after four?"

Teddy began slowly nodding and then said, "You got it. Now, go get some sleep! I have to go pick Sylvia up now."

Frank Moniarti closed the passenger-side door of the car and wearily made his way up to the front door of the house.

As he pulled his house keys out from the front pocket of his pants, he watched Teddy circle back around the fountain and begin driving back down the hill of his driveway. *This has been one of the longest nights that I can remember,* Moniarti thought to himself. *But at least we've found him. He may have eluded the police, but he won't get away from us.* Moniarti unlocked the front door of his house and was greeted by the dogs upon his entry. *Meg probably hasn't fed these poor guys in hours,* he thought to himself. *I'll take care of this, and then I gotta get to bed. I know that I don't want to still be this much of a mess by the time that Jimmy gets here on Sunday.* Frank walked into the kitchen and filled their food and water dishes. As the dogs began eating and drinking, Frank shook his head and loosely smiled. "If any of you have to go outside after this, it's gonna have to wait until the morning," he whispered and wearily looked up at the clock above the kitchen sink. It was now a quarter to five. "Oh wait, it *is* the morning already," he whispered to himself. He then began shutting off the lights in the kitchen before walking through the dark house toward the staircase.

Once Frank Moniarti made it up to the top of the stairs, he walked down to the bathroom to switch into his pajamas and brush his teeth. As he moved the toothbrush around in his mouth, he looked at his reflection in the mirror. His eyes were bloodshot and swollen, with thick bags underneath them. It had been days since he had known what a decent night of sleep had felt like, and that was even before Jimmy had any of his problems take place. Frank rinsed his mouth out and then spit down the drain before turning the faucet on to clean the sink out. Taking care of someone like Plemagoya was no easy or pleasant task. He knew that, Jimmy and Teddy knew that, and even Nicholas Malone knew that. Frank ran a small hand towel under some hot water and then placed the dampened towel over his face and felt the tension of the day beginning to escape from his body. *Out of all the places that might've gotten knocked over that day and out of all the people on the face of the planet that could've been a target for that sort of thing, why Fossgate's? Why then? And why Jimmy?* Moniarti thought to himself, as he pulled the dampened towel away from his face. He looked back at his reflection in the mirror and lowered his eyebrows. *I hope that I get the chance to ask Plemagoya that, along with whoever else that he was workin' with. Nobody threatens the safety of my family and then just casually walks away afterwards.*

Frank Moniarti turned the light off in the upstairs bathroom and then slowly and quietly began walking down the hallway toward the bedroom. *There's no way that Meg could've waited up this long for me,* he thought to himself. *After all, I specifically told her not to.* He opened the door to the bedroom and slowly pushed it open further. He saw his wife sleeping soundly on her side, facing away from him.

He smiled as he lifted back the covers on the bed. *Now, if I can just lie down without waking her up, I can avoid getting bombarded with all sorts of questions.* As he silently rested his head against his pillow, lying perfectly still, he began staring up at the ceiling. *It shouldn't take more than a couple more days before Malone calls me to tell me that the car's ready,* Frank thought to himself. *But that'll all work itself out. In the meantime, I gotta figure out what I can say or do for Billy Walker's widow. He wasn't quite as lucky as Jimmy was. Hell, Jimmy might not even still be with us if it wasn't for him.* Frank Moniarti rolled over on his side and looked over at his sleeping wife. *It looks like we're all pretty lucky compared to what had happened to Billy. Or compared to what's gonna happen to Plemagoya as a result of bein' so reckless. I can rest assured of that.* He closed his eyes, rolled over onto his back, and then fell fast asleep.

CHAPTER 19

Opportunity Knocks

Several blocks east from the campus of the University of Toledo, in the Old West End District, two men who were dressed in dark clothing drove down Bancroft Street in a Divco Milk Delivery Truck.

"Good thing they're payin' us a pretty penny to be drivin' all the way down here from Detroit in this heap of shit in the middle of the night," Leroy "Sly" Robinson said, as he shook his head in the passenger seat of the truck.

"There ain't no turnin' back now, Sly. Mr. Malone got his orders, and we've got ours. Just don't go slammin' the door on your way out, and we'll be all right," Doyle Reynolds said, as he pulled onto Robinwood Avenue and then put the milk truck into park in front of an old Victorian-style home. Sly Robinson looked through his half rolled-down window and saw a black 1959 Cadillac Coupe de Ville parked in a driveway across the street. The car in the driveway sat evenly, without any sort of a hill, which would make putting the car into neutral and pushing it out of the driveway a lot easier, without the fear of the car rolling backwards into another parked vehicle.

"Don't this car belong to somebody who owes quite a sizable gambling debt to Mr. Malone?" Sly asked, as he looked over to see Doyle nodding.

"That would definitely explain why he left us with a spare key to it the last time that he was around," Sly said.

"That's just how it goes sometimes. Opportunity knocks, and you take it," Doyle said, as he leaned down to check the side mirror, looking for any approaching headlights. "Looks like we're good to go. Better make this quick," Doyle said, as he turned off the engine to the milk truck.

"Roger that, Jack," Sly said, as he reached into the glove compartment and pulled out the duplicated car key and then placed it inside of his pocket. "Just a quick creeping in through the shadows of the trees, and she's all ours," Sly said, as he smiled over at Doyle and then patted him on the shoulder.

Sly Robinson reached into the back of the truck and retrieved a small toolbox and two sets of gardening gloves; and he then reached back again to grab two glass bottles of milk. "All right, just like we talked about," Sly said, as he put on a pair of gardening gloves. "I'll go first, and you wait until you see that I got the door open. Then, after I get in and put the car into neutral, just give it a push. And don't forget to give these suckers their milk. Something's gotta help to brighten their day after they find that their car's gone." Sly lifted his eyebrows and passed a pair of gardening gloves over to Doyle, and then he gently set the two glass bottles of milk down onto the floorboard of the truck.

"I swear you like doin' this sorta thing to people way too much sometimes," Doyle said, as he looked past Sly at the Cadillac with his mouth formed into a playful smile.

"Hey, it's just a matter of whistlin' while we're workin'. There ain't nothin' wrong with that," Sly said, as he gently opened the door to the truck and began to rapidly sprint up the driveway toward the house, careful to remain hidden within the shadow of the large tree that sat in the front yard of the property. Thankfully, the leaves that had fallen to the ground were still damp, and that helped to eliminate the threat of any sort of a crunching sound underneath their feet.

Once Sly made it up the driveway to the Cadillac, he remained hidden as he quietly set the small toolbox next to the car and pulled out the duplicate key. As he slowly pulled the door to the Cadillac open, he nodded at Doyle as he gently picked up the small tool-box from the ground. Doyle Reynolds quietly got out of the truck with the two glass bottles of milk in his gloved hands. He then cra-dled them up in his arms to prevent them from rattling against one another. He looked both ways before crossing the street, and he could hear the faint sound of a dog barking far off in the distance. He looked around to admire the colors of the autumn leaves that had collected on the lawns. *Damn, that looks like gold,* he thought to himself. Once he had made it up to the front end of the Cadillac, he silently set the two glass bottles of milk on the cement driveway; and then he saw Sly nodding to him through the windshield as the brake lights went on. There was a faint popping sound as the car went into neutral; and then Doyle gave the front end of the Cadillac a hard nudge with one of his broad shoulders, sending it rolling down the driveway in reverse. The car silently came to a stop in the middle of the street, and Sly watched as Doyle gently set the two glass milk bottles on the front porch of the house before rapidly walking back down the driveway. Doyle then wiped the sweat off from his forehead and positioned himself behind the car to push it a more comfortable distance of at least three houses away before allowing Sly to start up the engine.

After the car was a safer distance of about three houses away, Doyle walked up to the driver-side window and whispered, "You owe me a cheeseburger when we get back." Sly Robinson nodded to him and smiled before reaching down to start the car with the dupli-cate key. Doyle then sprinted his way back over to the Divco Milk Delivery Truck and drove around the block to follow Sly westbound down Bancroft Street. Once they were in a more secluded area, off from northbound Interstate 75, they would switch the license plates. A New Jersey dealership license plate would then be installed, and the old Ohio license plate would be soaked in turpentine and then get crushed up by a vice, before being neatly disposed of in Lake Erie on their way back to Detroit.

CHAPTER 20

Sunday, October 14, 1962
Psalm for a Fallen Hero

Teddy Pazzelli turned the dark blue 1955 Buick Riviera onto Pacific Avenue and parked down the street from St. Nicholas of Tolentine Church. Frank Moniarti turned around from the passenger seat to make eye contact with his son.

"I know that this isn't gonna be easy for you, Jimmy," Frank said. "But most of the police force are gonna be inside of there to pay their respects. Even if you don't feel too comfortable at first, at least know that you're gonna be safe. Okay?"

James Moniarti closed his eyes and then rapidly nodded. He turned to face the window before opening his eyes again and then said, "I just still feel really bad for his wife and his kids, ya know?"

Frank lowered his eyes and let out a sigh before saying, "That's perfectly understandable. But at least you're here to be able to say somethin' about that. As for the people who were responsible for doin' this, just leave that part up to us. We'll probably find a way to corner 'em before the police do."

Teddy turned off the engine to the car and then said, "Let's just avoid saying anything about that once we get out of the car, okay?"

Pazzelli smiled over at Frank and James, as he pulled the key out of the ignition.

"Yeah," James said as he looked down at his knees, "after this is over, we've got all the time in the world to figure everything else out."

Frank looked over into the side mirror to straighten his hat and then asked, "Everybody just about ready?"

James looked back up, made eye contact with his father, and then said, "Yeah, let's go get this taken care of." Teddy Pazzelli opened his car door first, and then the two other men got out of the car.

As the three men stepped out onto the sidewalk, Frank looked up at the sky. "It sure turned out to be a nice night," he said. The sun was now setting low in the sky, and the clouds were reflecting soft shades of orange and gold. James took a moment out to button up his brown sport coat that he was wearing over his light blue dress shirt before the three men began walking towards the church. The spires on top of the colossal cathedral had suddenly caused James Moniarti to stand in astonishment before crossing the intersection at South Tennessee Avenue.

"Ya still with us, Jimmy?" Teddy Pazzelli called back over his shoulder.

"Of course," James replied. He looked down from the golden crosses on top of the red roof of the stone structure and down past the large stained glass windows and then straight ahead toward the vast group of people who were filing in through the three pairs of large wooden doors. After they had climbed the front stairs leading up to the cathedral, Frank Moniarti held open the closest wooden door to them under the right-side doorway arch and lowered the brim of his hat down so that his face was momentarily concealed between his hat and the chest portion of his black trench coat.

There was a small draft while walking inside the church, and there was the faint yet sweet smell of burnt candle wax that had lingered in the cool air from the previous services that were held that day. People solemnly walked in single file lines, dipping their hands into holy water before doing the sign of the cross and kneeling to the altar before they were seated. The first three rows were filled with uniformed police officers, who all kept their hats stationed down in their laps. Frank Moniarti momentarily stopped in the center aisle as he caught a glimpse of Betsy Walker in the front row from behind. He then continued walking on, following James and Teddy to the first available row behind the uniformed police officers. Frank and the two other men followed the example of the police officers and sat quietly with their heads pointed downward, and their hats were all stationed down in their laps.

James Moniarti raised his eyes upwards to view the stained glass portraits that were contained within the semidome above the altar and then lowered his eyes back down to see a bald, heavyset priest making his way up to the podium on the left side of the altar. He wore a blue-and-white vestment and kept his eyes fixed down at a prayer book as he walked past the front of the altar.

He then cleared his throat before he stepped up to the microphone and said, "Thank you all for joining us this evening, ladies and gentlemen. My name is Father Henry McMillan, and we are gathered here tonight to honor the memory and the heroic legacy of Patrolman William Edward Walker."

James suddenly felt a lump growing in his throat and lowered his head back down in silence. Although he hadn't actually personally witnessed Patrolman Walker's life coming to an end, there was still an element of fear that had made itself known deep inside of him. He kept remembering all the terrible feelings of helplessness and uncertainty that had overtaken him during the robbery and began to sympathize with what Billy Walker must have felt like upon entering into the showroom of Fossgate's Fine Jewelry at that fateful moment.

James looked away from the podium and saw a table covered in a white cloth that held pictures of the Walker family, aged pictures of Billy serving as an altar boy in this very church and pictures of Billy's graduations from high school and the police academy, pictures from his wedding day, and a solid brass urn that contained his cremated remains. James moved his eyes back and forth across the contents of the table, studying all the portraits of the late policeman. His sandy-brown hair was neatly trimmed into a crew cut, with thick eyebrows above his clear blue eyes, which added a sense of radiance to a smile that served to enhance his round chin and sturdy jawline.

He was in the prime of his life and far too young to die, James thought to himself. *If only the robbers could somehow see what I see here tonight. They've caused so many people so much pain.* James then looked back over toward the podium to hear the priest's sermon.

After Father McMillan had concluded his introductory sermon for the service, he raised his head up to view the people in the congregation, and then he lowered his head in silence for a brief moment before he lifted his head back up and moved his eyes over to the right. He then lifted his arm up over the podium before speaking, "Now, we will hear a reading from the Book of Psalms by Police Chief Marty Albertson." The priest's voice echoed throughout the cathedral as Albertson made his way up to the podium. The police chief reached into the pocket of his jacket, pulled out his reading glasses, and turned a few pages in the prayer book, before looking up from the podium at the large group of people in attendance. His eyes then slowly lowered back down to the podium, and he began reading Psalm 55 from the prayer book:

> Listen to my prayer, O God.
> Do not ignore my cry for help!
> Please listen and answer me,
> For I am overwhelmed by my troubles.
> My enemies shout at me,
> Making loud and wicked threats.
> They bring trouble on me
> And angrily hunt me down.
> My heart pounds in my chest.
> The terror of death assaults me.
> Fear and trembling overwhelm me,
> And I can't stop shaking.
> Oh, that I would fly away and rest!
> I would fly far away
> To the quiet of the wilderness.
> How quickly I would escape—
> Far from this wild storm of hatred.
> Confuse them, Lord, and frustrate their plans,

For I see violence and conflict in the city.
Its walls are patrolled day and night against
invaders,
But the real danger is wickedness within the city.
Everything is falling apart;
Threats and cheating are rampant in the streets.

Marty Albertson paused as he looked up from the podium and focused his eyes on the dimly shadowed figures of Teddy Pazzelli and Frank and James Moniarti, who were seated three rows behind the uniformed police officers; and then his eyes moved over to Betsy Walker and her two young children. His eyes then quickly circled back towards the three sets of wooden doors and the stained glass windows near the pipe organ toward the back of the cathedral before returning to complete his reading of Psalm 55 from the prayer book on the podium.

After Police Chief Marty Albertson left the podium, there had been several other memorial speeches that were given by fellow officers and family members before Father McMillan returned to the podium with his final thoughts of comfort and the concluding prayer. As the people inside the church began rising to their feet, Frank Moniarti had spotted Chief Albertson and Mayor Antill seated further down in the front row from Betsy Walker and the two children. They had been separated from each other by over half a dozen uniformed police officers. As people slowly began to empty out of the cathedral, Frank began to make his way up to the front row.

He watched as Father McMillan came down to greet Betsy Walker with a hug and overheard him say, "Many blessings upon you, my child, and upon your loved ones during this incredibly difficult time. Please know that you are always welcome here if there is ever anything that we can do for you." He then nodded at the children and walked over to speak with the mayor and the police chief.

Frank Moniarti approached Betsy Walker slowly, keeping his hat gently pressed against his chest. "I am so sorry, Mrs. Walker." He began and then solemnly looked downward before continuing, "Twenty-three is way too young to have something like this happen."

He then lifted his eyes back up to meet with her veiled face before he continued, "My son was in there, too."

Betsy turned her head towards James Moniarti and saw him slowly nodding. "But he and several other people are still alive because of your husband's bravery," Frank said. "Nobody here tonight will ever forget what he sacrificed for their safety. I just thought that you should be made aware of that."

Betsy Walker remained silent for a moment, briefly looking down at her children who were next to her on the long wooden bench before returning her look towards Frank. "Thank you," she said in a trembling voice, and Frank Moniarti nodded respectfully before turning around to walk back down the aisle.

"We're all very sorry that this happened," James said, and then he and Teddy both nodded to her before turning around to follow Frank out of the church.

Marty Albertson then approached Betsy Walker, looking at her softly and warmly. He spoke in a radiant voice, "On behalf of the Atlantic City Police Department and the honest and hardworking citizens of this city, our most sincere condolences go out to you during your time of loss, Mrs. Walker." Betsy slowly nodded from behind her black veil. Marty Albertson reached back and took a small white box from Mayor Antill. "We wanted you to have this as a keepsake," Albertson said, as he passed the box over to her. "I want you to know that your husband not only once was but will always be hailed as a hero in our department."

Betsy Walker opened the small box to find an oval-shaped object that was concealed by a folded white silk cloth. As she gently pulled the cloth containing the object out from the box, it became partially unraveled. There was a faint gleam of metal that radiated from behind it, and she slowly pulled the cloth away to find that it contained her husband's police badge. It had recently been cleaned and polished right down to the center, where it depicted The Great Seal of the State of New Jersey. "His acts of bravery will never be forgotten," Albertson said and then leaned down to embrace her.

She then turned her head to face Mayor George Antill, who placed his hand on Marty Albertson's shoulder. "Come see us if you ever need anything, Betsy. We're always here for you," the mayor said.

And then, Betsy Walker slowly nodded before she watched both men walk side by side out of the cathedral.

CHAPTER 21

A Bit of Sound Advice

Natty Rosebrook looked out from the blinds in the front window of his office at the used car dealership and saw a pair of headlights circling around the parking lot before coming to a stop near the front door of his garage. He then saw the rear door of a taxi quickly swing open, and Tony Tyler stepped out onto the gravel in the front parking lot. Natty closed the blinds in the window and walked over towards the customer service entry door. The sound of Natty's hard-soled shoes against the cement floor of the entryway were overpowered by the sound of frantic knocking at the hardwood front door. Natty unbolted the lock and pulled the door open slowly.

"Tony? What are you doing here? We're closed!" Natty said, "If you're lookin' to buy a car, you're gonna have to come back tomorrow."

Tony Tyler firmly pushed his hand against the door. "Don't mess around with me right now, Natty!" Tony shouted, "I'm really in a lotta trouble here! And I need your help!"

Natty Rosebrook slowly pulled the hardwood door open a little further and then said, "All right, what's on your mind, Tony? I was just about to head on home for the night."

Tony stepped in through the doorway and rolled his shoulders in an attempt to shake his unbearable level of tension. "Have you seen Vinnie around?" Tony asked, as he was still struggling to catch his breath.

"That all depends on what you might be wantin' to see him for," Natty said with an inquisitive look. The two men walked side by side back into the office. "Is everything all right?" Natty asked.

Tony Tyler quickly shook his head back and forth and said, "No, not at all! Far from it! I went looking for him last night after someone stole my car, and I couldn't seem to find him around anywhere! He wasn't answerin' his phone up in his hotel room or nothin'!"

Natty's facial expression suddenly loosened, and then he said, "Geez, I'm sorry to hear that, Tony. Is that the same light blue 1961 Chevrolet Impala Bubble Top that I sold ya about six months ago?"

Tony lowered his head and began nodding; then he said, "Yeah, I had to take a cab back to the hotel and then woke Pedro up in the middle of the night to help me pay for the ride. It was pretty embarrassing."

Natty began slowly opening the wooden door located on the back wall to his office. "Keep on talkin'. I'm still listenin'," Natty said. Tony remained less than two feet behind Natty's right shoulder as he followed him into the back room.

The room behind the office had the same wooden paneling on its walls as the office. There was the linger of stale cigarette smoke in the air, and Tony could see a card table set up in the middle of the room, with two steel folding chairs positioned on opposite sides of it. There was a deck of playing cards sprawled out across the table and several more steel folding chairs sat it a closed position against the wall to his left. There was a maroon leather sofa straight ahead of him, and a small wooden stand held a dim lamp that radiated a soft lighting in the room. Natty stopped walking about a foot in front of the card table, and as soon as Tony Tyler fully entered into the back room, the door behind him suddenly slammed shut. Vincent Plemagoya swiftly and silently swung a baseball bat square against the center of Tony's back and then quickly turned the bat sideways, pushing it hard against Tony's body, forcefully ramming him forward towards the leather sofa that was located on the other side of the room.

Tony landed face-first into the backrest of the leather sofa with a grunt and immediately turned around to see Vincent Plemagoya repositioning the end cap of the Louisville Slugger against the thinly carpeted floor. He placed the palms of both his hands against the knob of the bat in order to support the weight of his body.

"So what brings you around here to this place so late into the night?" Plemagoya asked, as he lowered his head and raised his left eyebrow.

"Vinnie! What are you doin' here? Natty didn't say nothin' about you bein' back here! And last night, Pedro said that he hadn't seen you around, either!" Tony said, quickly grabbing for a pillow off from the sofa and placing it in his lap. He wanted the security of having something to pad his face with, just in case the baseball bat came back up from the floor. "Where have you been lately?" Tony asked. "Somebody stole my car last night, and when I came lookin' for you to try and get it back, you were nowhere to be found!"

Plemagoya lifted the end cap of the baseball bat back up from the floor and used it to push the brim of his white hat further up his forehead. "Maybe Pedro *had* seen me, and maybe he hadn't. That should really be the least of your worries right now, Tony," Plemagoya said. And then he rested the barrel of the baseball bat up against his right shoulder before he continued, "I don't know as if I exactly believe you when you tell me that your car had been stolen. Lost, yes. Stolen, no. If that happened, why didn't you go to the cops? What made you want to try to find me instead?"

Tony Tyler nervously cleared his throat and reached up to rub the back of his neck before he said, "Well, ya see, it all started when I was down at the pool hall. These two guys just kept on…"

Vincent Plemagoya raised his left hand, and Tony immediately ceased in telling his story. "Let me give you a bit of sound advice regarding where and when you should be placing a bet, and where and when you shouldn't. Please, allow me to use my Louisville translator here for better clarification," Plemagoya said, as he began to tap the baseball bat against the palm of his left hand.

"Whoa, Vinnie! Wait! I can explain everything that happened, if you'll only give me the chance!" Tony said, as he began squirming further back into the backrest of the leather sofa. Plemagoya quickly turned to his right and smashed the bat directly into the folding center of the card table. Playing cards and poker chips flew up into the air before scattering across the floor, and the card table buckled under the blow from the baseball bat. Tony quickly lifted his knees up in fright and shielded his face with the pillow from the sofa.

"Relax," Plemagoya said sternly. "I was only swattin' at a bug that was on the table."

Tony lowered the pillow away from his face and placed his feet back down onto the floor, and then he said, "Hey! Look, Vinnie, you still owe me the rest of my cut from the job that we did over at Fossgate's! If it wasn't for me, we would've gotten pinched for that already!"

Vincent Plemagoya looked over at Natty, who was still clinging to the wall, startled from the force of the card table collapsing. "Well, I've been holdin' out on him the whole time. Haven't I, Natty?" Plemagoya asked, as he watched Natty quickly begin nodding before returning his eyes over to Tony. "All righty then, if you wouldn't mind givin' me a little more time to gather up your money, I could probably have it for you in the next couple of days," Plemagoya said, and then he leaned his head back over his shoulder. "Now, Natty, if you want to show Tony back up front, I will even gladly give him a hand counting out what I owe him, once I have the whole amount with me again."

Natty Rosebrook began walking over towards the leather sofa and said, "All right, Tony, on your feet. We'll be able to sort all this out some other night. Hopefully, before whoever stole, or *won*, your car travels too far away with it."

Tony Tyler rose to his feet, keeping his eyes fixed on Plemagoya, and he said, "I still don't know if I trust you to deliver it to me, Vinnie. You said you'd have it in the next couple of days. That means that I should have what you owe me in my pocket by Tuesday night. And I won't have to hang around no more pool halls just tryin' to make enough money to stay alive with."

Plemagoya grinned and nodded and then said, "Just ask Natty. I always pay my debts on time, don't I?"

Tony looked over towards Natty. "Well, there is the matter of that one time when you…" Natty suddenly stopped speaking as he watched Plemagoya raise the baseball bat, swinging it hard against the base of Tony Tyler's neck, causing him to stumble, before loudly collapsing unconscious against the thinly carpeted floor.

"All right, Natty, I guess that I owe you a new card table. But how about it? Weren't you proud of me for that swing?" Plemagoya asked, as he turned to face Natty, who kept his eyes lowered on Tony as he remained motionless on the floor.

"Absolutely," Natty said, "we'll have to drag that table out to the dumpster together later on. But we can't just leave Tony here like this…Where do you plan on takin' him?"

Vincent Plemagoya's face grew into a wide grin, and then he said, "You just leave that up to me…I know of a place. Where'd you park your car?"

* * *

Natty Rosebrook pushed the button for the automatic garage door opener and then looked over at Vincent Plemagoya, who held tightly onto the steel handle of a large wagon. "Ya know, Vinnie, I usually use that thing for carryin' old blown-out tires out to the back area from the service garage. But never for anything like this," Natty said, as he looked behind Plemagoya to see the unconscious body of Tony Tyler resting sideways in the wagon.

"Just go unlock the car. I'll take care of the rest," Plemagoya said and then followed Natty across the gravel front parking lot. The wheels on the wagon left a trail in the dirt and gravel, and Vincent had to pull hard on the steel handle to get the wagon over towards the car. Natty had parked over a hundred feet away from the garage door, and Plemagoya could feel the strain in the muscles of his shoulders as he pulled the wagon with both hands. He kept his back turned towards Natty as he continued across the parking lot. "Couldn't you have parked a little bit closer, Natty?" Plemagoya asked, pulling his hat off and dropping it down onto Tony, before wiping the sweat off from his forehead.

"Hey, I didn't know what you had in store for us here tonight. I never really do, to tell you the truth," Natty said, as he pulled his car keys from the front pocket of his plaid pants. He unlocked the passenger-side door of his forest-green 1960 Pontiac Catalina four-door sedan with his keys and then reached back inside to pull the pin up on the rear door. He looked over to see Vincent lift his hat up off from Tony's body before placing it back on top of his head. Natty then opened up the rear-side door of the car and helped Plemagoya lift Tony Tyler's unconscious body from the wagon into the back seat. After they closed the door, the two men walked over to the other side of the car.

"Just keep headin' east on US 30. I'll tell ya where we're goin' along the way," Plemagoya said with a devious smirk, and he opened the rear-side door to climb into the back seat with Tony.

"Okay then," Natty said, as he pulled the car keys back out from his pocket, "this night seems to be full of all sorts of surprises."

* * *

It had turned out to be a mild evening outside as the temperature had continued to drop from earlier on that day. A tall, thin man with short blond hair stepped out from a bar onto the sidewalk near the corner of Mississippi Avenue. He put a pair of dark sunglasses over his eyes and reached down into his black leather vest to fetch a pack of cigarettes. Above the flame from his silver Zippo, he could faintly see a pair of headlights approaching through the lenses of his dark sunglasses. After the car came closer, he watched it pass by him before turning around in the middle of the street just before it would have reached the boardwalk. He looked down the road and watched the car revving before being thrown into gear, and then the tires loudly screeched against the dry pavement. The tall, thin man quickly pulled his sunglasses off and saw a forest-green four-door car briefly slow down in front of him, and the rear door flung open.

"*Banzai!*" a shrill voice shouted out from the back seat of the car, as a foot kicked a young man in a leather jacket out onto the sidewalk. And then the car door slammed shut, and the car quickly drove off into the night.

The tall, thin man with the short blond hair dropped his cigarette down onto the sidewalk and sprinted over to see if the young man was still alive. He stopped and stood over the young man's body and saw that he was still breathing. "Hey, buddy, are you okay? Looks like you just took one hell of a fall!" the tall, thin man said and watched as the young man's eyelids began to flutter. Tony Tyler awoke to see the tall, thin man standing over him and the blurred vision of a purple neon sign moving back and forth above the man's head. "Do you need help? Look, I really think you should see a doctor. I will call inside and get you an ambulance," the man said. As Tony opened his eyes further, he saw that the moving purple shape on the sign was an anchor that lit up from three different angles. It kept moving back and forth rhythmically, like a pendulum. The tall, thin man ran back over and flung the door to the bar open. "Hey! I need some help out here! Somebody just got hurt!" the man shouted into the bar. There were two men inside who walked away from playing a game of blackjack to come outside, and he watched as the bartender quickly picked up the phone from behind the bar, plugging his other ear, as he called for paramedics.

"Hello! Operator?! I need an ambulance sent over near the corner of Boardwalk and Mississippi Avenue right away! That's right! Send it to Maple's Anchor! There's been some sort of an accident!" the bartender shouted, and then he quickly hung up the phone and ran out in front of the bar to see the injured young man lying flat on his back against the sidewalk.

CHAPTER 22

Motivational Skills

It was a busy night on the other side of Lake Erie. In an abandoned warehouse that overlooked the Detroit River, the black 1959 Cadillac Coupe de Ville sat hoisted up three feet above the concrete floor. A shower of sparks landed around a welding helmet, as Sly Robinson put the finishing touches on what he was now considering to be one of his greatest achievements. His ability to remove any identifiable features from a stolen car quickly and thoroughly had been what had eventually earned him the nickname of "Sly" with most of his business associates. After turning off his blowtorch, he slid out from underneath the car and lifted up the faceplate to the welding helmet.

"Hey, Doyle!" Sly shouted. "Once I put this beauty back down onto the floor, give it a turnover for me, would ya? This thing should run even better than it did last night when we boosted her! And they say that it's the mileage that matters!" Sly let out a strong belly laugh that continued as he pulled the faceplate shut on his welding helmet. There was a bright flash as he reignited the blowtorch.

Doyle Reynolds sat back at a desk directly across from the driver-side door of the Cadillac, eating a bag of popcorn. He stopped eating for a moment and pulled a handkerchief out from the front pocket of his camel-hair coat. "All right, but you still ain't told me how we're gonna get this thing all the way over to the East Coast from here without attractin' too much attention to us," Doyle said. "We don't usually go that far. There's a lot that can go wrong with us headin' a distance like that."

Sly rolled out from underneath the car after he finished welding and said, "You just let me worry about that, old friend. I've got everything under control. All I need right now is for you to turn the engine over for me so I can make sure that everything is runnin' properly." Sly rolled back underneath the car and continued working.

The keys to the Cadillac were dangling from a nail in the wall behind the desk. Doyle got up from his seat and pulled them off from the wall. He was a large, muscular man, who had been working with Sly Robinson in the stolen automobile industry for just over three years now. It was absolutely essential to have additional muscle on your side in a business that was this risky. "So I guess that I'll just be findin' everything out as we go along," Doyle said under his breath, as he opened the driver-side door of the Cadillac. "All right. Just tell me when," he said, as he took a seat behind the steering wheel and stuck the key into the ignition that was located on the dashboard.

Sly rolled out from underneath the car and disappeared from Doyle's view behind the open hood. "Just one more little adjustment," Sly said. "And now!" Doyle turned the key over in the ignition, and the car started up with no hesitation. "Give it a good rev for me!" Sly commanded, and Doyle pushed his foot down on the accelerator. Even while the engine was revving, the car sounded quieter than it had the night before. A sudden look of jubilant satisfaction had begun radiating across Sly's face. "Yee-haa!!!" he shouted, as he clasped his hands together and lightly jumped up off the ground. He felt the back of his head connect with the bottom of the open hood. "Oww! Shit!" he yelled. Sly was still rubbing the back of his head when he walked up to where Doyle was seated in the car. "Okay, you can shut it off now," Sly said as he pulled a cigar stub out from the chest pocket of his light blue jumpsuit. He spit on the ground and then lit the cigar stub with a brass Zippo. He blew a thick cloud of smoke up towards the ceiling and looked back at Doyle who was still seated in the car. "This thing purrs just like a newborn baby kitten now!" Sly said excitedly. "As for gettin' this thing over to where it belongs, we're gonna be havin' some help with that. The first priority was gettin' this thing in proper runnin' order!" Doyle killed the engine and handed the keys over to Sly. "I'll be borrowin' a semi to pick this thing up here tomorrow," Sly said. He flicked the ash off from the end of his cigar before he continued, "In the meantime, let's call it a night. I'd say that we've worked hard enough for one day."

Doyle opened the door and got out of the car. "So when were you gonna tell me more about all these special features that we're havin' installed?" Doyle asked.

Sly let out a hard laugh and put his hand on Doyle's shoulder. "Patience, my friend," Sly said. "I'll be happy to tell you about all those things on our way over there. I want it to be almost as much of a surprise for you as it's gonna be for them. We've got a special stop to make along the way in Pennsylvania. And then this thing should be ready to go!" Sly walked towards the back of the car and pulled a gray tarp out from the trunk of the Cadillac. "You mind givin' me a hand with this thing?" Sly asked.

Doyle just shrugged and then began to help with covering the car. Then he walked back over to the desk, grabbed his bag of popcorn, and began turning out all the lights. "It must be somethin' mighty impressive," he said to Sly.

"We'll comfortably be able to tell our customers that this is our best work yet," Sly said and then began laughing, and they both disappeared through the doorway of the warehouse in a thick cloud of cigar smoke.

PART 2

Monday, October 15 to Thursday, October 18, 1962

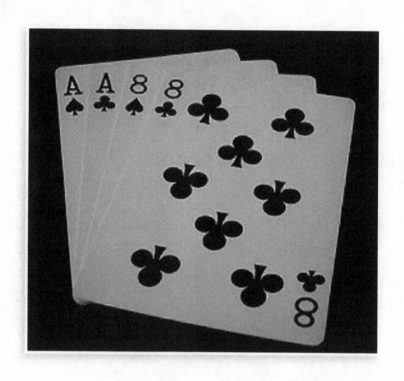

CHAPTER 23

Monday, October 15, 1962
Handle with Care

Sly Robinson gazed outside at the loading dock from a rusty window frame inside the old abandoned warehouse that overlooked the Detroit River. "They should be here anytime now," he said and then turned away from the window just before lighting up a cigar stub.

Doyle Reynolds sat behind a desk on the other side of the room reading a newspaper and said, "If they ran into any sort of a problem, I'm sure that we'd know somethin' about it by now."

Sly exhaled a cloud of cigar smoke toward the ceiling and then said, "I know. I'm just kinda nervous about them drivin' up to the loading dock in broad daylight like this." He turned back to face the window as he began pacing across the floor.

"Maybe that's the reason that they're runnin' behind schedule," Doyle said. "They're waitin' for the sun to start goin' down so that they can be more discreet about what we're doin' here." Doyle folded up the newspaper and then centered it on the surface of the desk.

"You're probably right," Sly said.

Doyle stood up from his chair and then stretched out his arms. "I can't say that I slept very well last night," he said. "Too much that's still left to do with this whole thing." Doyle motioned his head towards the tarp that covered the Cadillac and then said, "We still gotta uncover that thing before we try to load it up into the truck."

Sly quickly turned around and began nodding. "Yeah, I know," he said, as he walked over to extinguish his cigar in the ashtray that sat up in the window sill.

As Sly and Doyle pulled the tarp off from the black 1959 Cadillac Coupe de Ville, the body of the car reflected radiantly against the lighting from the fluorescent lamps on the ceiling of the warehouse. "Still sparklin' like a diamond," Sly said, as the two men fully removed the tarp from the car. "You watched me put a fresh coat of wax on her right after we got here, and I still don't see one single smudge."

Doyle set the tarp over by the desk. "Neither do I," he said, as he began walking back towards the car.

Sly abruptly looked over his shoulder at the dim rays of light from the setting sun that shone in through the window. "Either that's the tarp still crumpling against the floor or that's the sound of our truck pulling up along the gravel outside," Sly said before he rapidly turned around and darted over towards the window. His face suddenly grew animated with excitement. "Hey, Doyle! You'd better come take a look at this!" Sly said, and then Doyle walked over to the window and shielded the setting sun away from his view with his hand. They saw a silver Dodge semitruck slowly driving over the gravel path that led up to the loading dock of the warehouse. Sly patted Doyle on the shoulder and then said, "All right, this is our cue! They're gonna bring the truck up, pull it around, and then get their car out of the back of it. Then, all I need you to do is to back the truck up to the loading dock, and I will pull our car up into the back of the truck! Got it?"

Doyle slowly turned his head to face Sly and said, "But this isn't exactly *our* car. It's Mr. Malone's car, technically speaking."

Sly lowered his eyebrows and said, "Shut up! You know what I mean!"

Doyle slowly followed Sly across the warehouse to open the door to the loading dock. As the door slowly opened, the setting sun began filling the warehouse with a brilliant orange-and-red light.

There was a faint squeaking sound as the silver Dodge semitruck gradually came to a stop, and then two men in dark gray suits exited the truck and walked towards the back of the trailer. Doyle walked over towards the service door and down the stairs towards the truck, and Sly covered his eyes from the last rays of the setting sun. He squinted his eyes to see the two men in dark gray suits waving out from the window of a light blue 1961 Chevrolet Impala Bubble Top as it kicked up dust while they hastily drove back down the dirt road in front of the warehouse.

CHAPTER 24

Code of Conduct

Police Chief Marty Albertson stood behind his desk talking to Captain David Van Bulkem from across his office. "I need to see Detectives Jacob Farmers and Stanley Morris. Could you please send then both down here on your way home?" Albertson said.

Captain Van Bulkem nodded as he slowly sipped back the rest of his coffee from a foam cup before discarding it into the wastebasket next to Albertson's desk. "Way ahead of you, chief," Van Bulkem said. "I gave them a quick briefing when they got in this morning, but it's always better to have the same information twice than never at all."

The captain got up from his chair, nodded to his supervisor, and then closed the door behind him. Captain Van Bulkem hastily walked down the long corridor past the other offices and towards the staircase, listening to the shrill sounds of telephones ringing and broken fragments of conversations. After attending Billy Walker's memorial service last night, Chief Albertson wanted answers resulting in a logical sense of closure over what had happened at Fossgate's Fine Jewelry last week.

Captain Van Bulkem spun around the railing on the staircase as he made his way down towards the bottom floor of the police headquarters. He swiftly opened up the door to the bottom level, showing no signs of being out of breath, and shouted, "Morris! Farmers! The chief wants to see you upstairs, right away!"

Van Bulkem watched over the office cubicles as the two detectives quickly rose up to their feet. He nodded to them, and then he began to make his way over towards his own office to grab his belongings before leaving the police station for the day. After he put on his coat and placed his hat on top of his head, he looked down at his watch before picking up the phone. He quickly glanced around the corner to see the secretary methodically working away at a report on her typewriter, before turning his full attention back to his phone call. "Hey, Frankie, it's David. Listen, how about we go snag a cup of coffee tonight?"

As Stanley Morris and Jacob Farmers began making their way up the staircase, they encountered a news reporter coming down from the upper floor. "So, what do ya say, guys? The Yankees or the Giants this year?" the reporter asked. "We're already up to Game 7!"

Jacob Farmers snarled at the smiling news reporter and then said, "Get the hell outta here before I swat ya on the ass with your own newspaper!"

Stanley Morris ran his hand up through his hair and then reached for the doorknob once they were on the second floor of the building.

After the two detectives reached the end of the long corridor that led up to the police chief's office, Morris reached up and loudly knocked against the wooden door. The door quickly swung open, and Police Chief Marty Albertson poked his head out through the opening and said, "Ah! Hello, gentlemen, please come in and take a seat! I have some important matters of business to discuss with you!" Stanley Morris entered into the office first and took a seat to the right of the police chief's desk, with Jacob Farmers immediately following him to take a seat on the left. Albertson took a seat behind his desk and folded his hands. "I have been reading over your reports from what had happened at Fossgate's last Friday afternoon," Albertson said. "And I honestly have to admit that I am not too impressed with the way that the owner of the business was treated during his questioning." Albertson cast a stern look over towards Jacob Farmers.

"I was just doing my job, sir," Farmers said, and then he reached up to straighten his tie.

Marty Albertson began rising up from his chair. "Let me explain something to you, Jake. It's not a matter of whether or not you're doing your job," Albertson said. "The problem resides in the manner in which you are choosing to do your job. There's a professional code of conduct that needs to be followed here." The police chief walked around the left side of his desk to look down directly into the detective's eyes and then said, "Marvin Fossgate has been a very well-respected member of our community for quite a number of years now. That's part of the reason why I made sure that you and Stan stayed working on the case over the weekend. I was so disgusted by the way that Marvin Fossgate was treated after such a tragedy had occurred in his place of business that there was no possible way that I was going to give you the chance to treat Betsy Walker in that same sort of way." Farmers looked over at his partner and then cleared his throat. "Now, Stan and I have already talked a little," Albertson said. "I called him at home last night just so that he could give me an update regarding your mutual progress on the case."

Stanley Morris nodded and said, "Something tells me that there's been something more since then."

Chief Albertson broke his stern look away from Farmers and turned his attention over to Morris. "You guessed it, Stan," Albertson said. "We've gotten a lead on a potential meeting that's supposed to take place sometime tomorrow night between Tony Tyler and Charley Bennetti."

Morris quickly looked over at Farmers in surprise before returning his attention back to the police chief. "Where?" Morris asked dryly.

"Well, I can't exactly tell you that because technically speaking, we're not even supposed to know as much information as I've already told you," Albertson said.

Farmers lowered his eyebrows in anger and said, "Well, if you expect us to do anything about it, you *should* be able to tell us something!"

Albertson sat down behind his desk and then said, "Simmer down, Jake. If any further information regarding that happens to come in, you and Stan will be the first to know. But don't try to handle this all by yourselves. You'll probably just end up on a wild-goose chase if you do." The police chief pulled his reading glasses out from his coat pocket and placed them over his eyes. "That's all for now, gentlemen," the police chief said, and Farmers and Morris got up and left the office, and then Albertson leaned over next to his desk and began sorting through his filing cabinet.

CHAPTER 25

Dead Man's Hand

A dark blue 1955 Buick Riviera pulled into a car park, and the headlights went dark just before the engine stopped running. Frank Moniarti looked over at Teddy Pazzelli, and the only light in the car came from a dim streetlight that was nearly a block away from them.

"I'm still wonderin' if I should actually go through with this," Moniarti said, as he looked blankly out at the distant streetlight.

"The rest of us already did our homework, Frankie. Now, I'd say that it's time for you to do yours," Teddy said and turned his head to face over into the dark passenger seat of the car.

"Yeah, I know, Teddy," Frank said with a sigh. "I just wish that none of this had ever happened and that it hadn't come down to this, ya know?"

Teddy slowly nodded and then said, "That's perfectly understandable. But it's also important for you to remember that you've got people on your side. Come what may, you didn't get into this all by yourself, and you won't be dealin' with it all by yourself, either."

Frank Moniarti pulled his eyes away from the dim streetlight and looked over at Teddy and then said, "You've got a point. Let's go see what Nicky has in store for us, and then we'll take it from there."

The two men exited the car and walked around the other side of the block towards Lucky Nine's Pool Hall.

Frank Moniarti looked up to see the dim light bulb that hung above the faded old wooden sign of the business. "The outside of this place sure could use a makeover," he said.

Teddy Pazzelli shrugged and then said, "I think that it kinda gives the place a feeling of nostalgia."

The muffled voices from inside the pool hall became increasingly louder as they approached the front door. Teddy held the door open for Frank, who kept his head low, covering his face with the brim of his black hat. Moniarti looked up after they were inside of the pool hall and saw Ronny Steiner clearing plates and glasses off from the bar. Ronny briefly looked up and gave Teddy and Frank a nod before lowering the plates and glasses into a sink filled with steaming hot water. Moniarti carefully looked around the room for Nicholas Malone as he walked up closer to Ronny. He then took off his hat before resting his arms against the wooden edge of the bar.

"We're here to see Nicky. Do you know where he is?" Moniarti asked.

Ronny Steiner looked up at him from behind the bar and then leaned in a little closer. "He's in the cooler," he whispered, moving his eyes over towards the dark hallway that was located on the other side of the room. Frank and Teddy slowly began nodding in unison and then made their way over towards the dark hallway.

There was a small steel door to the left side of the hallway in the back of the pool hall, and it was marked with signs indicating that is was not an exit and it was for employees only. Frank hadn't even noticed it when he had been here last weekend. He pulled on the latch to the steel door, and he and Teddy entered into a small cooler to find rows of organized trays containing various foods that were stacked on the right side of the room, and across from the trays was a rack that contained a series of aged wine bottles, and over towards the far wall in front of them sat an untapped keg of beer. Frank Moniarti walked with Teddy past the rows of food trays and saw a large and thick steel door with a small viewing slit towards the top of it. Upon first entering into the cooler, the large steel door was carefully covered by the racks of food trays, and it sat in the corner of the room in between the food trays and the keg that was set directly upon the red tile floor. Frank Moniarti looked up at the door and then over at Teddy Pazzelli.

"So what are we supposed to do now?" Frank asked.

Teddy smirked and then patted Frank on the shoulder. "Just leave it all up to me. I know what to do," Teddy said and then walked up closer to the door and pounded hard against it with the bottom side of his fist.

The sound of the pounding reverberated through the large steel door, and then the small slit in the door made a faint screeching sound as it quickly slid open. "Moshi Moshi!" a nasally voice said through the small slit in the door.

"We're here to see Nicky," Moniarti said to the door in a low voice.

"Well then, I guess you'd better know the secret password," the nasally voice quickly replied.

Teddy Pazzelli took two steps closer to the door and then shouted, "*Terveydeksi!*"

There was a loud burst of laughter that came from behind the door, followed by the nasally voice enthusiastically replying, "Congratulations! You've been approved!"

Frank Moniarti looked over at Teddy from under the brim of his hat and said, "What the hell was that?"

Teddy turned back over towards Moniarti with a wide grin on his face and said, "It's the Finnish response to whenever someone sneezes." The large and thick steel door creaked on its hinges as it slowly began to move backwards. The musty smell of cigar smoke began trailing into the cooler from behind the door, and the two men stepped forward into the darkness.

There was a middle-aged man who was seated on a high wooden stool wearing a pair of khaki shorts and a light blue short-sleeve shirt that was covered with dark red palm trees. "Hi, I'm Roger Bradshaw. I'm the head of security here," the man said. "I just sit here on this stool all day and throughout most of the night, waiting for a couple of fine gentlemen like yourselves to knock on this door and interrupt me from doing my crossword puzzles. Mr. Malone even gave me a flashlight to work on them with, which also means that I can whack someone over the head with it if they decide to get outta line with me." Bradshaw lifted the flashlight up to the bottom of his face and smiled at Frank and Teddy. "Do either of you know of any good ghost stories?" Bradshaw asked. "It might help me to clear people outta here faster at closing time!"

Teddy Pazzelli laughed and patted Bradshaw on the shoulder and then said, "Nah, I'd probably just ask Santa Claus for a penny-whistle this year, if I was you."

Roger Bradshaw quickly lowered the flashlight away from his face and grabbed his sides laughing and then said, "You guys just be careful goin' down those stairs now, won't you, please?"

Frank Moniarti nodded at Bradshaw and then began leading Teddy down the long flight of wooden stairs that led into the lower level underneath the pool hall.

Once they made it to the bottom of the long wooden staircase, Frank and Teddy looked around the smoke-filled room and saw that it was filled with people dressed in fine clothing. Some were seated around poker tables, some sat in front of slot machines, and others were gathered around a large roulette table that was situated near the center of the room. *I'll be damned. So this is what Nicky's game room looks like. He's sure got me beat,* Frank Moniarti thought to himself and then slowly began trying to make his way through the crowd of people, with Teddy Pazzelli following closely behind him.

"This looks like it's quite a turnout for bein' a Monday night!" Teddy shouted to Frank over the loud sound of the crowd.

"Yeah, this joint's definitely swingin' tonight!" Frank shouted back over his shoulder. "Just keep an eye out for him, would ya?"

Teddy patted Frank on his arm and then began pointing his finger up over his shoulder. Moniarti stood up on the tips of his toes and saw a black wooden door closing across the room. He then watched as Nicholas Malone stepped out into the crowd, placed his cane against the wall, and then began to straighten his tie.

The two men continued walking forward through the crowd, and people began shifting around them as they made their way across the room. Teddy Pazzelli looked from side to side, viewing the cards that people kept hidden from the sight of their gaming opponents and wondering what the hands on the other side must have looked like. There was an exhilarating sense of excitement that filled the room, and people cheered and booed as cards were laid against the tables, and then they heard the rattling sound of the ball being set into motion in the roulette wheel just as they met Nicholas Malone near the center of the room. Frank Moniarti extended his hand over to greet him, and Malone shook his hand after placing the key to his office back into the right side pocket of his dress pants.

"So what's goin' on with that fruitcake that you've got watchin' over the door to this place?" Frank asked, as he looked back over toward the long wooden staircase.

"You'll have to excuse Roger. He served over in Okinawa during Operation Iceberg back in '45, and I'm still not really sure that he's completely made it back over here yet," Malone said and then motioned the two men to follow him back over towards the other side of the room.

As they walked back through the rest of the crowd that filled up the casino floor, Teddy stopped next to one of the poker tables as Malone and Moniarti continued to make their way back over towards the black wooden door. Teddy spotted a man in a black tuxedo sitting at the poker table, holding a hand with two black aces and two black eights. *Yikes! That poor bastard's got the dead man's hand,* Teddy Pazzelli thought to himself, as he slowly walked up closer to the table. He watched as the man in the black tuxedo reached across the table for another card. *The ace of diamonds! He's got a full house!* Teddy thought to himself. He then heard the man in the black tuxedo begin audibly laughing after everybody else at the poker table had revealed the cards that they had been holding in their hands. The man in the black tuxedo raked the pile of poker chips over into his direction with the sleeve of his overcoat.

"We win some, and we lose some," the man said, and then the card dealer cleared the playing cards off from the surface of the poker table before shuffling up the deck again.

Teddy Pazzelli looked over at Malone and Moniarti from the poker table and then mouthed, "I'll wait for you in the car."

Moniarti nodded to him, and then Malone pointed over to a long metal staircase that led up to a steel door at the end of a short walkway. Teddy found his way through the crowd and then began climbing the long metal staircase to exit the lower level of the building. Once he made it all the way up to the walkway, he opened the steel door and saw that it led back out into the alleyway behind the pool hall. *Funny how I never noticed this was here before,* he thought to himself. As he stepped out into the alleyway, he looked back at the other side of the steel door to find that it didn't have a handle on the other side. *Clever,* he thought to himself. *Exit only really means exit only.* He then began walking back over to the lot where he had parked the Buick Riviera, and after he got into the car, he started it up and pulled back around to wait in the alleyway.

Frank Moniarti and Nicholas Malone entered into the office through the black wooden door that was located at the far end of the casino. Malone quickly bolted the door shut behind Moniarti. Frank's eyes slowly circled around the room. Behind a long cherrywood desk that was located on the left side of the room, he saw that there was a large expressionist-style velvet tapestry that nearly covered the entire wall. The dark tapestry depicted the back profile of a faceless man standing over a green table and a series of wavy figures situated on the other side of the table, with several more people located in front of him. Frank Moniarti stopped to admire the obscured details contained within the portrait on the velvet tapestry. "That's really nice! Where'd ya find yourself somethin' like that?" Moniarti asked.

Malone walked over behind the long cherrywood desk. "This?" Malone asked, as he pointed at the large velvet tapestry that covered the wall. "I picked it up years ago on my honeymoon while we were staying in Monaco." Malone set his cane against the cherrywood desk and reached into one of the corner drawers and pulled out a dark and clearly aged bottle. "Do you want some bourbon?" Malone asked. "It's Old Timbrook Special Reserve from 1942. I picked it up back when I was over in St. Louis about fifteen years ago." Moniarti nodded and Malone pulled two small glasses out from another drawer in the cherrywood desk. "So how do you usually take it?" Malone asked, as he pulled the cap off from the bottle.

"Neat, if you wouldn't mind," Moniarti said, as he gently pulled a cushioned chair up in front of the cherrywood desk.

"Comin' right up," Malone said, as he began filling up the two small glasses.

Nicholas Malone carefully passed one of the glasses of bourbon over to Frank Moniarti. "A special occasion like this one calls for a little sip from a special bottle," Malone said, and then the two men clanked their glasses together over the cherrywood desk.

"I'd say that it does, too. So what have you got for me so far?" Moniarti asked.

"My associates have found you quite a fine automobile, Mr. Moniarti. A Cadillac with low mileage, and they just left Detroit with it earlier on today," Malone said and then took a large sip from his glass of bourbon.

"A Cadillac? Are you kiddin' me?" Moniarti said with a wide smile. "You really do want me to be rollin' around town in style, don't you?"

Malone smiled as he nodded. "When I said quality, I meant quality. I wasn't about to have 'em go boost you somethin' out of a junkyard. Not for that sort of a price." Nicholas Malone set down his glass, grabbed his cane, and then began walking over towards a safe that was located behind a mirror on the other side of his office. He gently slid the mirror off to the side and then began turning the knob on the safe. "I try not to do business transactions like this in front of the wrong kinds of people because I really don't want to have seven years of bad luck on my hands," Malone said. "This means that I'm puttin' my trust in you, Frankie." Malone turned back around holding a folded manila envelope in his right hand. He closed the safe before setting the envelope down onto the desk and then sat back down in his chair. He held the glass of bourbon up to his nose and gave it a strong whiff before setting it back down onto the surface of the desk. "Those are the directions to my warehouse over in Ocean City. There's an invoice in there, too. I don't usually accept CODs, but with somethin' that's this large, I'll make an exception for ya," Malone said and then swallowed down the remainder of his bourbon.

"All right," Frank said, "thanks for the directions, Nicky. And I really appreciate your level of understanding with this situation. I'll feel a lot better once this whole thing is over." Frank Moniarti finished off the bourbon that remained in his glass, grabbed the folded manila envelope off from the desk, and then stood up from his chair.

As Moniarti began making his way over towards the door, he heard Nicholas Malone's voice coming from over his shoulder. "Hey, Frankie, there's just one more thing," Malone said, as he remained seated behind the desk. "I know that you've got a driver of your own, but as an added bonus feature for your purchase, I'll be happy to send along my associate, Ronny Steiner, wherever and whenever you might need him." Malone lightly shrugged before continuing. "Roger Bradshaw can watch over the pool hall whenever Ronny's away. Over the years, experience has taught me that the more help that you can get with a job like this, the further ahead that you'll be," Malone said and then winked.

Frank Moniarti turned away from the door and then smiled. "Thanks, Nicky. That's very kind of you," Moniarti said with a nod and then reached down for the doorknob.

When Frank Moniarti opened the door to Malone's office, he was greeted by a thick cloud of smoke from the casino. As he made his way through the crowded room, he passed by a short elderly man wearing a tan leather Italian flat cap, who was seated in front of one of the slot machines. Marvin Fossgate placed fifty cents into the Mills Blue Bell High Top slot machine and then pulled the lever. Moniarti suddenly stopped and then looked over from the long metal staircase that led up to the exit and watched as Marvin Fossgate quickly placed a wooden bowl under the slot machine to help catch a portion of his jackpot winnings. Frank Moniarti smiled and then made his way up the staircase to the walkway and then slowly pulled open the steel door to exit the building.

CHAPTER 26

Making Blueprints

Teddy Pazzelli sat parked in the alleyway behind Lucky Nine's Pool Hall with the engine of the car still running. The hidden back door to the casino slowly opened up, and then Frank Moniarti began approaching the passenger-side door of the dark blue 1955 Buick Riviera. Teddy reached over and pulled up the pin to unlock the car door. Moniarti pulled it open and sat down in the passenger seat before closing the door.

Teddy raised his eyebrow at Moniarti in an inquisitive look. "Well, from the sounds of things, we should be all set," Moniarti said. "The car just left from Detroit a little while ago, and we're gonna meet Nicky over at his warehouse in Ocean City next Friday night to get all the other matters of business taken care of. And we've got some extra help available to us, if we need it. Nicky offered to send along Ronny Steiner to help us out whenever we might need him, as an added part of the deal."

A wide grin of excitement suddenly came over Teddy Pazzelli's face, and he said, "See? I told ya! Like I said, we've got this one in the bag. There's absolutely no place in the world that Plemagoya's gonna be able to hide from us now. This is precisely the right-sized can of bug killer that we're gonna need to eliminate that sort of a pest."

Frank Moniarti removed his hat from his head and gently set it down onto his lap. "Yeah, I know," Frank said. "But now, there's another issue."

Teddy lifted his hands up off the steering wheel and shrugged. "Such as?" he asked.

Frank slowly shook his head pensively and then said, "If we're gonna do this and run the risk of gettin' caught, I'm gonna need a few days to work out a way where we can do this the most effectively. Which means that now, I've got a few phone calls to make."

Teddy placed his hands back on the steering wheel before setting the car into motion. "I can certainly respect that," he said with a nod.

Frank placed his hat up onto the dashboard and reached into his pocket for a pack of cigarettes. "Tomorrow is my anniversary, and I wanna spend some long overdue time with Meg. I've been away from home for far too long, Teddy," Moniarti said. "And even when I'm there, she's usually long since asleep by the time that I get home. At least, that's the way that it's been lately." Moniarti lit a cigarette and then placed his hat back on top of his head.

The car rumbled over the grooves in the gravel as they reached the end of the back alleyway. Teddy turned the car left to head towards the expressway and then said, "You sure could use some time off, Frankie. I'm not gonna lie to you about that. We can always take some time before next Friday night to figure out what we're gonna do. Consider it like making blueprints."

Frank Moniarti exhaled smoke out from his nose as he rolled down the window and then said, "Well, I'm gonna need to work on makin' somethin' else first just to clear out my thought process. I'm tellin' ya, Teddy, now that this car is on its way over here to us, I feel more relieved than I have in a long time. And if Meg turns out to be in the mood for rest and relaxation as much as I am, I'm gonna drive it in like I'm killin' a vampire!"

Teddy Pazzelli lowered his head in laughter before quickly lifting it back up to concentrate on the road. He briefly looked over at Moniarti through the darkness. "That's perfectly understandable," he said. "Take as much time as you need over the next few days. We've just got a really important assignment to take care of once you've had some time away from your work."

Frank Moniarti slowly nodded and then said, "I really appreciate your level of understanding regarding that."

Teddy slowly turned his head to look over at Moniarti. "Hey, don't mention it. I should have ya back in Hoboken in no time at all," he said, and then their car began accelerating down the expressway.

CHAPTER 27

Tuesday, October 16, 1962
A Very Special Occasion

Frank Moniarti walked down the long hallway towards the bathroom on the upstairs floor of his estate, where he could hear the sound of radio static as Meg searched for the signal of a station. Moniarti peered through a small opening in the bathroom doorway to see the sky-blue tiles along the walls, and a transistor radio softly playing on the edge of the bathtub. Frank could see the slender locks of Megan's red hair against her white bathrobe as she powdered her nose in a round vanity mirror on the edge of the bathroom sink. Through the dissipating steam in the room, he could smell the powder whirling through the air, along with the gentle dabs of *Soir de Paris* that she had freshly applied to her neck.

"Are you almost ready?" Frank asked, as the corner of his mouth lifted up into a gentle smile.

"Just about," Meg said. "But as you know, certain levels of perfection take time." And then she placed the circular powder applicator back into its case. "It's been a long time since you took me out to a movie theater, Frank," Megan said. "And, the newspapers are all saying that the film that we are about to go see is nothing short of spectacular!"

Frank nodded. "I have read the same thing," he said as he entered all the way into the bathroom. "I know that you've been waiting for this to happen for a long time now," he said, as he leaned down and then gently placed his hands on her shoulders from behind. "And, just so you know, you look just as beautiful as the day that we were married!"

Megan suddenly began laughing and gently shrugged his hands off from her shoulders. "Oh, Frank, stop it and behave yourself, or we'll never make it to the show on time!" she said.

Frank placed his hands in his pockets and began rocking back and forth on the heels of his shoes. "There, happy now? I'm behaving," he said. Frank slowly began looking up toward the bathroom ceiling and said, "Can I come out of time-out yet?"

Megan began swatting at him from behind her back. "Oh, get!" she said. "And go let the dogs outside before we leave!"

Frank raised one hand from his pocket in a naval salute and said, "Aye, aye!" Megan squinted her green eyes and playfully pursed her lips at him in the vanity mirror.

Frank left the bathroom and began walking down the long upstairs hallway. "Could you hang my green dress up on the door when you come back up?" Meg asked from the open bathroom door.

"Of course, dear," Frank said from near the top of the staircase. After he made his way down the stairs, his dress shoes made a clomping sound against the hardwood floor as he walked from the foyer into the living room. He clapped his hands together, and then three sleeping dogs lifted their heads and arose to their feet. They followed him into the dining room, and then he let them out into the side yard through a double door that was next to their long, antique dining room table. After the dogs came back into the house, Frank Moniarti walked down the driveway and then inside of his large garage. He then pulled his dark gray 1956 Rolls-Royce out from the garage and parked it right in front of their luxurious home. He then went back inside to make sure that Meg would have her green dress hanging from the bathroom door upstairs. Today was a very special occasion. Not only was it their twenty-seventh wedding anniversary but also because Meg had been excited about going to see a movie in the theater since last summer.

CHAPTER 28

Sunset Outside the Matinee

Frank and Megan Moniarti walked hand in hand out from underneath the large marquee sign that covered the doorway to the Fabian Theater in Hoboken. "Thank you for such a wonderful afternoon, Frank," Megan said, as she walked down Newark Street holding onto her husband's arm. "I think that everything has definitely been well worth the wait."

Frank looked over at her and smiled and then said, "Twenty-seven years of marriage is a long time to be together, but I feel like we've made the most of every day. And I'm really glad that we could finally take some time out together. Especially after how much time I've been spendin' away from home lately."

Megan leaned her head over onto Frank's shoulder and then said, "Don't trouble yourself with any of that now, dear. Life picks up, and then life slows back down again. Sometimes, it's just all a matter of how we choose to hitch a ride."

Frank nodded and then said, "I'm really thankful that you understand that." He looked down at his feet as they continued to walk.

Megan gently shook his arm and then said, "So, Frank, tell me what's next! I don't feel like going back home right away!"

Frank lifted his eyes towards her with a gentle look and said, "We don't really have to go home right away. Feel like walkin' a bit further over towards the pier?"

Megan smiled, and her green eyes seemed to become even more radiant, reflecting the soft green color of her dress. "Sounds like a marvelous idea!" she said and then hugged onto his arm as they continued walking together down Newark Street.

As they reached the pier, there were a series of large cargo ships crossing over the Hudson River. When they walked over the grass towards the coastline, they saw the gentle glow of the setting sun reflecting against the Manhattan skyline. Frank wrapped his arms around Megan's waist and slowly rocked her back and forth with his head gently resting against the back of her shoulder.

"It's such an incredible view from here," Megan said softly, and Frank leaned over and kissed the back of her neck.

"I'd say it is, too. Who needs Venice if we've got somethin' like this?" Frank said, and Megan laughed softly as she leaned her head back against the brim of Frank's hat. Suddenly, one of the cargo ships on the river blasted its horn. They both stood perfectly still for a moment, and the echoing sound of the horn startled a flock of seagulls away from the coastline.

Megan turned around to face her husband, leaning in closer. Frank then leaned in and kissed her softly on the mouth.

After their kiss broke away, Megan raised her cheeks as she smiled and then quickly turned away from him. She then pulled out a pocket mirror from her purse to fix her lipstick.

"We'll have to save the rest of that sort of behavior until we get back home, Frank. We have too much of an audience here," she said and then applied another thin coat of lipstick to her upper lip. After Megan placed the mirror back in her purse, Frank wrapped his arms around her waist again.

"Maybe that's what the ship was honkin' for," he said. Megan began laughing and then rocked her hips back and forth, and Frank placed his head back on her shoulder.

Frank Moniarti began to gaze out at the Manhattan skyline. *Okay, tonight, I get to play. But then I go back to work tomorrow,* he thought to himself. The sunset began reflecting radiantly against the glass on the buildings across the Hudson River. Frank squinted his eyes against the glare before closing them tightly.

He suddenly heard the phone ringing from inside his den and the sound of Jimmy's voice speaking frantically into the receiver, *Dad, I need your help! Something went terribly wrong today!*

Frank squeezed his arms harder around his wife's waist. He then saw the smirk on Nicholas Malone's face after he had pulled the broken cigarette out of his hand, the sharp glare of Teddy's headlights piercing through the falling rain in the alleyway, the somber look on Betsy Walker's face from behind her black veil. He held Megan closer and sighed into her ear.

"Frank, are you okay?" Megan suddenly asked, and Moniarti opened his eyes as she began to turn around to face him.

His mind suddenly turned towards standing at the steel door alongside Teddy in the cooler at Lucky Nine's Pool Hall last night. He faintly heard Teddy's voice shout, *Terveydeksi!* And then, sitting parked in the Buick Riviera in the back alleyway. *Like I said, we've got this one in the bag...* Teddy Pazzelli's voice then began trailing away.

"Yeah, just learning to savor every moment while it lasts," Frank said and then tenderly kissed his wife on the forehead. His face gave away into a gentle smile of satisfaction, and then they began walking their way back over to the parking lot by the movie theater.

CHAPTER 29

All Past Regrets Aside

Randy Wyman pulled his white 1957 Ford F-100 custom pickup truck into the parking lot around the corner from The Golden Sandbox and carefully checked his hair in the rearview mirror. *This is the third late night out in less than two weeks,* he thought to himself. *If Scotty finds out about this, I just might be out of a job. But she's worth it. Every little risk that I am taking, that we are taking, in doing this is worth it.* He pulled the key out from the ignition of the truck and waited. Suddenly, there was the gleam of headlights slowly approaching in his side mirror. A silver mist 1958 Buick Roadmaster 75 four-door hardtop pulled up into the parking space beside him, and he saw Melanie Hillsdale smiling and waving at him from behind the steering wheel. Randy nodded and then got out of the pickup truck.

Melanie rolled down her window and then said, "So where do you feel like goin' tonight?"

Randy smiled at her playfully and said, "Anywhere that isn't here, as long as I'm goin' there with you."

Melanie laughed and then said, "Hop on in. Let's go grab a bite to eat."

Randy Wyman said, "Now you're talkin'." And he walked over to the passenger-side door of her car.

The Buick Roadmaster pulled out from the parking lot, and Randy rolled his window down partway with the hopes that some fresh air might help to settle his nerves. "So where are we goin' to eat?" Randy asked.

Melanie glanced over at him and said, "Let's just go back to my place. I'll cook something for you there."

He looked back over at her and smiled. "If you say so. It's less chance that we'll be spotted together in public. I mean, normally, I'd be perfectly okay with that. But if Scotty ever spotted us together somewhere outside from work, that could spell big trouble for the both of us."

Melanie Hillsdale laughed and patted Randy on his leg and then said, "You're such a little worrywart! Just learn to relax. Even if he did spot us out together, as long as we don't broadcast that we're privately seeing each other outside from work while we're *at* work, then we should be perfectly fine. I mean, what do you honestly think that he's going to do to us? Fire us if we ever got caught shopping together at the same grocery store? That sort of thing gets a tad bit ridiculous after a while."

Randy rolled his window back up and then said, "Yeah, I know it does. But still, I look at Scotty as a friend, besides being our boss, ya know?" Melanie slowly shook her head and then merged onto the expressway.

Once they made it back to Melanie's apartment, she began making sausage patties, scrambled eggs, and toast in the kitchen. Randy went into the bathroom to straighten up his hair in the mirror. After he came back out, he entered the kitchen and stood behind Melanie as she prepared their food.

"I really appreciate you doing this for me. I don't really have anything left in my refrigerator back home," he said, and Melanie nodded while pointing over at a glass of milk that she had poured for him that sat on the kitchen countertop.

"Don't mention it. I really appreciate you throwing those two yucky little rodents out of the club last weekend after one of them tried getting a little too friendly with me. What I do there is business, after all," she said and then turned the pilot off on the stove before scooping the food onto two separate plates.

"So is what you're doing here for me right now simply a matter of business?" Randy asked, as he playfully raised one of his eyebrows.

Melanie set the plates onto the dining room table and then playfully swatted at his arm. "You should know better than that by now, Randy!" she said.

He nodded as he made eye contact with her and said, "Of course, I do." They both pulled back their chairs at the table and then began eating.

After their meal together, Randy helped her to clear off the table and clean up the dishes. "I should probably get you back now," Melanie said. "We both have to work tomorrow, and if we are both falling asleep on the job, Scotty just might start to suspect something."

Randy laughed and shook his head, before saying, "If you say so."

Melanie rolled her eyes at him. "Please, don't start in with that again. Why do you always say that to me? Here, let me grab your coat, and then we can be off on our way," she said and then grabbed his coat off from the back of the chair at the dining room table and handed it over to him.

"And so just like that, you're throwin' me out?" Randy asked playfully as he put his coat on.

"Oh, stop!" Melanie said. "You should know better than that by now!"

Randy Wyman began to laugh and said, "See? You say that to me all the time." Melanie slowly shook her head and then led him out of the apartment, before turning around to lock the door behind them.

As the Buick Roadmaster pulled back into the parking lot around the corner from The Golden Sandbox, Randy looked across the lot at his pickup truck. "I really should get that thing washed one of these days," he said. "I'd never want to take you camping somewhere with it being in the condition that it's in now."

He looked over at Melanie, as she began to snicker. "Does that mean that I already have you thinking about some of the days still yet to come? With us being together not so secretly, perhaps?" she asked with a soft tone in her voice.

Randy shrugged and then said, "Well, somebody's got to keep the wild animals away from you. Now, don't they?"

Melanie put the car into park next to his truck and kept the engine running as she turned around to face him. "You know what I mean, Randy. With all past regrets aside, do you really feel like there is any sort of a future in store for us here?" she asked with an inquisitive look.

Randy gazed out into the darkness. "We're just gonna have to wait and see on that," he said. "We've got something really great going on here between us, but we can't let it interfere with any of the other responsibilities that we have around here. At least not for Scotty's sake."

Randy Wyman opened the passenger-side door to the car. "I gotta go get some sleep," he said and then stepped out onto the gravel parking lot. After he closed the door, he made it two steps away from the car before he turned around. He looked down at Melanie through the opening in the passenger-side window and heard her say, "Wait." He watched her door swing wide open, and then she quickly came rushing over to the other side of the car. "You're not getting away *that* easy!" she said.

Randy suddenly raised his eyebrows and then asked, "What'd I forget?"

Melanie leaned against the back door on the passenger side of the silver mist Buick Roadmaster. "You forgot this," she said softly. And then she grabbed hold of the collar of his coat, gradually pulling him in closer to her. As her mouth softly met with his, she slowly lowered her hands down from Randy's collar and gently began to caress his shoulders; and then their heads slowly and rhythmically began to sway back and forth.

CHAPTER 30

Friendly Competition

Tony Tyler stood in the middle of a gravel parking lot around the corner from The Golden Sandbox with his leather jacket zipped up to try and conceal the thick white brace that was wrapped around his neck. A taxicab pulled up to a nearby curb, and Charley Bennetti passed the amount of the fare over to the driver from the back seat, with a generous tip included. Tony Tyler kept his hands inside the pockets of his leather jacket as he watched Bennetti approach him. Charley's wing tip shoes loudly scraped across the surface of the gravel, and he kept the brim of his hat tilted downward towards the ground as he walked across the parking lot.

"Thanks for comin' out here tonight, Charley. I'm glad you could make it," Tony said, as he took his hands out from his pockets and unzipped his leather jacket. He held the sides of his jacket open to show that he was unarmed.

"Spare me the small talk, Tony," Charley said in an irritated voice. "Things have become somewhat complicated on my end lately, and my time has suddenly become very valuable."

Tony lowered his eyes toward the ground and narrowly shook his head over the neck brace before saying, "You don't even want to know about some of the things that I've been through lately."

Charley lifted his hat off from his head and wiped the sweat off his forehead with a handkerchief and then said, "Yeah, you're right. I probably don't. But would that happen to be why you've been so hard to reach over these past couple of days?" Bennetti placed his hat back on top of his head and double-checked the parking lot for headlights.

Charley Bennetti then turned to face Tony Tyler once again after he saw that the parking lot was completely dark except for the dim ambience that came from the streetlights. Tony placed his hands back into the pockets and then began restlessly pacing back and forth. "Well, it seems that I also might have ran into just a *few* situations that complicated things considerably over this past weekend," Tony said. "Vinnie was supposed to give me my share of the money the other night. But instead, he hit me in the back of the neck with a baseball bat, and then he and Natty decided to throw me out of a moving car onto the sidewalk right in front of Maple's Anchor." Tony suddenly stopped pacing, and then Charley's eyes grew wide with disbelief.

"They dropped you off *where?*" Charley asked, as his mouth grew into a loose smirk, and Tony's facial expression began seething with agitation.

"You heard me, Charley, and I don't really feel like repeating it!" Tony shouted. "It still isn't very comfortable for me to talk too loud with this thing wrapped around my neck!"

Charley Bennetti placed his hand on Tony Tyler's shoulder. "And you just got outta the hospital this morning? Yeah, it sounds to me like you've been through a lot lately, too!" Charley said and then let out a loud laugh as he removed his hand from Tony's shoulder and then folded his arms over the sides of his maroon overcoat.

Tony quickly pulled Charley's folded arms away from his sides. "Shut up, Charley! Just shut up!" Tony said through gritted teeth. "I didn't ask for you to come all the way out here just to make fun of me!" Tony suddenly winced in pain and reached up towards his neck brace.

Charley Bennetti tried to look sympathetic and said, "I'm sorry, Tony. I just can't help it sometimes. And here I was thinking that *my* boss was unreasonable. Please, go on. I'm still listenin'." Charley Bennetti caught his breath and began to stand upright again.

Tony Tyler scowled and then turned his look away from Charley and began looking around the parking lot. "So anyway." Tony began. "Past what happened to me the other night, all this stuff in the papers lately about the death of that cop, and now the whole city seems like it's suddenly on high alert…"

Charley Bennetti suddenly raised his hand to cut Tony off. "Wait a minute," Charley said with an inquisitive look. "Are you tellin' me that you're the one that killed Billy Walker?"

Tony ran his hand up through his hair and exhaled a long breath, and then his voice began to get choked up as he said, "Look, I really didn't mean to, all right? It was just a stupid accident. That *wasn't* supposed to happen!"

Charley Bennetti took off his glasses and cleaned the lenses with a handkerchief before he placed them back over his eyes. "That's *some* stupid accident, Tony," Charley said. "The cops are even taking a closer look at our team now. Needless to say, you've caused just a few trust issues with your recent behavior." Charley Bennetti's eyes then began wandering off into the distance.

There was a short moment of silence, and the two men could faintly hear the soft buzzing sound coming from the streetlights. Tony suddenly broke the silence with his voice, trembling and uneasy, as he said, "Well, it hasn't just been *my* behavior that has caused all these trust issues with the cops. Things just might've happened a little bit differently than what the cops probably think that they did."

Charley Bennetti raised his eyebrows as he suddenly leaned in closer before saying, "Would you possibly care to explain that a little bit further for me please? I'm sure that Mr. Moniarti would also like some peace of mind right about now. After all, you idiots endangered the life of his son, on top of causing us some extra problems with the cops."

Tony Tyler's eyes suddenly grew wide with disbelief. "Oh shit!" Tony shouted, "Nobody told me nothin' about that!" He broke away his eye contact with Charley and looked down at the parking lot. He began tracing circles in the gravel with the sole of his shoe before he softly cleared his throat and went on. "Look, all I know is Vinnie's supposed to meet me here with my share of the money. I was gonna use it to pay off a debt to get my car back. But now, I want you to take it, just so that you guys can get the cops off your backs. As for my car, I can always figure somethin' else out."

Charley Bennetti lowered the brim of his hat as he gave Tony Tyler a curious look and then asked, "So you lost your car, too? You *really* have been on a roll lately, haven't you?"

Tony Tyler loosely shrugged and then said, "Hey, everybody has some sorta hard luck sometimes! So do ya want the money or not?"

Charley lowered the brim of his hat towards the ground and then slowly walked around behind Tony. He suddenly spoke in a quiet voice filled with deep contemplation, "Well, my boss just might somehow get the mistaken impression that I took some sort of a bribe from you, and that could look really bad on my end. You've caused us *way* too many problems as it is already, Tony. I hope you realize that now. I guess that I could ask Mr. Moniarti if it might somehow be enough to compensate him for some of his recent inconveniences, but I can't really promise you anything. Besides, just how much money are we talkin' about?"

Tony Tyler's head remained still as Charley stood behind his back. "It should be about ten grand, if he comes here with the full amount," Tony said.

Charley Bennetti slowly walked back around to meet with Tony Tyler face-to-face. "I'll see what I might be able to do for ya. So what else do you know that you're not tellin' me yet?" Bennetti asked, and his facial expression hardened. "I mean, what do you honestly feel like you've got left to lose at this point?"

Tony Tyler turned to his side and then began pacing again. He suddenly stopped and made eye contact with Charley and then said, "Well, Natty Rosebrook was in on the job, too. He was the one who went in there yellin' at everybody. We had that old lady faint on us, and then Billy Walker must've made it in through the back door without any of us seein' him. Vinnie was the one guardin' the front door, and Pedro was supposed to be watchin' the back door. But then Pedro suddenly got careless! He must've got too excited after he cut the phoneline or somethin'! Because next thing that I'm hearin' from Pedro is that some witness got away! And that's on the same day that I'm readin' about this cop's funeral in the newspaper, and all the while, I'm lyin' in a hospital bed! How would you feel about all that if you were me, Charley?"

Bennetti looked down at the ground and slowly shook his head. "Well, now that you mention it, I'm pretty thankful that I'm not you!" Bennetti said, "But regardless of that, it still doesn't solve any of the current problems that you've caused for us lately, now, does it?" Charley slowly raised his eyes back up and saw the look of desperation on Tony Tyler's face.

"Well, no, not exactly. But Vinnie should be here with the money anytime now!" Tony said, "And after that, you can count it, just to make sure that it's all there! And then after that, you can call whoever you need to and then get back in touch with me."

Charley Bennetti leaned in closer and raised his finger towards Tony Tyler's chest before saying, "Whoa, hold on a second! You're gonna be the one countin' it to make sure that it's all there, pal! And if anything unexpected happens during the process, you're all on your own! Those are the terms! Understood?"

Tony Tyler raised his hands up in the air. "Yeah, sure. I gotcha, Charley. I gotcha," Tony said in a nervous voice. "I just wish that I could get this whole thing to go away."

Bennetti shook his head without breaking his eye contact with Tony and then said, "It's a tad bit too late for that. All we can do now is hope for some level of disaster control, Tony, and that's about it. There have been way too many levels of trust that have been violated lately. And if anybody sees me here, my goose is gonna be cooked for sure. So I'm gonna go walk across the street and wait behind that wooden fence over there for Vinnie to show up with the money. And about ten more minutes is all that I'm gonna be allowed to give ya. So, let's just try to relax and hope for the best. Okay?"

Tony Tyler lowered his shoulders in an attempt to unwind and then said, "Yeah, let's just be patient and hope for the best. I will have to find some way to signal over to you once I got the money with me and Vinnie's gone."

Charley Bennetti walked up and patted Tony Tyler on the cheek. Tony winced as he drew back in his neck brace. "Now you're learning how to play by the rules a little bit better," Charley said. "I suppose that it's better late than never." And then he slowly shook his head. "There's nothin' wrong with a little bit of friendly competition," Charley said, and then he began softly whistling to himself as he walked across the street to hide behind the wooden fence.

A few minutes later, Charley Bennetti saw a glare from a pair of headlights through the boards of the fence and heard the soft hum of a running car engine. He slowly peered up over the fence to see a forest-green 1960 Pontiac Catalina four-door sedan pull up in front of where Tony Tyler was located in the parking lot. The passenger-side door opened, and then Bennetti saw a man in an ivory-colored suit get out of the car, but he remained situated behind the open door of the car.

Charley could hear Tony Tyler's nervous voice saying, "Vinnie, I'm really glad that you could make it. Did you bring all the money along with you?"

The man in the ivory-colored suit slowly nodded, tilting the brim of his hat. "Here, kitty, kitty! I brought along a little midnight snack for ya!"

Bennetti heard a nasally voice speaking loudly, before he heard the faint sound of a laundry bag softly ruffling as it landed against the gravel in the parking lot. Tony Tyler took a few steps forward before three reports from a pistol suddenly echoed out into the night. Charley Bennetti quickly ducked away from the wooden fence and took shelter behind an aluminum garbage can in the dark alleyway.

* * *

Across the other side of the parking lot, Randy Wyman quickly grabbed Melanie Hillsdale by the waist and tackled her onto the gravel upon hearing the sudden sound of the pistol reports. "Stay down," he sternly whispered to her. "And don't try to get up until I do."

Melanie silently nodded and then turned her field of vision underneath their two parked vehicles to see the body of a young man wearing a leather jacket lying motionless on the ground. There was the shrill sound of laughter, and then she saw a man wearing an ivory-colored suit pick up a bag from the parking lot and then get back into a forest-green car, before it sped away in a cloud of spit-up gravel.

* * *

After the car sped away, Charley Bennetti ran out from behind the wooden fence to see Tony Tyler's dead body lying next to a dark pair of fresh tire tracks that had been dug into the gravel of the parking lot. Bennetti struggled to catch his breath after he made it over towards Tony, and he looked down at his body in shock.

"Oh no! Oh my god!" Charley said as he panted and then lifted his forearm up to cover his mouth. He slowly began to catch his breath and then pulled his arm away from his face.

A few moments later, there was suddenly the sound of another car slowly approaching across the gravel of the parking lot. A light blue 1961 Chevrolet Impala Bubble Top pulled up without its headlights on, and the driver shut the engine off after the car was parked right next to where Tony Tyler's body was located.

Ronny Steiner casually got out from the driver seat of the car and looked up at Charley Bennetti through his thick glasses and then said, "Hey, kid, would you mind givin' me a hand with this? My back ain't quite what it used to be."

Bennetti's eyes grew wide, as he watched Ronny open up the trunk of the car and grab a hold of Tony Tyler's lifeless arms, before pulling his body across the loose gravel of the parking lot. Ronny Steiner suddenly stopped dragging Tony's body a few feet away from the car.

"Hey, look, Tuesdays might be my days off, kid, but that doesn't mean that I still don't have a schedule to keep," Ronny said and then curiously looked down at the pair of Converse shoes that he had been dragging through the loose gravel. Charley Bennetti quickly walked over towards the car and lifted up Tony Tyler's feet. After Ronny had closed the trunk, both men got into the vehicle, and then the car slowly drove away into the distance.

CHAPTER 31

Trouble in Paradise

Melanie Hillsdale quickly wrestled herself out from underneath the weight of Randy Wyman's body and felt the gravel separating under her knees as she made it onto her feet.

"Don't get up!" Randy whispered forcefully and then looked over in the direction of the gunfire, "What are you doing?"

Melanie brushed the dirt off from her blue jeans. "I'm going to go call for help. Somebody's got to," she quietly said in an uneasy voice. She extended her trembling hand down to Randy to help him back onto his feet.

"Just remember to stay down!" Randy commanded. "And let's not come out from behind any of the parked cars if we don't have to!" His voice was stern, yet quiet. If whoever had fired the shots had still happened to be anywhere within the vicinity, the shooter's ears would hopefully still be ringing enough from the gunfire to cover up the sound of their voices and their footsteps across the gravel.

Once Randy made it onto his feet, he held Melanie by the waist behind the cover of their two cars. Both their breathing and heart rates had quickened, and Randy could feel Melanie's body steadily quivering as he held her. He heard a muffled sniffling sound against his shoulder, and after their embrace broke away, she wiped a teardrop away from her cheek.

"There will be plenty of time for all that stuff after we find a pay phone," she softly said and then tightly grabbed Randy by the wrist as she led him through the shadowy parking lot. They both stopped a few feet away from the edge of the parking lot and saw that there were no vehicles and no people left at the scene of the crime that they had just witnessed.

"We're gonna have a pretty difficult time trying to explain this one," Randy said, as he took the lead and pulled Melanie out into the clearing by the road.

There was a gas station about a block away that had closed down for the night, and a phone booth sat in a dimly lit portion of the parking lot. "There's a phone," Melanie said with a mixture of relief and enthusiasm. "Do you happen to have a dime on you?"

Randy Wyman reached into the side pocket of his jacket and pulled out a handful of loose change. "There must be one in here somewhere," he said with a shrug, and then he tightly closed his hand around the coins as they quickly ran across the street to the phone booth.

It was nearing one o'clock in the morning, and the road was completely empty. Once they made it up to the darkened phone booth, Randy passed a dime over to Melanie. "You go ahead and make the call. I'm gonna stay out here until the police arrive. That way, I at least know that you're safe," he said and then looked back over towards the parking lot for any possible approaching headlights.

Melanie looked down at the dime in her hand before quickly closing the door to the phone booth. The inside of the phone booth was dark and reeked of stale cigarette smoke. Her hand was trembling as she loosely dropped the dime into the payphone. She looked over her shoulder to see Randy briefly nod to her before giving her a thumbs-up. "Hello!" she yelled frantically. "Operator, can you give me the police, please?!"

A low and dry voice answered the other end of the phone, "Atlantic City Police Department."

147

Melanie turned her view away from Randy as she spoke into the phone, "We're over at the gas station just around the corner from The Golden Sandbox! There's been a problem over here! Someone's been shot! I can explain more to you once you get here, but I need help sent over here right away!"

The voice on the other end of the phone did not change its mellow tone, even in the current state of emergency, "Just try to remain calm, ma'am. We'll send some help over to you right away."

Melanie closed her eyes and exhaled in relief. "Thank you," she said softly before she hung up the phone and pulled open the door to the phone booth.

Randy stood off to the side smoking a cigarette. "Well, at least we're still alive enough to be scared," he said, shrugging.

Melanie shook her head at him. "Shut up!" she shouted. "They said that they should be here any minute!"

Randy extinguished his cigarette down into the gravel of the parking lot and then said, "All right. Well, I say that we stay right where we are until they get here."

CHAPTER 32

A Late-Night Questioning

Inside of a cold and dark interrogation room at the police station downtown, Melanie Hillsdale sat alone at a hard wooden table with her eyes closed. She couldn't help but wonder to herself why it was that she had ended up here at this hour of the night and why time seemed to be going by so slowly. The minutes seemed to pass by like hours. She felt as though she had remained pretty calm during the whole ordeal, with all things being considered. That was, until she and Randy were asked to come down to the police station. *Things weren't supposed to have turned out like this,* she thought to herself. *It was all just a matter of being in the wrong place at the wrong time.* The door to the interrogation room suddenly opened behind her, and she could hear the sharp sound of approaching footsteps against the cement floor, but she didn't dare turn around. She opened her eyes to see a man in his early thirties with light brown hair and sharp eyebrows. His gelid blue eyes were fixed down on a thick photo album as he walked over to the table and sat down across from her.

"Hello, Melanie. My name is Detective Stanley Morris. I realize that you have already been through a lot tonight, but I was wondering if you might be able to do a bit of a favor for me," he said and then slid the thick photo album across the table, and the scraping sound that it made caused Melanie to tense up against the wooden chair that she was seated in.

"Look, I only really heard what happened. I didn't really see much of anything or anybody, for that matter," she said. "So asking me to look through these photos to see if I can identify anyone from them probably isn't going to get very far."

Stanley Morris locked his eyes on her without blinking. "I can understand why you would be hesitant to look at any of these photos right away," he said. "It's very common for people to go into shock after they witness a murder and not really remember any of the details about the perpetrator until several hours, if not several days, after the crime has been committed." His eyes started to soften as he saw a teardrop begin to roll down Melanie's cheek.

She buried her face into the palm of her hand. "I just told you that I didn't see anything!" she shouted. "I only heard some shots ring out in the parking lot, and that's it! Looking at pictures right now isn't going to help me to remember anything! I had never even seen any of these people before! Not the guy who got shot, nor the guy who did the shooting! They were absolute strangers to me, and they still are! And quite frankly, I'd kinda like to keep it that way!" She began searching through her white leather purse for a tissue. She wiped the teardrop away from her cheek and then slowly turned her head away from the table to blow her nose.

When Melanie turned her head back forward, she suddenly saw the door open behind the detective's shoulders. A tall older man wearing glasses suddenly stood on the other side of the interrogation room. He was wearing a dark brown suit with a red shirt underneath it and had a gradually receding hairline. His mustache reflected the same amount of silver hair that had grown along the sides of his head. His feet loudly connected against the cement floor as he walked over closer to the table.

He came up and whispered into his partner's ear, "I can't seem to get anything out of this other guy either." And then he pointed his thumb up over his shoulder.

Morris exhaled deeply in frustration and then ran his hand up through his hair as he turned away from the table. He began to rub the center of his forehead in circles when he turned back around. "Melanie Hillsdale," Morris said in a dry and raspy voice, "I'd like you to meet my partner Detective Jacob Farmers."

Melanie gave Farmers a piercing look of frustration as she bit into her lower lip before pushing the package of tissues back down into her white leather purse.

Morris placed his hand up on his partner's shoulder. "Excuse me, Jake," he said. "I'm going to go down the hall and get some water." Farmers nodded to him before returning his attention back to Melanie. "I just got off the phone with your father, Melanie," Farmers said. "He should be here to pick you up within the next few hours." With her father driving in from Philadelphia to Atlantic City at this time of the night, the definition of *within the next few hours* could mean three to four hours. That was an eternity to be spending in a place like this, and it was also a statement that would cause the time to go by much slower than it already had been.

There was a brief moment of silence in the room, and then Jacob Farmers hardened his gaze and squinted his gray eyes, as he leaned in towards her. "Now, just a minute. I overheard you telling my partner that you didn't really see anything or anybody. And the next thing that came out of your mouth is that you had never seen either of the men involved in the shooting before. The microphones around here work like a charm." Farmers raised his eyebrows up behind his glasses. "So which is it?" he asked.

Melanie shook her head and sniffled as her deep feeling of bewilderment suddenly intensified. "Which is what?" she asked. "I already told your partner that I don't know anything, and now you are treating me as if I was the one who had shot this guy!"

The light reflected off his glasses as Farmers looked down at the photo album that had been placed in front of her, and then he looked back up into her eyes. "So you *weren't* the one who shot this guy?" Farmer's asked.

Melanie's eyes widened in shock. "What?! Are you crazy?!" she shouted. "What are you even talking about?! I don't even own a gun! How could that even be possible?" Her wide eyes suddenly hardened into a piercing stare of rage.

Just then, Stanley Morris returned from his trip down the hall. Farmers just casually shrugged and then said, "Well, that answers that. But somebody has got to get to the bottom of all this, now, don't they?" Melanie rolled her eyes and then looked away towards the floor. Farmers lifted his cheeks up into an eerie smile that made Melanie squirm back into her chair. "Look, I will go down the hall now, and I'll bring you back some coffee," Farmers said. "We can take as long as you'd like, and we can go over all the facts as many times as you want to, but this case needs to make some level of progress here tonight." Stanley Morris nodded over his partner's shoulder. "Just give it some thought," Farmers said, and then he turned around and began walking towards the interrogation room door. Morris watched Melanie's eyes shut tight as the door loudly closed, and the echoing sound of footsteps gradually began fading away down the hall.

CHAPTER 33

Out Past Curfew

As the minutes continued to slowly pass by like hours, Randy Wyman and Melanie Hillsdale sat quietly in the lobby of the police station with the two detectives. They both ignored the detectives as they silently looked over at the door for each of their rides back home to arrive. Melanie had received the benefit of having a detective phone her father. On the other hand, Randy Wyman had been forced to break down and call his boss, Scotty McCormack, in the middle of the night to humbly ask him for a ride home. Neither one of their cars were allowed to leave from the parking lot at the scene of the crime until the police had finally wrapped up their investigation. Melanie kept silently wondering to herself, *Are we witnesses or are we suspects? Because all night long, they have been treating us like we are suspects.* She turned her head towards Randy and blinked before she gently placed her hand upon his knee. Randy sat silently in a chair with his arms folded as he pensively stared down at the floor. Upon feeling her touch, he slowly raised his head and his facial expression began to soften.

"It's going to be okay," she softly whispered. "It's not like they can keep us here forever." Randy shrugged and then stretched before leaning back in his chair to blankly stare up at the ceiling tiles. "Did you find a ride?" Melanie asked quietly.

Randy nodded and then said, "I had to call up Scotty." Melanie's tired eyes suddenly grew wide with surprise. Randy pulled his sleeve back to look at his watch and then said, "He should be here to pick me up in about a half hour."

Melanie slowly leaned in closer to Randy until he could feel her breath against his chin. "Does he know that I'm here?" she asked.

Randy locked his hands together behind his head and looked back up towards the ceiling. "Nah, I didn't say anything about that. Not yet, at least," Randy said. "But you know that if we're both forced to ask for the day off in order to go to court together, he's bound to find out eventually, right?"

Melanie slowly nodded and then turned away from him. "I guess that something like this was bound to happen to us eventually," Melanie said, as she blankly stared at the door. "I mean, you know how Scotty is. If you try keeping any sort of a secret from him, he's eventually going to find out about it."

Randy lowered his head back down to look over at her and then said, "Well, he didn't say anything about firing me for having to pick me up from the police station in the middle of the night. So I wouldn't worry about it too much just yet. Let me talk to him first. And once he finds out what's going on here, I got a feeling that we'll both be fine. I mean, it's not like we could've controlled any part of what happened to us tonight."

Melanie quickly spun around in her chair to face him. "Yes, we could have!" she said, raising her voice. Randy quickly placed a finger up to his mouth to signify her to speak more quietly. "My father is going to go through the roof the moment that he walks in through that door," she whispered curtly. "If I were you, I'd ask those cops if I could go to the bathroom now. Because if you don't have to go just yet, you'll certainly have to by the time that my father gets done screaming at everybody. He's driving in all the way from Philadelphia to get here."

The two detectives stood at a counter with their backs turned to them as they quietly went over the contents of a thin manila folder.

Randy cleared his throat before he began to speak. "Excuse me," he said nervously. Detective Jacob Farmers slowly turned away from the counter. "Where are your restrooms located?" Randy asked, and Farmers silently point down the hallway to their left before turning his attention back to the contents of the manila folder. "Thank you," Randy said and quickly got up from his chair.

Melanie swatted at his behind as he stood up. "Fraidy-cat!" she said and then folded her arms as she looked back over towards the door. She could faintly hear the detectives speaking to each other as they went through the contents of the folder on the counter. *Are they ever going to be able to catch whoever did this?* she wondered to herself. *Or are Randy and I going to be the only targets of their investigation from this point on because they don't have anybody else to question?* She nervously shook her head in annoyance and avoided making any sort of eye contact with the detectives as she waited for her father to arrive.

A few moments later, Conrad Hillsdale forcefully pulled open the door to the lobby of the police station with his shoulders hunched up inside of a thin navy-blue denim jacket. The knees to his jeans were brown with dirt, and his gray hair looked frayed and unkempt. The surefire signs of a concerned parent who had been woken up in the middle of the night with a phone call. His voice boomed into the quiet lobby, "Okay, I made it over here, just like I promised that I would! Now does somebody want to tell me what the hell is going on here!"

Farmers raised his hand calmly and then said, "Now, hold on just a minute there, sir."

Conrad lowered his eyebrows down into a scowl and said, "Don't' you call me *sir!* I don't wear a badge! If anything, that's what I'm forced to call you guys whenever I get caught drivin' down the expressway with a headlight out, if I'm not mistaken!" His breathing was heavy, and his teeth were clenched together with rage.

"No, you're not mistaken...with some of us," Farmers said calmly. "But we're not those kinds of police officers. I'm Detective Jacob Farmers with the homicide division, and this is my partner, Detective Stanley Morris."

Conrad's eyes lowered at both the detectives as Morris turned his attention away from the contents of the manila folder on the counter. "Homicide?!" Conrad shouted. "Everybody here looks perfectly alive to me! So what the hell does any of this have to do with my daughter?!"

Stanley Morris closed the manila folder and looked up at Conrad. "She's been a witness to a murder," Morris said, "along with someone else."

Conrad walked a few steps closer and then asked, "Someone else?! Who?!"

Melanie quickly got up from her seat and then said, "Daddy, please calm down!"

Behind the door to the men's restroom, Randy Wyman was splashing cold water from the faucet over his face to help keep himself awake. He could hear the muffled sound of Conrad Hillsdale's voice booming through the empty lobby of the police station. He turned the faucet off, dried his face with a paper towel, and then looked at himself in the mirror.

"It's now or never," he said to his reflection. "You've got a responsibility in this sort of a situation." Randy noticed that his breathing was suddenly becoming fast and heavy. He exhaled deeply and then reached over for the handle to the restroom door. As he walked out into the lobby of the police station, he saw Melanie and her father standing face-to-face with the two detectives.

Conrad Hillsdale shook his finger angrily at the detectives as he shouted, "You've got a lot of nerve holding my daughter down here if she hasn't done anything wrong! You easily could have called her a taxi back home in the time that it took me to drive on over here from Philadelphia! At least that way, I would've known that she was safe! And where in the hell is her lawyer?!"

Randy Wyman began walking faster as he approached the counter. "Excuse me," Randy softly said.

Conrad looked over behind the detectives and said, "Who in the hell are you? Don't tell me that *you're* her lawyer!"

Melanie rubber her father's shoulder before kissing him on the cheek and then said, "That would be the man who saved my life."

Randy's eyes grew wide as Conrad's look of fury suddenly began to become less threatening. "You?" Conrad asked, "You mean to tell me that you did the same job that the police in this city were supposed to be doing?"

Randy Wyman cleared his throat and then said, "Well, sir—"

Conrad held his hand up to cut Randy off in the middle of his speech, and then he said, "You don't have to call me *sir!* In fact, you don't really have to call me anything! All I care about right now is the fact that my daughter is safe!"

Melanie walked over toward Randy's side and began to caress his arm. "I *am* safe now!" she said. "But all because of him!"

Randy raised his hand up to Conrad, and then he said, "My name is Randy Wyman, and I work as a security guard protecting your daughter, Mr. Hillsdale. I would never intentionally let anything bad happen to her. I can safely promise you that now and in the future."

Conrad's facial expression began to soften, and his eyebrows lifted up in curiosity. "All right then," he said as he shook Randy's hand. "But I'm gonna be gettin' her outta here right now and back home to her apartment where she belongs. It sounds like she and I have a lot to talk about along the way."

Melanie let go of Randy's arm and walked past her father, lifting her arms and shoulders up in a gesture of frustration as she made her way over towards the door. Conrad nodded at Randy, and then the corner of his mouth lifted up in a loose smirk before he turned around and followed his daughter out the door.

"So when does your ride get here?" Farmers asked Randy with a growing smile.

"Any minute now," Randy said and then walked back over to take a seat across the lobby from the two detectives.

CHAPTER 34

Wednesday, October 17, 1962
Remembrance from Times Past

Charley Bennetti entered in through a revolving door off from Illinois Avenue that led into the lobby of The Skyline Hotel. He had his head hung down low as he approached the front desk.

"I'm here to see Sandy Granger," he said to the man at the front desk. His blue eyes and thick dark eyebrows were barely visible between the brim of his hat and the rims of his glasses.

"Has she been expecting you, sir?" the man behind the desk asked in a calm voice. Charley could see that he was a tall, thin man, probably in his mid-sixties, and was used to people coming in for late-night appointments.

"Not exactly. But I know that she'll be happy to see me," Charley said and then reached up to rub the back of his neck.

"Very well, sir. I shall keep it our little secret," the man behind the desk said, and then he pulled a room key off from a hook on the back wall. "Room 417. Please, remember to return the room key to us once you are through with your meeting. That happens to be Miss Granger's policy as much as it is ours," the man said with a thin smile, as he passed the room key over the counter to Charley.

"Yeah, I gotcha. No worries here, pal," Charley said. "It's just been awhile since I came in here to see her, and I kinda feel like we've got some catchin' up to do. I'll have it back to ya by breakfast time, at the very latest."

The lobby of the hotel was nearly vacant. All that seemed to remain at this hour of the night were a select few travelers, who sat patiently waiting for their taxicabs to bring them to the airport to catch a late-night flight. Charley had counted a total of three men in the lobby when he left the front desk. Two of the men appeared to be reading newspapers, and the third one sat facing away from the others, eating a bag of peanuts, and listening to a recap of the day's sports scores on the radio. None of the men even seemed to have taken any notice when Charley entered in through the revolving door. He reached down next to the holstered pistol that was under his left arm and down into the inside of his jacket pocket. He could feel a small envelope filled with money. The envelope contained $500 in all, and next to it was a ticket for his flight out to Denver in the morning.

The heat had definitely been coming down all around lately, and Frank Moniarti had given him the money and the ticket, along with the suggestion that he go on a skiing trip until certain recent events had blown over. Charley had never been one to argue in a situation like that. Moniarti always seemed to know what was best for all those involved in his organization. If he told Charley to take a vacation, he instinctively knew that it was meant to be for his own good. Still, Bennetti knew deep down that he wasn't going to be able to just up and leave town without paying one more visit to Sandy, even if it was only for comfort's sake.

He walked down the hallway to the two brass elevator doors, which stood out against the blue velvet wallpaper that covered most of the walls that were located on that floor. The buttons to summon the elevator on this floor had grown faded with repeated use. Especially the ones with the arrows pointing up. The buttons pointing down from the lobby elevator led down into the parking garage below, and they were rarely used from this level. Charley pushed the button to go up and eagerly paced in front of the doors until he heard the bell ring to signify that the elevator doors were about to open.

He entered into the elevator to his right and pushed the button for the fourth floor with a trembling hand. He hated the feeling of being nervous, hated the feeling of uncertainty, and definitely hated the thought of things not going according to plan. Charley knew that this was the only thing, the one course of action that could subdue his anxiety and help him to not be this much of a nervous wreck while he was at the airport in the morning. He needed the company of a woman. And not just any woman. Sandy Granger had always been a familiar acquaintance to Charley, and she had helped him to get through some very difficult times. But this was major in comparison to the other times that he had sought comfort from her.

The last time that Charley had privately visited The Skyline Hotel to see Sandy had been shortly after he had been arrested while driving a moving truck that had been filled with stolen pinball machines. But that had been child's play compared to this. And now, he was soon to be flying away to another state in order to avoid any of the professional and legal ramifications that were about to unfold. Suddenly, he heard a bell ring, and the elevator doors slowly opened on the fourth floor. Charley Bennetti walked cautiously down the hallway, keeping a watchful eye on each door that he passed, until he stood directly in front of the door to room 417.

His anxious nerves prevented him from whistling to break the silence. He reached up and knocked on the door. *Hurry up!* he thought to himself. *If anybody sees me here, I am a dead man! Do you understand that?! A DEAD MAN!*" The door opened, and Sandy Granger stood in the doorway in a black silk nightgown. He could smell the sweet coconut odor of her shampoo floating in the humid air.

"Charley?" she whispered. "Why didn't you tell me that you were coming over here to see me?"

He looked up into her dark brown eyes, which had become filled with concern. "I didn't really have the time to explain anything, and I honestly still don't," he said in a dry voice.

"Come on in. I just ordered some coffee to be sent up," she said, as she opened the door a little further. Charley removed his hat and wiped the sweat off from his forehead as he entered her room.

Bennetti closed the door and began looking around the room. As Sandy began walking over to the closet, the smell of her shampoo was quickly replaced with the smell of clean linens; and his eyes traced the dark red walls of the room, past the marigold sheets on the queen-size bed, and over to the wooden table that was positioned next to an opened window.

"Here, Charley, let me take your coat," Sandy said in a soft voice, as she slowly approached him with a wooden coat hanger. The contours of her bare frame were visible through her black silk nightgown, which clung to her body in the humid air like a second layer of skin.

Charley let out a slow, delicate sigh. *I must be dreaming right now,* he thought to himself, but this was certainly no dream. The aching in his shoulders as he removed his overcoat and the way that his hat had clung to his forehead when he removed it had reminded him of that. "I'm really tired, Sandy," Charley said in a trembling voice before he cleared his throat. "Is it okay if I sit down?"

Sandy gave him a warm smile. "Be my guest. I think that the fresh air might do you some good," she said, as she extended her arm towards the wooden table.

Charley Bennetti took off his holster and set his pistol down onto the nightstand before he pulled one of the chairs away from the wooden table over by the window and sat down. His knees were still shaking, and he tried to hold them still under the table with his hands. He watched Sandy take a seat at the table in the other chair across from him. Her black silk nightgown made a faint rustling sound against the hardwood seat of the chair, and once she was seated, she pulled her thick dark brown hair back over behind her shoulders.

"So what brings you around?" she asked as she reached over the table to caress his hand. Her tender touch sent a familiar wave of comfort throughout his body, and he slowly began to feel his nerves unwinding. "Take your time, Charley. We've got all night," Sandy said, with her dark brown eyes shimmering in the dimly lit room.

Charley shook his head and then said, "I don't know what I've gotten myself into lately, or why it's been so long since I've been here to see you, *or* why exactly it was that you chose to stop working for us!" Sandy Granger's eyes grew wide, and she nervously ran her teeth along the side of her lower lip. "I mainly came here to see you tonight because I wanted to," Charley said. "But Silvia Pazzelli has also been wantin' me to keep an eye on you lately." Bennetti leaned in closer to her and then said, "She said that workin' for Plemagoya might be bringin' you in more customers for now but that your job has gotten to be a lot more dangerous than it used to be."

Sandy Granger lowered her head and squinted her eyes shut. Charley saw a teardrop run down the side of her nose before she slowly picked her head back up. "I'm so sorry, Charley," she said. "I really didn't have any sort of a choice in the matter." Her lower lip suddenly began trembling, and then she said, "Just know that, through it all, I never stopped…" Her voice trailed away, and she suddenly broke off her eye contact with him.

"Never stopped *what*? Loving me?" Charley asked, lifting his eyebrows inquisitively, and Sandy slowly began nodding. He got up from his chair and walked over to hold her as she cried.

"Just promise me that you don't hate me now," Sandy said in a muffled voice, as she pressed her face into his shoulder. The coconut smell of her shampoo entered into his nostrils again, and her skin felt warm and soft through the silk of her black nightgown.

"No," Charley said softly as he shook his head, "business will always be business, but what we share together is personal."

There was suddenly a muffled knock at the door. "That must be the coffee," Charley said. He quickly got up from the table and threw his hat over the pistol on the nightstand and then walked across the room into the bathroom and quietly closed the door. Sandy Granger wiped the tears away from her eyes and got up from the table.

"I will be right there!" she said loudly as she pulled a bathrobe off from a hook on the wall to cover up her nightgown.

Charley Bennetti heard Sandy taking the chain off the front door from the inside of the bathroom. He gently removed a towel from the rack next to him, pulled off his glasses, and began wiping away the beads of sweat that had collected on his face. *It's sure gonna be a long night,* Charley thought to himself, as he pulled the towel away from his face and made eye contact with his reflection in the mirror. Sandy Granger had changed a lot over the years; but somehow, to him, she would always remain the same girl that he had grown up around the corner from in Camden. Back in those days, money was tight, and time was valuable. Now, it seemed as though things were the other way around.

CHAPTER 35

An Unexpected Guest

It was a slow evening for business at The Golden Sandbox, even for a Wednesday night. There appeared to be less than a dozen customers out at the tables on the floor. A five-block radius that had included the club had been closed off the previous evening so that the police could try to solve a murder, and apparently, word traveled fast around this town, even though the story had been kept out of the late edition of last night's newspapers. Melanie Hillsdale arrived right on time for the beginning of her shift at seven o'clock that night, which was somewhat of a miracle. She hadn't slept properly for several days now and found herself applying more cosmetics to her eyes than usual to cover up the bags that were starting to collect under them. She yawned with her mouth closed and then stopped walking towards the dressing rooms once she looked over past the bar and saw Randy Wyman leaning up against the far wall with his arms folded. She slowly began approaching Randy but avoided maintaining eye contact with him. She kept her eyes looking from side to side because it was one of the tricks that she had learned over the years to help her stay awake whenever there reached a point when she had become this exhausted. Randy gave her a gentle smile once she reached him.

"You look tired, Mel," he said. "How you holdin' up?"

She leaned in close to whisper to him in the hopes that he could still read her lips, even if he couldn't clearly hear everything that she was saying to him. "Not too good," she replied. "It's been a long week so far. And having us get interrogated by a couple of relentless police officers last night didn't really seem to help matters too much."

Randy put his hands on her shoulders and looked straight into her eyes. "Well then, you probably should've taken tonight off," he said. "As you can see, there aren't really a whole lot of customers after what happened around here last night."

Melanie nodded blankly as she set her white leather purse up on the bar. "I know, Randy," she said. "But I really needed to get out of the house. I needed to be able to take my mind off things for a while. Even if it meant coming back here. The more active that I stay right now, the better off I think I will be." She pulled a cigarette out from her purse and held it up to her mouth. Randy ignited his Zippo and held it up to her cigarette, which was now being held by her trembling hand. "Thanks, Randy," she said. "I'm gonna go get ready to go on stage now, but I'm gonna need a moment alone just to collect myself."

Randy gave her a gentle smile and then said, "Hey, you know that I can definitely understand that." Melanie nodded to him and then drearily made her way down the back corridor towards her dressing room.

Once she was inside of her dressing room, she pulled a small .38 Special from her purse and set it inside of the safe that she kept below her vanity table. *I absolutely hate the fact that I have to carry this thing around,* she thought to herself. *But if I don't, who knows what might end up happening to me.* She reached back into her purse and pulled out an envelope containing the bus ticket back to Philadelphia that her father had given to her, along with the pistol, after they had left the police station last night. She set it inside of the safe and angled it to cover up the pistol. Then, she closed the door to the safe and spun the knob around a couple of times to ensure that it was fully secured.

There was suddenly a loud knock at her door. "Randy, I told you that I needed a moment alone to collect myself," she said as she slowly pulled the door open.

"Melanie Ann Hillsdale?" she heard a man's voice asking. Melanie's eyes widened with surprise. The man on the other side of the door pulled a badge out from the inside pocket of his dark brown suit. "I'm not sure if you remember me from last night, or not," he said. "But I'm Detective Jacob Farmers from the Atlantic City Police Department. I was wondering if I might be able to ask you just a couple more quick questions."

She let out a sigh of annoyance as she rolled her eyes. "Yes, I remember who you are!" she shouted. "Weren't you the one who kept on antagonizing me while I spent several hours answering the same questions over and over again? What do you want with me?"

The detective tucked his badge back into his coat and then said, "Just to talk to ya, if that's all right."

Melanie slowly pulled the door to her dressing room open further and stepped out into the hallway. She briefly wrinkled her nose a little as she stepped closer to the detective and caught a whiff of his cheap aftershave. "I really don't have anything left to say to you that I didn't already talk to you and to Detective Morris about last night!" she yelled. "What the hell do you guys want from me?! Don't you realize that showing up like this to question me again while I am working, after I have honestly already told you everything that I know, constitutes harassment?!"

Jacob Farmers reached his left hand into the pocket of his pants and pulled out a plastic bag that contained a familiar-looking diamond earring. The dim light that radiated from the ceiling caused a reflection on it that created a gleaming light against his dark red shirt as he held it up to her. "I am here to see you tonight because that conversation you had with me and my partner was before we found this little beauty lying in the same parking lot as the three shell casings from the murder. We went back to scour over the area again later last night," Farmers said, and he raised one of his eyebrows at her inquisitively before he continued, "you know, just lookin' for clues and doin' my job. The usual sorta stuff that you'd come to expect from a guy like me. Anyways, we found this earring lyin' over in an area that was pretty close to a three-foot-long blood trail that went across the very same parking lot. You sure that you don't have time to talk to me? Even if you're in the clear, it's pretty safe to say that your life could be in danger here."

Melanie raised her shoulders and put up her right hand to cover his face from her view as she turned away. "Look, as I have already told you, you guys already got everything that I know out of me last night while I was at the police station! I really don't understand why you can't just accept that!" she shouted.

Farmers smiled at her as he put the plastic bag containing the earring back into his pocket. "Okay," he said, "but even after I have shown you that, it might be wiser for you to learn to cooperate with us, rather that thinking that you and Randy can handle something like this all on your own."

Melanie turned around and faced Farmers with a blank look, but the tone of her voice failed to conceal her level of agitation. "If I should somehow happen to miraculously think of anything that I didn't already tell you guys at the police station last night, I will be more than happy to give your partner a call," she said and then began closing the door to her dressing room.

Farmers leaned in closer to the door as it was nearly shut. "What time do you go on tonight?" he asked. "The working day is almost done for me! I get off duty in about an hour!"

He leaned closer to the dressing room door after it had closed and heard her muffled voice say, "Screw you!"

Farmers laughed under his breath. And as he turned around, he came face-to-face with Randy Wyman. Their eyes meet, and the detective's mild look of playful amusement quickly dissipated into a blank stare. "Is she always this difficult?" Farmers asked, as he pointed his thumb up over his shoulder towards the dressing room door.

Randy shook his head. "I honestly don't think that you'll ever know the half of it when it comes down to something like that. I would say that your work here is finished. Have yourself a nice night, Officer," he said to the detective and then followed him back across the club and over towards the front door.

CHAPTER 36

Outside Sources

Vincent Plemagoya and Pedro Navilla sat at a table inside of a dimly lit bar near the coastline of the Atlantic Ocean with two female companions seated in between them. Plemagoya lifted his hat up off from the table and then motioned at Pedro towards the door with his head.

"Where are you going?" one of the women asked, as Plemagoya got up from the table.

"Don't worry about where I'm goin'," Plemagoya said. "You should be a lot more worried about whether or not I'm ever comin' back again." He then winked at her before placing his hat on top of his head.

Pedro looked at him, shaking his head in annoyance, and then looked at the woman who was seated next to him. "I'll be right back," Pedro said as he leaned in towards her. "Just gimme a minute or two."

The woman slowly nodded, and then Pedro left a small amount of money on the table to cover the drinks that they had ordered before he followed Plemagoya outside of the bar.

The two men walked around the corner from the bar and then got into the silver 1954 Ford Crestline that was parked in a lot behind the building. "This won't take too long," Vincent said, "because I know that we've got company waitin' on us."

Pedro looked over at Plemagoya with a visible expression of agitation on his face. "You're damn right, we do!" Pedro shouted, "So whatever this is about, it'd better be good!"

Plemagoya gave Pedro a piercing glance and then said, "You mean you didn't hear about what happened to Tony Tyler last night?"

Pedro shrugged, and the irritated look on his face began to loosen. "Yeah, I sure did," he said. "Natty told me about it earlier today. But that situation sounds like it's a lot more your problem than it is mine, hombre! I didn't have no part in that!"

Vincent Plemagoya shook his head and laughed and then said, "It don't matter to me if you had any part in what happened last night or not! I'm tellin' ya, Pedro! Charley Bennetti's really gotta go! And I mean right now! All I'm doin' is askin' for you to help me! He's the only one who saw what happened to Tony last night!" Plemagoya looked over into the side mirror of the car to see if any headlights were shining in the parking lot, and then he said, "It's time for us to squash him like the scared little rat fink that he is! I've already set up one trap for him. I know that he's over at The Skyline Hotel. If you'll just set the other trap up, I bet that he'll be off our hands before the night's over." Plemagoya placed his hand on Pedro's shoulder and then said, "Pretty please, muchacho? I'll even make sure that your pretty little senorita sticks around until you get back."

Pedro quickly shook his head and then said, "Damn it, Vinnie! All right! But no more favors after this! Remember what I said last weekend about learning to control yourself a little better?"

Vincent Plemagoya laughed. "Sure do!" he said and then pushed a folded-up piece of paper into the front pocket of Pedro's shirt. "That's the name of the detective that you wanna try and reach," Plemagoya said, and then he got out of the car, as Pedro started the engine.

* * *

Police Chief Marty Albertson sat awake at home in his den near a desk lamp going over the officer's reports from Tony Tyler's murder last night. *What in the world am I going to tell the mayor the next time that I see him?* he thought to himself. *Just last weekend, there was quite a sizable problem at Fossgate's, and now we've got this to deal with. Lately, my job has been to somehow convince him, and so many other people, that crime has gone down in this city over the past few months. Nobody's gonna believe me anymore.* He organized all the police reports into a pile before tucking them back into a manila folder, and then he neatly set the manila folder on the lower right-hand corner of the desktop. Tomorrow would be a very long day if no new leads would break loose with this case.

* * *

Pedro Navilla pulled the silver 1954 Ford Crestline into the parking lot of a gas station just off Interstate 95 and then quickly got out of the car to walk up to a phone booth that was located on a dimly lit side of the building. He nervously struck a match to light a cigarette and then threw the extinguished match outside of the phone booth. He exhaled smoke that swirled around inside of the phone booth in a blue cloud, as headlights from a passing car on the interstate briefly shone into the parking lot. Pedro dropped a dime into the pay phone and dialed the number from the paper that Plemagoya had stuck into his pocket. He then pulled a handkerchief out from his pocket and wadded it up in order to muffle the receiver. Once there was an answer on the other end of the phone, Pedro began to speak slowly in a low-toned and distorted voice, "I have some information concerning the whereabouts of Charley Bennetti."

* * *

Detective Jacob Farmers sat with his feet propped up against the top of his desk, as Stanley Morris stood against a cubicle sipping a cup of black coffee. "Tried gettin' all the leads gathered up that I could after what happened last night," Farmers said. "And so did you. We've still got virtually nothing to go on right now, except for a few clues and two very tightlipped witnesses."

Morris rolled his eyes towards the ceiling and then said, "Don't remind me! I still don't really understand how a dead body with three bullet holes in it is somehow capable of just getting up and walking away like that!"

Jacob Farmers smiled and then said, "Well, that's what we do around here, now, isn't it? We solve mysteries. Now, you know just as well as I do that a body doesn't just up and disappear like that. Not unless somebody stuffed it into the back of a car, that is."

Suddenly, the telephone on his desk rang. He quickly landed his feet back against the floor and picked up the receiver. "This is Detective Jacob Farmers," he said, as he watched his partner slowly begin walking away. "No shit? You've got a lead on Charley Bennetti?" Farmers asked, waving his partner back towards his desk. Stanley Morris quickly turned around and walked back towards his partner's cubicle. He watched as Jacob Farmers frantically scribbled some notes down onto a pad of paper on his desk and then hung up the phone receiver.

CHAPTER 37

Sudden Complications

Charley Bennetti awoke to Sandy Granger softly kissing his forehead.

"I am going down the hallway to get a bucket of ice," she said in a soft and soothing voice.

Charley smiled with his eyes shut and then rolled over onto his left side. Through half-opened eyelids, he could see a blurred vision of the rear side of Sandy's bare figure disappearing into the bathroom, and he watched the light go on underneath the door. He could then faintly hear the squeaking sound of the faucet turning on as she had begun to brush her teeth. He slowly drifted back off to sleep before Sandy gently and quietly opened the bathroom door, dressed once again in a bathrobe over her black silk nightgown. She took the room key that Charley had left on the nightstand beside the bed, along with the ice bucket, and quietly closed the door before locking it.

She walked quickly down the dimly lit hallway towards the ice machine that was located near the center of the fourth floor of the hotel. Down the other end of the hallway, across from room 401, the door to the staircase softly and slowly opened, and Detective Jacob Farmers watched as Sandy Granger began filling a small bucket with ice.

"Okay, let's go," Farmers whispered to Morris, and the two detectives sprung from the doorway and began rapidly walking down the hallway towards Sandy.

The ice bucket in her hands was nearly full, and then she heard a low voice coming from behind her left shoulder, "Excuse me, ma'am. Is it all right if we have a word with you?"

She rapidly spun around to see the smiling face of Jacob Farmers, as he and Stanley Morris both pulled out their badges. Her eyes grew wide in shock as her mouth fell open; and she suddenly dropped the ice bucket on the floor and covered her mouth.

Stanley Morris came up from behind Jacob Farmers, while reaching behind his back to grab his handcuffs. Farmers smiled, and his teeth glimmered eerily in the dimly lit hallway. "Do you like jewelry?" he asked, "because we brought ya a pair of matching bracelets. Sorry that we didn't think to bring you a pair of matching earrings to go along with 'em." Stanley Morris locked the handcuffs tightly around Sandy's wrists and then picked the ice bucket up off from the floor.

"Come on, let's go find Charley. I have been waiting for the chance to catch up with him lately," Farmers said, as he reached deep into the right-side pocket of Sandy's bathrobe to grab the hotel room key. The two detectives then began to escort her back down the dimly lit hallway, and she kept her head hung low so that her dark brown hair covered her face.

Jacob Farmers looked over at his partner and said, "Ya know, Stan, I've got some vacation time comin' up. I just might decide to take on off to Florida for a little while after a catch like this one. Keep her here in the hallway for a quick second. I'll go in first, and then I'll motion for ya once I know that the coast is clear." Stanley Morris slowly nodded. "Is there anybody else in the room with you two?" Farmers asked. Sandy Granger narrowly and rapidly shook her head, and Morris watched as a loose teardrop came off from the tip of her nose. Once they reached the door to room 417, Farmers lifted a finger up to his mouth and softly said, "Shhh…" He slowly and quietly began to unlock the door.

Charley Bennetti suddenly awoke to the feeling of something cold and metal tightly pressed under his chin. "Rise and shine, lover boy!" Detective Jacob Farmers said through gritting teeth, "If you so much as move a muscle, the cleaning ladies in this place are about to start workin' overtime! Understood?"

Charley Bennetti blinked hard and quickly looked over to see that the holstered pistol that he had placed over on the nightstand earlier was now gone. His eyes then suddenly moved down towards the foot of the bed and were met with an unrelenting stare from Detective Stanley Morris. Jacob Farmers lifted Charley Bennetti up off the bed and began frisking him. Farmers smiled thinly as he pulled out his handcuffs and then said, "And there are no other weapons on ya this time, Charley. Good boy."

Stanley Morris then pulled out a notebook from the pocket of his gray overcoat. "Charles Lloyd Bennetti, you are under arrest," Morris said. "You have the right to remain silent. Anything you say can and will be used against you in a court of law. You have the right to an attorney. If you cannot afford an attorney, one will be appointed to you."

Farmers let out a soft chuckle and then said, "I'm sure that he probably knows the routine by now, Stan."

After his rights had been read and the handcuffs had been firmly secured around his wrists, Charley Bennetti lifted his head and came face-to-face with Sandy Granger. "I'm so sorry, Charley," she said, as she shrugged.

He noticed that her hands were also firmly secured behind her back. "It looks like bad luck has really gotten the best of us."

Jacob Farmers leaned up over Bennetti's shoulder and said, "Save it for when we get down to the station, cupcake! You've both got a lot of explaining to do!"

"Could the two of you please give us just another moment?" Farmers asked, as he gently smiled over at his partner and their other suspect. Stanley Morris slowly nodded and led Sandy Granger out of the hotel room. Jacob Farmers then immediately came around to meet with Charley face-to-face. Farmers still had one side of his face locked into a loose smile, as he looked down at his watch. "Well, it might be too late for the two of you to be on the eleven o'clock news tonight," he said. "But it's just in time to make the early edition of tomorrow's paper. Are you willing to cooperate with us?" Charley kept his face low but maintained a disdainful level of eye contact with the detective. "Oh, and before I forget, here's a little room service that comes compliments of Frank Moniarti," Jacob Farmers said, and then he lifted his right arm up and hit Charley Bennetti with his elbow—twice in the chest and then once in his left eye. "Get up, champ! Let's go find you a lawyer," Farmers said, as he lifted Charley back up off the mattress. Farmers reached over onto the wooden table by the window and grabbed Charley's glasses off from it. "Oh, and uh, here you go. Just in case you were wondering, I've never really believed in hitting a guy with glasses," Farmers said and laughed, and then he quickly led Charley Bennetti out of the hotel room.

CHAPTER 38

Thursday, October 18, 1962
A Small Favor

Frank Moniarti and Teddy Pazzelli pulled up on South Tennessee Avenue in a dark blue 1955 Buick Riviera just down the street from the city jail, which was located on the second floor of the city hall building.

"Thanks for taking me down here on such a short notice, Teddy," Moniarti said with his head lowered. "I'm hopin' that if Mayor Antill has already been down here to talk to Charley that he was more gentle with him than what I'm gonna be."

Teddy Pazzelli nodded and then said, "As for the ride, Frankie, you're welcome. As for Charley, try not to do anything too rash that's gonna get you thrown in there right alongside of him. I've heard that the food that they serve up in that place is *terrible*! Not only that, but then we'd both have a whole lot of explaining to do to Meg once I got you back outta there. So just keep that in mind once you get outta the car. All righty?"

Moniarti lifted his head up to make eye contact with Pazzelli and then said, "Thanks for the reminder, Teddy! I'll keep that in mind! But if I'm bailin' his ass outta here, then he owes me! I told him to stay away from The Skyline Hotel no matter what! Especially, after Sandy traded sides on us! Even if he somehow still trusts her—and *clearly*, he still does—that's too dangerous of a place for him to go! I tried tellin' him that already! And, I *thought* that I had gotten my point across to him! But apparently not!"

Teddy kept his hands on the steering wheel as he shrugged and then said, "Just try to have some level of understanding about the situation. All right, Frankie? I mean, I gotta eat, you gotta eat, and even poor little Charley's gotta eat, sometimes…"

Frank Moniarti quickly flung the passenger-side door of the car open with his foot. "Yeah, yeah!" he said. "Just remember that this bail money ain't comin' outta *your* pocket!"

Teddy Pazzelli casually nodded and then said, "I'll remember that, Frankie. I'll remember that. I'm just gonna go on down near the pier and feed the pigeons for a little while so that I don't end up gettin' a parking ticket. I'll be back in about a half hour."

Frank Moniarti adjusted the brim of his hat in the side mirror. "All right. Well, this shouldn't take too long," he said and then got out of the car.

* * *

Charley Bennetti lay silently asleep in his cot on the second tier of jail cells located on the second floor of city hall. A guard suddenly began loudly rapping his nightstick against the bars of the holding cell. "All right, Bennetti! On your feet! You've got a visitor!" the guard shouted, and Charley snapped his eyes open before quickly rolling off from his cot and onto his feet.

"Don't I even get to brush my teeth first?" Bennetti asked.

"Not unless you're plannin' on kissin' somebody," the guard scoffed. "Besides, after the compromising situation that you got caught in, I don't really think that this one's your type. Now get movin'!"

Charley quickly buttoned his shirt up and then straightened his hair in the mirror. He noticed that his left eye was starting to bruise as he picked his glasses up off from the sink and placed them back onto his face.

"What're ya doin', Charley? Gettin' ready for prom? I ain't got all day!" the guard barked.

"Don't get mad at me because I'm more popular than you are," Charley said from the mirror. "Besides, this person is here to see me right now because they want to. You and I aren't here to see each other right now because we want to. It's because we have to. See the difference?"

The guard raised his finger up through the bars and said, "One more word outta you, and I'll have the boys down in the kitchen, serve ya up some cold beef stew with a cigar butt stickin' out of it tonight! You got that?" Charley Bennetti silently nodded, and then the guard slowly opened the door to his cell before they began walking together down the cement path of the cell block.

* * *

The guard led Charley into the visitation room and walked him over to the wooden chair next to the table that faced towards the entry door. After Charley sat down, the guard walked back over to the door and began quietly talking to someone on the other side of it. Charley slowly began to rise up off from the wooden chair to see a dark gray hat moving from behind the head of the short, stocky guard. The guard lifted his hand to take something from the person before quickly nodding and stepping through the doorway to exit from the room. Once the guard had left, Charley Bennetti's eyes grew wide with surprise to see Frank Moniarti standing in the doorway to the visitation room. Bennetti slowly sat back down into the wooden chair and then swallowed hard. He suddenly felt an overwhelming sense of nausea well up in the pit of his stomach as he watched Moniarti walk in through the doorway.

"Hey ya, Charley," Frank said. "How's the food in this place?"

Charley Bennetti cleared his throat and then softly said, "Not too good, actually."

Moniarti removed his hat as he approached the table. "I just gave the guard a hundred bucks and told him to go take a coffee break so that we could have a moment alone to figure things out,"

Frank said calmly before taking off his overcoat and pulling up a chair at the table.

Frank Moniarti placed his hat off to the side and then laid his hands flat against the hardwood surface of the table. "So do you mind tellin' me exactly what happened before I decide whether or not I'm gonna spring you outta this place?" he said. "Your lawyer already told me about your intention to plead no contest, and he also said that your next hearing has been set for about two weeks from now." Charley Bennetti's lower lip began to tremble, and he remained silent for a moment. "How do you expect me to help you, if you won't talk to me?" Frank asked. "You're in a lot of trouble here, Charley! Now, spill it!" Bennetti rolled his head around over his shoulders. His neck still felt sore from the way that he had slept.

"The judge set the bail at fifteen grand, and—" Charley suddenly stopped speaking.

"Fifteen grand?! Hell, I'm amazed that the judge allowed you any amount of bail at all!" Moniarti shouted, "The money is the least of my worries right now! What I wanna know right here and right now is what in the hell you were doin' meeting up with Tony Tyler! And why you then saw it fit to head on over to The Skyline Hotel and start rollin' around in the sheets with that cheap, dime-store floozy after I had specifically told you time and time again to stay away from that place!" Frank Moniarti lowered his eyebrows in a piercing stare.

And Charley suddenly leaned his shoulders back against the hardwood chair and then said, "Look, Frankie, it was never anything personal. But if I hadn't met up with Tony from time to time to get information from him, you and Teddy never would've known how to find Plemagoya. And it was Tony Tyler who ended up pullin' the trigger on Billy Walker. I figured that you'd wanna know about that." Charley paused to clear his throat before continuing, "Like I told you, I was planning on leaving for Denver this morning, just like we had talked about. But after I watched Tony get shot, well, let's just say that I had some dirty work to do after that."

Frank Moniarti pounded his fists against the table and then said, "I'd say ya did, too! What part of 'don't go over to The Skyline Hotel for any reason' didn't sink in through your thick skull, Charley? You could've gotten yourself killed goin' down there!" Frank Moniarti broke away his eye contact with Charley and then began shaking his head in frustration.

There was a moment of silence between the two men before they made eye contact with each other again. "Yeah, Jacob Farmers was thoughtful enough to remind me of that before he took me in," Charley said and then began rubbing at the swollen spot underneath his left eye. "I guess that we should've upped his holiday bonus last year…"

Frank Moniarti suddenly sprung up from his chair at the table and quickly grabbed Charley Bennetti by the collar of his shirt. Bennetti's glasses fell to the floor, and Moniarti kicked them underneath the table. He forcefully slammed Charley's body up against the brick wall behind the table and then violently poked his finger directly into the center of his chest. Moniarti was pressing his finger straight into the bruised part of Charley's chest, and it caused his shoulders to visibly hunch up against the cold brick wall that was directly behind his head. As Charley quickly turned his head to the side, the light green paint on the bricks seemed to cause his degree of nausea to elevate to an increasingly unbearable level.

"Now you listen to me, you little bastard!" Moniarti shouted, "I'm about to do you a favor, and then it's gonna be time for you to do me a favor in return! Do you understand that?!" Moniarti's eyes were in a seething blaze of passionate fury. His face was red and contorted, and his saliva was spraying in a forceful mist as he screamed. Charley had to wince in order to keep any of it from going into his eyes.

"Yes!" Charley whimpered, "Yes, I understand that!" He turned his head away in a shameful retreat from the terrifying look on Moniarti's face.

"Good, because I am about to get you outta this place just before they try to pin Tony Tyler's murder on you! On top of all the other charges that you've been slapped with! After this is over, don't you ever question me on anything that I ask you to do from now on! After I get done payin' your bail, your ass belongs to me!

Permanently! Do you understand *that*?!" Moniarti leaned in closer as Charley whimpered and nodded. "You told me that you had some dirty work to do after Tony Tyler got killed!" Moniarti continued, "Well, I'm afraid that you don't even know the half of it, buddy! You can forget all about your trip to Denver! And that little girlfriend of yours is gonna end up rottin' away in this place, I'm sorry to say! But once you're officially outta here, I'm gonna expect you to call up Teddy and find out everything that this little favor is gonna entail!" Frank looked over his shoulder towards the door and then began to lower the tone of his voice. "He won't be able to say exactly what the favor is over the phone, but look for an envelope in your mailbox once you get back home that has a red geranium stamped on the back of it." Moniarti said, "No questions asked, no complaints muttered, no backing out of the deal, just a small favor. Then, after this is all over, consider yourself relieved from your duties. I'm gonna go find another bookkeeper." Moniarti quickly turned around and grabbed his hat and overcoat from the table and chair and then walked out the door.

Charley began to tenderly rub the bruised spot in the center of his chest and then began quietly weeping as he collapsed down onto the cold cement floor.

CHAPTER 39

Making a Pit Stop

Doyle Reynolds looked over at Sly Robinson as the semi that they were riding in passed by a sign that read Monroe County. They had been on the road for close to eight hours now, and the fact that they had been mysteriously heading too far north in the State of Pennsylvania had sparked Doyle's curiosity.

"So do you mind finally tellin' me what all this is about?" Doyle asked. "We've been on the road for a *real* long time now."

Sly laughed over in the passenger seat. "Ya know, I gotta hand it to ya for your patience," he said, as he reached into the glove compartment of the semi to pull out a folded-up road map. "We're headin' to a little town around the way called Tobyhanna. There's an army depot base located up over there, and we're just gonna leave the car in their care for a couple hours while we go put some gas into this hog of a semi and go grab a bite to eat. I even brought along a deck of cards, you know, just in case you might wanna play a game of cards at the truck stop or somethin' while we wait."

Doyle kept both hands on the steering wheel as he shrugged and then said, "That don't bother me none. But don't you think that unloadin' a stolen car onto government property is just a *tad* bit risky? I mean, don't you think that the FBI might wanna have a few choice words to say to us after we go and do somethin' like that?"

Sly squinted his eyes as he kept them focused on the road ahead of them. "Nah, that stuff's all been taken care of," Sly said. "Trust me. It was all in the work order that Mr. Malone had given to us. I didn't wanna say nothin' before we left because I figured that you probably would've stayed behind knowin' that we were gonna be doing somethin' like this. But Mr. Malone is a *lot* more connected than you probably think that he is! I mean, how many politicians in Washington do you think are wearin' his suits right now?" Both men started to laugh, and then Sly began to unfold the road map.

After Sly looked over the map of their current location, he looked next to him and saw Doyle stretching and yawning behind the wheel. "We should be just about there," Sly said. "Then after that, we've got about three more hours of road time ahead of us before we reach Ocean City."

Doyle Reynolds shook his head, and then he said, "Three more hours of drivin'? And that's after they get done fixin' this car up? You told me that they were gonna be hangin' onto it for a couple of hours. But you still ain't told me what they were gonna be doin' to it."

Sly rolled down his window to let some fresh air circulate throughout the cab of the semi. "That's right! I didn't!" he said. "Back in Detroit, all I was doin' was fixin' up the muffler and the exhaust system to make sure that the car would accelerate silently. Over here, they gonna be installin' some bulletproof glass, craftin' up a bullet-proof body, and givin' that thing a whole lotta extra acceleration!"

Doyle raised his eyebrows as he looked over at Sly and then asked, "And how they gonna do that?"

Sly folded the map over in his lap and then asked, "How they gonna do what?"

Doyle focused his eyes back on the road and then asked, "Make the car go faster?"

Sly smiled as both men looked out of the windshield, and then he said, "That's a hard thing for me to explain to you because you really don't know nothin' about cars. I've always been the one takin' 'em, and you've always been the one keepin' a watch out for me. But some scientist over here has been workin' on some sorta new water injection system that uses methanol that we're gonna be tryin' out on this car. He says that he's done enough experiments to the point that he knows that it works!"

Doyle Reynolds slowly shook his head and then asked, "You sure about that?"

Sly lowered his eyebrows as he looked over at Doyle and then said, "Yeah, of course, I'm sure! And so's the scientist! And, so's Mr. Malone! Otherwise, we wouldn't be comin' out here all this way!"

Doyle smirked and said, "Like I said to you earlier, I guess that I'll just be finding everything out as we go along."

Sly began laughing and then said, "You got that right! Our turn is comin' up! So just try to act natural! This part of the deal will all be over with soon enough! And then, we're gonna be rich!"

Doyle nodded and then clicked on the turn signal before he began turning the semi down a long service road.

CHAPTER 40

Unethical Practices

Melanie Hillsdale stepped out onto the sidewalk from the passenger seat of Scotty McCormack's gold-colored 1962 BMW 3200 CS and entered into the front door of the downtown police station. She walked up to the clerk at the front counter and set her white leather purse up next to the glass window. The clerk had her back turned towards Melanie as she talked with the secretary who sat only a few feet away from the clerk. The secretary saw Melanie standing at the counter and nodded at the clerk before pointing over to Melanie.

"Hello, may I help you?" the clerk said.

Melanie stepped up further towards the glass and said, "I would like to request a formal complaint form to file against one of your officers here who works in the homicide department."

The clerk quickly turned around and looked back towards a door located at the beginning of a short hallway that was directly across from the secretary. "Please, excuse me for a moment, and I will try to find someone who can help you with that," the clerk said.

Melanie rolled her eyes and then turned her back to the glass before folding her arms. *Geez, all I did was ask you for a simple piece of paper,* she thought to herself. *If it takes more than one person to handle that, I don't think that this is going to go very well.*

185

The sound of Melanie's pacing footsteps echoed throughout the empty lobby until she saw a door next to the service window suddenly open. Captain David Van Bulkem stepped out into the lobby. He was a tall, thin man with short red hair, bright blue eyes, and a clean-cut face with a square-but-rigid-looking jaw. "Hello, my name is Captain David Van Bulkem," he said in a deep voice.

"My name is Melanie Hillsdale, and I—" She began.

"Please," Captain Van Bulkem interrupted and then extended his arm towards a single row of chairs that sat against the wall of the lobby. Once they were seated side by side, Captain Van Bulkem lifted a clipboard up into his lap and said, "I understand that you are here to file a formal complaint against one of our officers?"

Melanie stared at him blankly and then said, "Yes, you see, I feel as though my rights and, more importantly, my privacy has been violated lately, and I felt this was the only way that—"

Van Bulkem cleared his throat before interrupting her again. "I see…So, which officer is it that you were wanting to file a complaint against?"

Melanie lifted her leather purse up off from her lap and then set it down on the floor next to her chair. "Well, I believe his name was Detective Jacob Farmers," she said. "You know him. Tall, wears glasses, has a mustache, wears clothes that barely fit him, along with some of the most horrid aftershave that I've ever smelled on anybody in my life."

Captain Van Bulkem placed his reading glasses onto his face and then pulled a pen out from the pocket of his shirt. "We are here right now to get to the root of a potential problem, miss," he said. "We can always discuss people's personal hygiene at another time and in another location. Now, please, carry on with why you feel that filing a formal complaint against this officer might be absolutely necessary." Van Bulkem slowly lowered his head and then looked at Melanie over the frames of his glasses.

She could feel an uncomfortable stare coming from the police captain, the clerk, and from the secretary off to the side. She briefly looked down at her hands, which were folded in her lap, before looking back up to make eye contact with the police captain. "Well, you see, I was held here and questioned the other night without the presence of an attorney." She began. "And then after that, he proceeded to come into an *extremely* restricted area at my place of employment and then tried to harass me even further. As it stands now, I'm planning on leaving on a bus for Philadelphia right after this, just to get away from this whole mess. But I will be happy to return to town to testify as a witness, if and when a trial date gets set either for the murder case, or better yet, for this detective's level of unethical practices. And I will even have a *lawyer* with me when the time comes down for that!"

Captain Van Bulkem passed the clipboard over to Melanie and then looked silently down into his lap. "I'm sorry," he said. "You're not the only citizen that's been having problems with this particular detective lately. Granted, he has been with this department for a substantially long period of time, and experience is supposed to make people better at what they do. However, better doesn't always mean perfect."

Melanie went over the form on the clipboard with a pen. "I realize that," she said without looking up. "But I wanted to take care of this before he had the chance to treat anybody else this way."

Captain Van Bulkem sighed and then said, "I understand. You are welcome to leave the form with the clerk, and I will see to it that the chief of police gets it before I head on home."

Melanie slowly looked up at Van Bulkem and then said, "But this form requires your signature, too. I can see it right here at the bottom. These forms don't get used around here very often, do they?"

Van Bulkem smiled as he shook his head and then replied, "It would be a lot more concerning to all of us around here if they did."

Melanie finished filling out the complaint form and then passed it over to Van Bulkem. He pushed his lower lip out as he looked down through his glasses at the form before signing it. "There," he said. "We should be all set. But don't hesitate to call us if there's ever anything further that you need." He passed over one of his business cards to Melanie, and then she thanked him before she placed it into her purse and walked back out of the police station.

* * *

Scotty McCormack dropped Melanie off early at the bus station over on Atlantic Avenue. She sat quietly with her luggage positioned next to and in front of her seat in the lobby, waiting for her bus to depart in about fifteen minutes. She sipped at a foam cup filled with black coffee, as she heard the muffled sound of a male voice on the intercom announcing the departure of other coaches. The moments seemed to be going by much faster now than they ever did while she had been sitting at the police station. *I can't wait to get out of here,* she thought to herself. *I will try to find a way to make it back here once all this is over with. But I know that deep down, Randy understands.* She began collecting all her luggage bags and then looked up to see Randy Wyman racing towards her. In her brief moment of surprise, she dropped her two duffle bags and her suitcase. He was out of breath by the time that he had reached her.

"Sorry that I didn't make it here sooner," he said. "I went by your apartment to see if you were there, and then I had the cab driver drop me off here." He looked down at the luggage bags that were sprawled out on the floor. "Here, let me get those things for you." He picked up her bags, and then they began walking side by side towards the bus terminal. "I couldn't just let you leave without saying good-bye to you. Even if this situation only lasts for a little while, I couldn't just let you go back to Philadelphia without any sort of company before you left."

Melanie looked over at Randy and smiled as she wiped a teardrop away from her eye. "Well, that was really sweet of you," she said. She looked down blankly at the ground as they continued to walk. "I just had Scotty bring me down to the police station one more time."

Randy's eyes suddenly grew wide in surprise. "For what?" he said. "Did you forget somethin' while we were down there?"

Melanie shook her head and then said, "Not that I can think of. I just filed a formal complaint against the detective that you had to shoo away from my dressing room last night."

Randy suddenly lifted the corner of his mouth in a smirk and then said, "Yeah, I gotcha. That guy was just a tad bit outta line doing something like that."

Melanie sighed as they continued to walk and then said, "You're telling me. I really don't want to be going where I'm going, but for my own safety, I really don't think that I have any sort of a choice in the matter."

Randy nodded and then said, "That's right, you don't."

Melanie looked back up at Randy and said, "I will try to make it back here at some point before too long—"

Randy cut her off from speaking as they reached the line for the bus terminal and said, "Don't bother coming back here! Not ever again!" He looked around at the other boarding passengers and then lowered his voice before continuing, "It's *way* too dangerous here right now. I will come to you." Melanie began to weep as they reached the doorway to the bus terminal. Randy quickly set her bags down to hold her and tenderly kissed her face as the tears kept rolling down her cheeks. He held her close to his chest and then spoke to her over the loud engine of the bus, "*This will all be over with very soon! And, once it is, I will come to find you! I promise! But, don't leave your father's house until I make it there!*" Melanie pulled away to look Randy in the eyes before she slowly nodded and tightly closed her eyes. Her tears continued to run down her face as she reached down to pick up her luggage. She entered onto the bus and climbed up to the top of the stairs, and then she paused. Melanie suddenly turned around and softly blew Randy a kiss from the top of the stairs inside of the bus, just before the doors closed.

CHAPTER 41

Off Duty

Detective Jacob Farmers walked slowly down the long corridor that led to the police chief's office. He kept his head positioned low to avoid making eye contact with anyone who might potentially turn around any given one of the corners of the corridor and try to strike up a conversation with him. Things were not going to go well for him during this meeting, not today, and he was preparing himself for the worst. There had been a few too many people talking within the department lately and far too many rumors out on the streets. He knew that some of his more recent behaviors had been unethical and, in some cases, illegal. However, his goal whenever he was assigned to a new case had always been to take the routes that he figured would be the most effective, regardless of the consequences. His methods had oftentimes produced results, brought about confessions from criminals, and had led to the solving of a lot of difficult cases.

There was a wooden door at the end of the corridor with an engraved brass sign labeled "Martin J. Albertson, Chief of Police." Jacob Farmers stopped in front of the door, breathing heavily, and then quickly placed a few breath mints into his mouth. He began chewing them and then reached up and loudly knocked against the door.

"Come in," Albertson said from behind the door.

"I just got a message downstairs that said you wanted to see me, sir?" Farmers said, as he began pushing the door open further.

"That's right, I do. Come in and make sure that you pull the door closed behind you," Albertson said, as he looked up from a manila folder that was centered on the desk in front of him. Jacob Farmers entered into the office, pulled the door closed behind him, and then pulled a chair up in front of Albertson's desk.

Marty Albertson pushed the manila folder off to the side and pulled his glasses off from his face before looking up to make eye contact with Farmers. "So what's with these formal complaints regarding your lack of professional conduct that have come to my attention here since last night?" Albertson asked as he began rising up out of his chair. "We've got some terrified showgirl claiming that you had entered into her place of employment without a warrant and then knocked on her dressing room door in order to continue on with a dead-end interrogation," Chief Albertson said and then raised his eyebrows as he sat up on the corner of his desk directly in front of Farmers. "She had no lawyer present for the questioning, by the way." Albertson folded his arms as he looked down at the detective, before continuing, "And then we've got a sworn statement of police brutality from none other than Charley Bennetti, whom you had personally arrested and booked last night on charges of racketeering, soliciting, illegal possession of a firearm, and resisting arrest. He's all lawyered up, and eventually, he's gonna end up walkin' out of court a free man if the judge believes any part of his sob story after he has his next arraignment hearing." Albertson reached back over his desk and then turned around to wave the manila folder in front of the detective's face, as he said, "Your days of pullin' a fast one behind all our backs around here is about to come to a screeching halt, Jake." The police chief stood up from the desk and began walking back over towards his chair.

Farmers looked down into his lap and cleared his throat before looking back up at the police chief. "Is it okay if I take a moment out to try and explain myself?" he asked. "Or would that sort of thing not be allowed at this given point in time?" Albertson slowly began shaking his head. The detective's eyes suddenly wrinkled behind his glasses as he smiled at his supervisor. "Shouldn't *I* have a lawyer present during a time like now?" Farmers asked.

Albertson let out a sigh before picking up the phone on his desk. "Hi, Judy. Yeah, it's Marty," the police chief said into the phone receiver. "Could you please send him up here now? Thanks." The police chief hung up the phone after he had finished speaking into it and then returned his attention over to Detective Farmers. "I do have one other surprise in store for you," Albertson said. "And he's on his way here right now. Whatever might happen after that given point in time is really up to you."

The two men sat together in silence for a moment before there was suddenly a knock at the door. "It's open!" Albertson shouted from behind his desk. A man with wavy brown hair wearing a black suit with a dark blue dress shirt walked into the police chief's office and quietly closed the door behind him. Marty Albertson raised his right arm towards the door to his office, and Jacob Farmers turned his head around over his shoulder to see who had entered in through the door. "I'd like for you to meet Agent Benjamin Jordy," Albertson said. "He's with the Internal Affairs Bureau and has been sent over here from the County Prosecutor's Office with some paperwork for you to sign regarding the formal complaints before you are indefinitely suspended from duty, pending a further investigation."

Jacob Farmers let out a snicker of arrogance. "So that's it?" the detective asked. "I'm out, just like that? No matter what sort of leads I've got on any of my cases, they're all gonna go cold after this?"

Agent Benjamin Jordy pulled up a seat at Albertson's desk next to Farmers. "I'm afraid so or, at least, as far as your services with this department are concerned," Jordy said, as he turned to face Farmers. "I'm sorry that it has to be this way, Jake. I'd offer to give you something for the pain, but from the way that you smell, I'm guessing that you already took a few sips to numb that off before you got here."

Farmers looked at Agent Jordy defiantly and then asked, "What else did you happen to have in mind?"

Jordy smirked at that question as he placed his briefcase down next to his chair. "Well, most of us around here prefer to have something like donuts for breakfast," Jordy said. "That's usually something that doesn't involve a flask or a shot glass. Most of us save the booze for our days off, not right before we are about to go on duty."

Farmers lowered his eyebrows in fury. "Now, you listen to me…" Farmers began before Chief Albertson raised his hand to cut him off.

"This would hardly be the time or the place for that sort of thing, Jake!" Albertson shouted sternly.

"Yeah, well, how about the parking lot?" Farmers quickly replied.

"All right, that's enough!" Albertson barked from behind his desk.

Jacob Farmers shrugged at the two other men and then asked, "So what happens now?"

Albertson raised his eyebrows as he looked over at Farmers. "Well, just so you know, if there is ever any questionable behavior on the part of any of our officers, and we don't take any action right away, it doesn't mean that we didn't notice," Albertson said. "It simply means that we are patiently waiting until we can see if the officer's behavior is gonna get better or if it's gonna get worse. In this given case, we've seen that it's gotten worse." Farmers tried to open his mouth to reply, and Albertson simply raised his hand up before looking away. "You've had your chances, Jake," Albertson said. "Or at least, as many chances as I'm gonna be allowed to give you. I just need you to sign the paperwork and then turn over your gun, your handcuffs, and your badge, and we'll call you a taxi because the car is staying here. That's Stan's car now." Farmers looked over to see Agent Jordy slowly nodding.

Jacob Farmers placed his badge, handcuffs, and car keys onto the police chief's desk before pulling off his overcoat to expose his gun holster. He raised his arms up and locked his hands behind his head, and then Agent Benjamin Jordy slowly removed the revolver from its holster.

"Is this the only one?" Jordy asked, and Jacob Farmers began quickly nodding with his eyes shut.

"Thanks, Ben," Chief Albertson said, and Jordy began to empty the bullets out from the cylinder of the revolver as Farmers signed the paperwork that was on the desk.

"Don't forget these. They belong to you," Jordy said and then dropped the six bullets from the gun into Jacob's open hand.

Farmers then abruptly stood up and said, "Don't be so sure of yourselves that you're gonna get away with this! The first thing that I'm gonna do once I leave here is have a meeting with my lawyer!"

Jordy slowly looked up into the disgraced detective's eyes and then said, "I might consider saving myself that sort of a hassle if I were you. Who says you can't go home? I mean, even if it's just to think things over for a little while. It's not exactly like you've been the first and only person in this department that's ever made any sort of a mistake before. However, when it comes down to officers of the law with true honor and integrity, we weren't born to follow in the footsteps of bad examples such as yourself. Especially not any of us who happen to work in Internal Affairs. Consider us to be your watchdogs."

The disgraced detective lowered his head and scowled at the two men. Albertson laughed and then said, "Try not to take any of this too personally, Jake. This is how I know the mayor and the city council are on a quest to clean things up around this city."

Farmers fixed his stare on the police chief. "This isn't the end," Farmers said in a dry voice.

"I beg to differ," Jordy said with a smile. "Your former partner is now looking at a reassignment starting first thing tomorrow morning. Have a nice day and try to remember everything that we were just talking about here because we don't want to have any more trouble or any more paperwork regarding you."

Marty Albertson nodded at Agent Jordy and then stood up to walk across the office, before he opened the door to let Jacob Farmers back out into the hallway.

PART 3

Friday, October 19 to Sunday, October 21, 1962

CHAPTER 42

Friday, October 19, 1962
Waterfront Property

Charley Bennetti yawned as he slowly walked down the carpeted staircase in the boardwalk apartment building that he lived in. He really
hadn't slept well during his time in jail, and after Frank Moniarti had
come to visit him yesterday, Charley felt as though he had officially
worried himself to the point of exhaustion. He turned around the
corner from the bottom of the staircase and walked up to the area
next to the front door where the tenant mailboxes were located. He
slowly turned the key in the lock on the vertical metal door of his
mailbox. He found a cream-colored envelope in the mailbox with
a red geranium stamped across the back of it, which was sealing it
shut. He tucked the envelope into the inside pocket of his maroon
overcoat and then made his way back upstairs to his apartment. He
closed the door and then grabbed a letter opener off from his desk
before he walked over to sit down at his dining room table.

* * *

Nicholas Malone sat reading a newspaper behind an old wooden
desk in a dimly lit room inside of his warehouse in Ocean City. The

room was so quiet that he could hear the continuous ticking of his Rolex watch as he gazed over yesterday's sports scores. He turned his wrist to look at the time. It was now just past midnight, and Frank Moniarti and Teddy Pazzelli should be arriving any minute to begin their business transaction. Two hundred and fifty thousand dollars was a great deal of money, and if Malone had things his way, the car that was about to be purchased would have already been here by now. Things had a tendency to get rather complicated when there were a series of middlemen involved. However, Malone had not received any phone calls regarding there being any sort of complications involving his two colleagues getting arrested along the way, or having any delays with the work on the car in Pennsylvania, or having the delivery truck run out of gas along the way. So all in all, things seemed to be running along rather smoothly. The security around the warehouse had been instructed to allow the dark blue 1955 Buick Riviera to enter onto the property after both men in the vehicle had shown their identification cards upon approaching the gate.

A few moments later, Malone was interrupted from reading his newspaper when he suddenly heard the muffled sound of a knock at the service door that was located a few feet down from the entrance to the loading dock. Malone quickly folded up his newspaper and then grabbed his cane off from the side of the desk before walking across the warehouse to look outside the loading dock window towards the staircase that led up to the service door. He squinted his eyes to see Frank Moniarti and Teddy Pazzelli standing outside the service door. He could hear their muffled voices, and then a loud burst of laughter came out of Teddy as Malone walked over to unlock the door.

Nicholas Malone slowly opened the heavy, rusty metal service door and then nodded to the two men before stepping aside from the doorway. "You guys are right on time," he said and then extended his right arm to welcome both men inside of the warehouse.

"Thank you," Frank Moniarti said, as he removed his hat upon entering. He was carrying a large, black leather briefcase that he held tightly to the side of his long, black overcoat.

Teddy looked all the way around the empty space of the ware-house and then said, "Hey, if somebody yodeled inside of here, do you think that it would echo?"

Malone raised his eyebrow over at Teddy and replied, "Well, now that you mention it, we've had much louder sounds than that happen in here before. And to answer your question, yes, loud sounds do have a tendency to echo in a building like this one. This building has been here since 1885, and with it being as old as it is, it's needed some work over the years. You know, an update on the electricity and plumbing, extermination of a few pests, and even some work to make the building a little more soundproof. But it's really a fine piece of waterfront property. I've always thought so."

Frank leaned over towards Teddy and said, "I think that what he's trying to tell you is that some of the pests that he's exterminated over the years have gotten just a little bit noisy."

Teddy Pazzelli began to laugh and then said, "I guess that means that I should probably wipe my shoes off on the doormat over here."

Nicholas Malone closed his eyes and quickly nodded. "I prefer to try and maintain a clean house around here. It helps to keep the rats away," he said. "Now, if you wouldn't mind, let's head on back into my office for just a moment. It's a little more private there." The two men then began to follow Malone across the warehouse.

After the three men made it back into Nicholas Malone's office, Teddy Pazzelli and Frank Moniarti both took a seat in front of the wooden desk. "So have you heard any word from the delivery guys yet?" Moniarti asked, as he set his briefcase on the floor next to his chair.

"No. But that's usually a good sign," Malone said. "The less phone communication that goes on beforehand, the smoother that things have a tendency to go in the long run."

Moniarti began to slowly nod and then said, "Yeah, I gotcha. So we'll give 'em about a half hour before we really start to worry. Is that how this usually works?"

Nicholas Malone nodded as he began to unfold his newspaper. "I'll try to make all this just as quick as I can," he said. "It's been a long day so far, my hip is startin' to bother me, and I wanna rest up because tomorrow's my birthday."

Frank Moniarti slowly nodded and then said, "I can understand that. Happy birthday, in advance. My wife and I just celebrated our twenty-seventh wedding anniversary on Tuesday."

Malone looked up from his newspaper at Moniarti from behind the desk. "No kidding?" he said. "Twenty-seven years is a long time. It's been about fifteen for me, but it'll be twenty-seven years before I know it."

Teddy Pazzelli lowered his head and chuckled in the other seat and then said, "Yeah, and, uh, Frankie here just mighta killed off a vampire the other night."

Malone quickly turned his eyes to focus his view over on Teddy, and his eyebrows went up in curiosity, and then he said, "Excuse me?"

Teddy Pazzelli began laughing even harder after Malone's inquiry. "Don't mind him," Moniarti said. "It's an inside joke."

Malone quickly nodded and then said, "Yeah, I gotcha. They should be here with your car any time now. They didn't call to say anything about havin' any sort of trouble, or getting lost along the way, or anything like that."

Teddy Pazzelli began to chuckle and then said, "Yeah, well, I guess that good quality *does* take time."

Nicholas Malone nodded and said, "And servin' up a high level of quality has been what's kept me in business all these years."

The three men got up from their seats at the wooden desk and then made their way across the warehouse to the loading dock.

CHAPTER 43

Honk Three Times

Doyle Reynolds pulled onto a long gravel alleyway in the gray over-size Dodge semi-truck with a sigh of relief. *Whew! We made it!* he thought to himself. *After comin' all this way, we've finally made it!* He approached a tall chain-link fence with barbed wire all across the top of it, which signified the entryway into the warehouse. This was the designated meeting place where he and Sly could finally dispose of the merchandise that was neatly hidden in the back of the semi. Hopefully, everything would run smoothly from this point forward, and the business transaction would take place without any unneces-sary complications. It had turned out to be a very long trip, with a few close calls in regards to their main goal of remaining inconspicu-ous and not attracting any sort of unwanted attention to themselves. Driving straight through the night had been a task for Doyle, and the coffee that he had purchased at the last truck stop was beginning to wear off.

At the end of the alleyway, he had finally reached the sliding gate within the tall chain-link fence. After he had stopped the truck, he took a handkerchief out of his pocket and wiped the sweat off from his face. Now was the time for him to remain alert toward his surroundings and keep his senses clear for any potential dangers that might cause him to have to double back and make an emergency exit from the alleyway. He scanned his eyes around the parking lot of the warehouse and then immediately looked back through both of the long side mirrors on the truck. There were no signs of any sort of police activity. He didn't see any marked cars around anywhere or anyone who appeared to be a police officer. And there didn't seem to be any other vehicles in sight with their motors running. In fact, he got the sudden impression that he was the only visible person around here right now.

He took his hands off from the steering wheel and forcefully pushed on the horn three times. The sound of the horn was so abrupt in breaking the quiet of the night that he could hear each honk of the horn echoing off into the distance. Instinctively, he reached over into the glove compartment of the semitruck and removed the Colt .45 Automatic that he had stored in there. He had brought it along with him just in case they would run into any problems with the law along the way. He carefully placed it back into the holster that he was wearing underneath his overcoat, just so it would be readily available if he ran into any unexpected problems in delivering the Cadillac. Doyle took one final look through each side mirror and didn't see anyone approaching the truck from the rear. He suddenly felt the tension in his shoulders begin to relax as he reached up and rubbed his eyes.

He looked straight ahead to see two men in dark gray suits walking out of a dimly lit building that sat about two hundred feet away from the gate of the fence. Doyle rolled down the window and could feel the cool night air against his face. It had been a long journey across several states, but the fresh air was now helping him to feel more awake than he had felt since they had reached the Pennsylvania state line. Once the two men had reached the other side of the fence, the one that was over to the left side of the truck looked Doyle directly in the eyes and then scanned his view all the way back across the length of the semi.

"What brings you all the way out here at this time of the night?" the man asked with an intensely suspicious look.

"I'm here for the lodgings," Doyle said, responding exactly how Malone had instructed him to last week over the phone. The man to the left side of the truck nodded and then signaled over to the other man on the right, who pushed the release button for the gate.

Once the gate to the warehouse fence was fully open, the man on the left side pointed past the building that they had come out from and down to another building that was approximately three hundred feet away. "Head on down to the loading dock of the warehouse and pull up to the delivery door. They've been expecting you," the man said.

Doyle nodded to him and then put the semitruck back into gear and slowly proceeded across the long gravel parking lot that surrounded the two buildings. *They're probably gonna frisk me once I get in there,* he thought to himself. After the two men in the dark gray suits had disappeared from his sight, he quickly and carefully placed the Colt .45 Automatic back into the glove compartment of the truck.

* * *

Frank Moniarti looked out from one of the square windows on the delivery door of the warehouse. "Here they come. Get ready with the door," he said, nodding over to Teddy Pazzelli.

"And you probably thought that they were never gonna arrive," Teddy said and then reached over to push the release button on the door. The headlights from the oversize truck cast a bright light all throughout the warehouse, and the sound of it approaching across the gravel parking lot caused Moniarti to feel a deep sense of anticipation that he hadn't felt for quite some time.

Frank and Teddy both stepped back as the semitruck entered in through the delivery door. Doyle kept his eyes ahead and only focusing his attention on Nicholas Malone, who was standing near the far back wall, directing him into the warehouse.

Doyle stuck his head out from the window of the truck and asked, "Do I have enough space now?"

Malone nodded to him and then began slowly walking up to the window of the truck. He kept his cane to the side of him as he stood near the driver-side door. His feet were now beginning to hurt him. He had been in the warehouse for nearly three hours now, preparing for everybody's arrival. The two teams had been designated separate arrival times for this occasion to avoid any potential suspicion from the authorities.

"You've done a real good job, Doyle," Malone said with a smile. "You've done a damn good job." Doyle shut off the engine to the truck now that it was in the proper position, and Frank Moniarti signaled over to Teddy to hit the button to close the delivery door.

After the delivery door was closed, the men all suddenly heard the muffled sound of a car horn honking from the back of the truck. Malone walked around to the back of the oversize semi and hit the release latch on the door to the trailer and then lifted it open. Teddy and Frank each grabbed a long steel tire ramp from the two opposite sides of the delivery door. They could both hear the steady humming sound of the engine of the Cadillac idling in the back of the truck. Frank and Teddy quickly installed the ramps onto the back of the semi, and then they quickly moved over towards the driver's side of the oversize truck.

As the men all looked towards the back door of the semi, there was a gruff rumbling sound from the trailer of the truck as the car inside of it went into motion. It came zipping down the ramps, and the tires of the Cadillac made a loud screeching sound as they connected with the concrete floor of the warehouse. Sly Robinson was frantically bouncing up and down with excitement in the driver seat, as he pulled the car around in a circle in the middle of the warehouse. Once the Cadillac had come to a stop, its front end was facing towards the delivery door again.

He leaned his head out of the driver-side window and shouted, "Honky, honk! Honk! Honkies!" His loud laughter echoed through the empty space inside of the warehouse. "You wanted a late-night special delivery, and you got a late-night special delivery! This here's one of our custom designs!" Sly said, as he got out of the car. He walked up to Malone and gave him a wide smile and then said, "You probably thought that we were never gonna make it here, didn't you?" Sly reached his right hand up and patted Doyle Reynolds on top of one of his broad shoulders. "Well, we did it!" Sly said. "We made it through the trip! We even made that special pit stop for ya! All thanks to my associate, here!"

Frank smiled out of the corner of his mouth and then said, "I'm really glad that you guys made it out here okay."

Sly looked back and forth at Frank and Teddy, who seemed to be allowing their tension from the sense of unfamiliarity to slowly dissipate. "I think that a toast just might be in order for an occasion like this!" Sly said, "What do you guys say?" Sly quickly walked back over to the Cadillac to open up the trunk. He turned around holding a six-pack of beer cans. After he had pulled one off for himself, he passed one over to Doyle, Teddy, and Malone. He held the offering up to Moniarti, who just shook his head. Sly smiled at Frank and then said, "Are you sure you don't want one? Don't you know that Schlitz is the beer that made Milwaukee famous?"

Moniarti lowered his eyebrows and gave Sly a stern look. "Let's just save that whole song-and-dance routine for another time!" Moniarti said, "How do I know that everything that I asked for on this car is functioning properly? Has everything already been tested just to make sure that it works?"

Sly recoiled from Frank's untrustworthy glance. "Of course, it has!" Sly shouted, "We wouldn't have come all this way with it if we hadn't done all that shit first! That really wouldn't have been a very customer-friendly way of doin' things. Do you have any idea what this thing is actually capable of now? You've got a bulletproof body and windows on this thing! Plus, you've got a new, state-of-the-art methanol-based water fuel injection system that I know that the person that you're gonna be chasin' with this thing isn't gonna have! After all, you were the one who had ordered all the special modifications, weren't you?"

Frank nodded slowly and then said, "Yeah, just makin' sure. Is it okay with you if we test-drive it around before makin' any sort of a purchase?"

Sly's eyes grew wide with excitement, and then he said, "Yeah, sure, there ain't no way that we're goin' all the way back to Detroit unless we know for a fact that we've got ourselves some fully satisfied customers!"

Sly held out the keys, and Malone took them as he turned over to look at Frank and Teddy. "So who wants to be the one to bring this thing out for a trial run?" Malone asked.

Teddy looked over at Frank and then took a long pull from his can of beer. "That would be me," Teddy said. "I figure that you and Frankie can do a little catchin' up together here while we're out and about. How's that sound?"

Frank looked over his shoulder and made eye contact with Teddy. "Fair enough," Moniarti said, and then he looked back over at Sly and Doyle and pointed towards them. "And you two are goin' along with him. Just make sure that you guys don't end up demolishin' this thing while you're out and about."

Teddy Pazzelli took the keys from Malone and then said, "Don't worry, Frankie. I won't put a scratch on her, and if this thing's really been built with the *meant-to-last* guarantee, I doubt if it's even gonna be possible for me to do that."

CHAPTER 44

Along for the Ride

Teddy Pazzelli set his empty beer can on the folding table that sat about ten feet away from the front of the semi. "You guys ready to go for a ride?" he asked.

Sly and Doyle made eye contact with each other. "I hope you know what you're doin'," Doyle said through his teeth, and Sly lifted the corner of his mouth in a confident smile. They both looked back over at Teddy and nodded in unison.

"Okay," Teddy said. "Well, I'll leave it up to the two of you to argue over who is gonna sit where. But since you're not from around here, it would probably be better if I led the way." Teddy walked over to the Cadillac and opened up the driver-side door. Sly walked up to the passenger-side door, and Doyle made his way over to the rear-passenger side of the car. As Teddy started up the engine, he looked over at Sly and smiled; then he said, "Now, we're gonna be hittin' the boardwalk in style!" Sly nodded at Teddy and then quickly turned around and nodded at Doyle.

Once the front gate of the chain-link fence was securely closed behind them, Teddy slowly drove down the gravel alleyway until he reached the paved service drive. "So I will gladly show you guys around this area while I inspect the work that's been done," Teddy said. "How does that sound to you, Leroy?" He looked over at Sly, who was now rolling down the passenger-side window. "Do you mind if I call you *Leroy?*" Teddy asked, as a smile began to widen across his face.

"Yeah, sure. Whatever. Just take it easy with this thing until we're onto a straightaway," Sly said, and then he looked back over his shoulder and saw Doyle pull a small bag of popcorn out from his jacket pocket. "Damn! Is there ever a time when you ain't hungry?" Sly asked and then shook his head before looking back out of the windshield.

"It ain't my fault!" Doyle said, "I got low blood sugar! If I don't eat, I start gettin' all dizzy! Besides, you're lucky that I'm still even awake after a trip like that!"

Teddy looked over at Sly and then back at Doyle through the rearview mirror then said in a calm voice, "Now, now, you two. Don't fight. I'm tryin' to drive here." He put on his blinker to turn right off the service drive and then began heading down through the industrial area that led over towards Route 52.

Sly looked around at the scenery and then said, "Man, all these factories are startin' to remind me of home. What about you, Doyle? You gettin' homesick, yet?"

Doyle nodded as he loudly crunched the popcorn in his mouth. "I ain't goin' back home without a nap, though," Doyle said. "I can safely say that much." His eyes looked bloodshot even in the dark.

Sly just shook his head. "Well, you better wake your ass up!" he commanded. "We ain't even booked a place to stay for the night yet."

Doyle shrugged and then said, "I'm doin' the best I can right now." He yawned and then rubbed his eyes. "I should still be good for a little while, at least," he said, as he looked out of the open rear-side window. As the night air rushed inside of the car, the smell of the ocean began to override the smell of the bag of popcorn that was in his lap.

Teddy Pazzelli turned the car off from the Black Horse Pike and went onto Atlantic Avenue. "How are we enjoying our little joyride so far? Is everybody still awake?" Teddy asked, as he looked around at the other occupants inside of the car with a smile. He then made a right turn onto Chelsea Avenue and said, "We're almost there."

Sly looked over at Teddy curiously. "So far...we're almost where?" Sly asked.

Teddy looked back at Sly and said, "We're almost in an area where we can have some real fun." Two blocks later, the avenue came to an end, and then the car quietly sat facing the boardwalk. Sly and Doyle looked all around the surrounding area and saw that they had finally reached the oceanfront.

Teddy fastened his seat belt over his waist and then slowly drove over the curb onto the boardwalk. He then casually looked over at Sly and said, "You might want to consider putting on your safety belt, Leroy." Teddy hit the gas and made a sharp left turn before Sly could reach for his seat belt. "The acceleration seems pretty nice," Teddy said, as the Cadillac continued gaining speed. Sly nervously placed his hands up on top of the dashboard, and then said, "Hey, man, take it easy goin' down here! I ain't about to end up sleepin' in the ocean tonight!"

Teddy let out a gleeful sounding laugh. "A little swim might do you some good!" Teddy yelled, "As long as you haven't eaten anything within the last couple of hours! I wouldn't want you to suffer from any cramps!"

Sly looked over at Teddy as he fastened his seat belt and then said, "That shit ain't funny, man! I'm tellin' ya to go easy with this thing!"

Teddy looked up into the rearview mirror and then said, "Okay, no swimming tonight. How about you? How you holdin' up back there? You ain't gettin' no cramps yet, I hope."

Doyle's eyes grew wide as he saw Teddy forcefully turn the steering wheel to the right to head straight towards an aluminum garbage can. He closed his eyes to avoid looking out of the windshield and then leaned over in his seat.

"Oh shit!" Sly screamed and then covered his face with his arms just before the Cadillac collided into the aluminum garbage can.

Teddy looked over at Sly and shrugged. "Whoops! Well, at least, the body seems pretty sturdy! I really like that! I really like that a lot!"

Teddy shouted, "You guys sure know how to do some exceptionally good quality work!" Teddy lifted his right hand off from the steering wheel and patted Sly on the shoulder with it.

"Both hands on the wheel, damn it!" Sly shouted as the path of the Cadillac quickly corrected itself.

Teddy let out a devious chuckle. "As you wish," he said, and then he placed his hand back onto the steering wheel. "Hey, look, you guys! I think we've got a pretty decent view of the stars from right here!" Teddy said, as he leaned his head out from the window and once again pulled the steering wheel hard to the right. The Cadillac connected with a metal railing, instantly creating a shower of sparks.

"That's it, man! Now, I'm really gettin' homesick!" Sly said and then looked over into the back seat of the car to see Doyle still lying on his side. The bag of popcorn that had been in his lap had spilled all over the back seat and down into the rear floorboards of the car.

Teddy looked down at his watch and then smiled. "All right, it's gettin' late," he said. "I guess that I can let you guys off the hook now." He began to slow the car down before he took the final left turn down the boardwalk. Despite the recklessness of the test-drive, the body of the Cadillac remained perfectly intact. Teddy turned the car left down Madison Avenue and then followed it onto Atlantic Avenue, which led them back towards the Black Horse Pike.

There was very little discussion among the occupants of the car on the ride back to the warehouse. The men in the dark gray suits had been waiting for them to return, and they quickly opened up the gate to let them back in. Once they had returned to the inside of the warehouse, Teddy was the first one to exit from the vehicle. He walked around the Cadillac to look for any damages that might have occurred during the joyride.

"How's it run?" Frank Moniarti asked, as he began to approach the vehicle.

"Like a charm, Frankie! Like an *absolute* charm!" Teddy said and then smiled at him from over the roof of the car.

"Okay, good," Moniarti said, and then he looked over at Sly and Doyle after they had exited from the car. Frank Moniarti looked around the inside of the car and saw the popcorn mess that still lingered in the back of it. "Just make sure that you vacuum that shit up out from the back seat before I hand over the briefcase," he said. "And then you've got yourselves a deal."

CHAPTER 45

Saturday, October 20, 1962
Ours for the Taking

There was a soft and calming sunset that dimly lit up the evening sky in Newark, with the temperatures having reached up into the high sixties earlier on that afternoon. The air was starting to cool off as Angela Malone rolled down the rear passenger side window of a limousine to watch her husband slowly making his way out of Military Park. She had promised to give him a moment alone to remember his fellow servicemen who never made it back from Normandy after D-Day. As Nicholas Malone walked back to the limousine, he kept his head low, with the brim of his hat pointed down towards the ground. This had been his first trip back to see the Wars of America sculpture in that park for several years. It had also been one of the last places in New Jersey that he had chosen to visit after receiving notification of his drafting for military duty by the Selective Service System. A mild breeze blew in through the window and caused Angela Malone's soft blond hair to brush up against the sides of her cheeks.

"Here he comes. You might wanna get out and open the door for him," she said to the chauffer from the back seat.

The chauffer gave her a nod and then got out of the limousine to open the door that was located across from her. As Nicholas

Malone approached the rear of the car, he heard the aging chauffer ask in a deep voice, "So where do you wanna go now, Mr. Malone?"

Malone carefully placed his cane into the back of the limousine and then said, "How about takin' us on over to The Blue Mirror Lounge?"

The chauffer nodded and said, "Anything you say, Mr. Malone. I hope that you're havin' a pretty good birthday so far."

Malone turned his body around to make eye contact with the chauffer and then said, "Yeah, just takin' some time out to remember a few old friends. One of them once had a birthday today, too." He then turned around to get into the limousine and closed the door.

Nicholas Malone looked over at his wife after the limousine had begun moving. "Forty-three years old today," he said. "I honestly never thought that I would've made it this far in life when I went overseas to fight." His head suddenly turned back forward as he looked down reflectively at his lap.

"I know, Nicky," Angie said. "But remember what you said to me right after you got back? Right after I agreed to marry you, you said to me that this world was ours for the taking..."

He turned his head back to face her. "Yeah, I know I did," he said. "And it has been, hasn't it?" The sides of his face gently lifted up into a smile. "Now, we've got a nice house, these nice quiet evenings together, this fancy clothing store chain and friends in all sorts of different places in society...Ya know, I never would've dreamed of havin' a life quite like this one back in 1944."

Angie placed her hand onto his right leg. "Life has a way of working itself out...Well, most of the time, anyway," she said. "And I'm glad that you and Ronny have remained so close for all these years. I mean, he's really done a lot for you, hasn't he?"

Nicky began to slowly nod, and then he said, "He sure has. I tell ya, I would've been eatin' outta garbage cans when I was a teenager if it hadn't been for him." Malone turned his head sideways to look out the window of the limousine. "Ronny's a good guy," he said. "And most importantly, he taught me that life goes on, even after the war was over."

The limousine slowly pulled up to the side of the street in front of The Blue Mirror Lounge. Angie gave her husband a playful smile and then said, "Wow, you haven't taken me here since we were still dating! You *are* on a quest to take me on a trip down memory lane tonight, aren't you?"

Malone shrugged and let out a soft laugh before saying, "This world is ours for the taking, remember? Now, let's just hope that the college kids haven't claimed our old table from us. It's a Saturday night, after all."

Angie lowered her head and leaned in further towards her husband. "So what are you gonna do if they have?" she asked.

Malone grabbed the handle to his cane as the chauffer was opening his door and then said, "Claim it right on back!" Angie covered her mouth laughing, as Malone stepped out into the street and walked around the back of the limousine up to the curb. The chauffer then came around and let Angie out so she could meet up with her husband on the sidewalk.

"We've both certainly come a long way," she said, as she embraced him and looked up into his dark blue eyes.

"Yeah, we have. Now, let's just hope that I don't have to shoo any young punks away from our old table," Malone said, and he winked at his wife before turning away to open the front door to the nightclub. "After you, as always," he said, and Angie lifted the corner of her mouth in a gentle smile as she stepped inside.

The Blue Mirror Lounge was somewhat tranquil for being almost seven o'clock in the evening on a Saturday. Nicholas Malone removed his hat as he walked into the lounge, and he held it down by his right side, as his left hand lifted up his cane.

"It looks like our old table is still open," he said. "We'll have the waiter seat us over there and then bring us a couple of martinis. How'd that be?" Angie looked back at her husband and nodded. Nicky leaned in a little further with a smile on his face and then said, "At least, we can afford to be drinkin' those things now." Angie laughed and playfully swatted at her husband's shoulder.

The waiter then suddenly appeared and asked them, "Just the two of you this evening?"

Malone nodded as he shifted his hat underneath his left arm and held onto his wife's hand. "Yeah," Angie said, as she leaned over closer towards her husband. "It's somebody's birthday today. But I don't want to have anybody start singin' to him just yet because that'll be my job tonight."

The waiter lowered his head and softly began to snicker and then said, "Yes, ma'am, I fully understand. Please, follow me." The waiter grabbed two menus and turned around, meeting eye to eye with Nicholas Malone.

"Could we have the table next to the bar with the mirror over to the right of it?" Malone asked, and the waiter slowly nodded, before leading them over towards the table.

After they were seated, the waiter asked, "Can I start the two of you off with something to drink?"

Malone placed his sport coat against the back of his chair. "How about a vodka martini with three olives? You guys haven't started waterin' the red-eye down in this joint, have ya?" Malone asked. The waiter shook his head, and then Malone continued, "Good. Then, could you please bring me the water along in a separate glass with some ice in it?"

The waiter smiled and then said, "Yes, of course, sir. And for you, ma'am?"

Angie pushed her purse over towards the side of the table with the large round mirror. "I'll take the same thing," she said.

The waiter jotted the drink order down on his notebook and then repeated it back for confirmation, "So I have two vodka martinis and two ice waters." Angie nodded to the waiter, and then he stuck his notebook back into his pocket. "Very good. Those should be coming right up," the waiter said, as he turned around and quickly walked over towards the bar.

Angie looked over at the waiter as he stood at the bar and then back over at her husband and then asked, "Am I the only one who looks at people and wonders whether or not they've ever shopped at any of your stores?"

Malone shook his head as he looked back down at his menu and then said, "Not at all. I wonder that exact same sorta thing all the time whenever I'm stopped at a traffic light."

Angie reached over and pulled Malone's menu down with her index finger. "Ya know, Nicky," she said. "Before our drinks end up gettin' here, there's somethin' that I was meanin' to do to you at this table a long time ago, but I didn't have the nerve to do it back then."

Malone looked up into her sparkling green eyes and then slowly nodded. They stood up from their chairs simultaneously and met over the table with a kiss in front of the large round mirror. The waiter suddenly appeared in the corner of Malone's vision.

"Don't mind me. Two vodka martinis and two ice waters," he said, keeping his eyes down on the beverage tray.

"You're still able to meet me halfway after all these years," Malone said, as he ran his hand through his wife's hair.

"And it'll only get better from here!" she said. "Your birthday surprises ain't over with yet, Nicky! You'll see!" They were both blushing when they sat back down in their chairs.

"It's okay. Take your time," the waiter said. "That's the greatest thing that I've seen here all night." He set the drinks down and then walked off toward another table located at the other side of the room.

CHAPTER 46

For Old Time's Sake

Angela Malone slowly pushed a key into the lock of the large wooden front door with an unsteady hand. The first vodka martini that she had with her husband at The Blue Mirror Lounge had eventually led to four more of them. Her total of five martinis compared with his total of seven certainly reminded her of their personal differences when it came to alcohol tolerance; but they were home now. As the large wooden door creaked wide open, Angela held it open for her husband to enter into the house, and then the chauffer in the limousine politely waved to them before pulling back out of their driveway.

"Thanks. I must've left my keys upstairs," Nicholas Malone said, as he gently placed his hat and overcoat on the coatrack next to the door, and then he shrugged and exhaled deeply. "Ya know, for being an old man, I feel like I can still hold 'em down pretty good," Malone said and then lifted his left eyebrow and smiled as he made eye contact with his wife.

Angie slowly shook her head and gently placed her arms around her husband's neck in an embrace. "Nicky, you know that you never have to worry about impressing me when it comes down to that sorta stuff," she said. "You impress me a lot more when it comes down to other things, much more important matters."

Malone pushed the large wooden door to the front of the house closed and leaned in closer to his wife. "Yeah?" he asked. "And what sorts of important matters are those?"

Angie closed her eyes and then kissed her husband tenderly on the lips. The lamp from the downstairs hallway cast a soft ambience upon their bodies, and Nicholas Malone felt every nerve inside of his body tingle before their kiss broke away. He stood still for moment, silent and breathing heavily.

"Make yourself comfortable down here," Angie said in a whisper. "I'm gonna go upstairs and freshen up a little bit, but I'll flicker the upstairs hallway light on and off a few times once I'm ready for you to come up. Okay?" Nicholas Malone nodded and then pulled his arms away from his wife's waist, and she slowly turned around and began walking over towards the staircase.

Nicholas Malone reached down and loosened up his blue-and-gray striped tie and unfastened the top button of his dress shirt. "I will fix us up a couple of gin and tonics in the kitchen and wait for your signal," he said.

Angie quickly turned around and walked back over to her husband. "Hold on a second!" Angie said with great excitement. "Gimme your hat and that tie! You won't be needin' those things anymore tonight!"

Malone passed his tie over to her and then reached on top of the coatrack to retrieve his hat. "I kinda hoped that I wouldn't be," he said and then softly laughed.

Angie's green eyes sparked in the dim lighting of the room. "Well, you've been on a quest to take *me* on a trip down memory lane tonight," she said. "Why shouldn't I do the same thing for *you*?" She squeezed her thick lips together into a kissing motion and then turned back around to make her way up the staircase. Nicholas Malone took a handkerchief out from his shirt pocket and began wiping away the beads of sweat that had collected on his forehead. *Somethin' tells me that I'm really in for it tonight,* he thought to himself, as he walked through the dining room into the kitchen.

Malone turned on the kitchen light and placed his cane against the kitchen counter. He then walked over and grabbed a bottle of gin from the liquor cabinet and two tall glasses out of the cupboard. He opened the refrigerator and fetched a bottle of tonic water and a tray of ice cubes from the freezer. He looked out the kitchen window and saw a black alley cat lazily crossing the road under the dusky glow of a streetlight. *A black cat just passed by me from left to right. That's supposed to be a sign of good luck. Especially if it's walkin' away from me. Well, I hope that he has a bit of good luck tonight, too. Must be all this warm weather that we've been havin' lately,* Malone thought to himself, as he placed three ice cubes into each one of the glasses. He then filled each glass one-third of the way up with gin and slowly poured in the tonic water to keep the fizz in the glasses from over-flowing onto the countertop. Malone grabbed the glasses off from the countertop and slowly walked out of the kitchen with his cane under his left arm. He stopped in the doorway and then turned the kitchen light off with his pinky before making his way back into the living room. He set the drinks onto a couple of cork coasters on the mahogany coffee table in front of the sofa, and then he sat down on the sofa and lit up a cigarette. He blew out the match and set it into the ashtray on the coffee table, and then suddenly, the light in the upstairs hallway began to flicker on and off.

Malone grabbed the drinks off from the coffee table, left his cane against the sofa, and kept the burning cigarette in his mouth. *That's my cue,* he thought to himself. He slowly walked across the living room and made his way up the stairs with his right foot guiding his left foot. Once he made it to the top of the staircase, he turned to the left and saw that their bedroom door was wide open with a lamp on the nightstand softly lighting up the room. He could smell the fragrant odor of perfume as he walked down the hallway towards the bedroom. He could suddenly hear Angie's muffled voice softly coming out from behind the closed door of the bathroom.

"Just go on in and make yourself comfortable. I'll be right there."

Malone looked over towards the bathroom door and said, "Anything you say, my darling. Anything you say." Once he entered into the bedroom, he set the drinks on the nightstand next to the lamp and flicked the long ash off from his cigarette into the ashtray.

He took a long drink from his gin and tonic and then extinguished his cigarette. He watched as the hallway was briefly illuminated from the light inside of the bathroom; and then he saw Angie's arm quickly slide a phonograph record player across the wooden floor and around the corner from the bathroom doorway.

The light inside of the bathroom suddenly went off, and Malone could hear the faint scratching sound of the record player starting up. Angie stepped into the doorway of the dimly lit bedroom, wearing only the thin veil of a black silk shawl to cover her naked body, and her hips began swaying back and forth to the sound of soft jazz music as she carefully put on Malone's tie and hat. Nicholas Malone's eyes grew wide as he placed the ashtray back on top of the nightstand without looking over at it. Angie playfully tossed his hat into his lap, as she continued to sway her hips. She suddenly flung the black silk shawl across the bedroom, and began to quickly flap his tie against her chest. She quickly spun around in a circle, nearly losing her balance. Malone rolled over on the bed onto his good hip, ready to catch her if she fell. She then pulled his tie off and tossed it over the bed and past the nightstand.

"Come here, Angie," Malone said and wrapped his hands around her waist to pull her onto the bed.

She could feel the breath from his nostrils against her neck as he hovered over her. "Ya see, Nicky? I *still* got it!" she said.

Malone began running his fingers through her hair and kissed her passionately. He pulled away from her to rapidly unbutton his shirt. "Yeah, I'll say you do!" he said. He then flung his dress pants off from the bed, and his belt buckle loudly connected against the wall. "Let's make this one for old time's sake, eh?" Malone said, and Angie began laughing loudly. As he began to kiss her neck and chest, Angie pulled the covers over their bodies, and then she reached over to turn off the lamp on the nightstand.

CHAPTER 47

Easy Come, Easy Go

Teddy Pazzelli and Frank Moniarti pulled up in the black 1959 Cadillac Coupe de Ville alongside Scotty McCormack's gold-colored 1962 BMW 3200 CS in the parking lot of a closed-down drive-in movie theater. Scotty McCormack sat in the driver seat of the BMW, and Randy Wyman was over in the passenger seat. Both men in the car remained looking forward until the Cadillac came to a complete stop next to them, and then Teddy turned off the engine. Scotty and Randy both exited from the BMW and then met Frank and Teddy behind the two parked cars.

"I don't usually allow people to come along with me on jobs like this," Frank said. "Except maybe for Teddy. But he's been workin' with me for a good long time now."

Teddy nodded and then said, "For over twenty years."

Frank briefly looked over at Teddy and then back over at Scotty and Randy before continuing, "But what happened to your business, with the mess that you both went through, I know that this situation has also become an intensely personal matter for the both of you."

Randy Wyman nodded and then said, "That's very kind of you, Mr. Moniarti. I'm really glad that you not only understand but appreciate that."

Scotty McCormack then said, "I'm really thankful that you understand that, too. Plemagoya's little trigger-happy mishap damn near cost me my business. I don't know if I can just let somethin' like that slide. Plus, there's that whole mess that he got some of my staff members into." Scotty looked next to him and motioned his head over at Randy. "I just wanna make sure that we're all sleepin' better at night after this is all over with," Scotty said.

"Oh, we will be!" Teddy Pazzelli said, "Follow me. I've got some merchandise to show you guys over here." Randy Wyman began walking over towards the Cadillac, and Scotty McCormack followed him.

Scotty McCormack stopped behind the Cadillac and reached under his checkered brown-and-white flannel overcoat to pull up the waistband on his oversize yellow dress pants. He was a tall and heavyset man with a soft pair of dark blue eyes, and he had shortly trimmed brown hair that was neatly kept and a double chin that covered a good percentage of his neck. He often wore expensive cologne to cover up the smell of his cigar-smoking habit, and had a loud, booming voice. However, tonight was a different story. He kept his voice down low whenever he spoke and planned on saving his cigars until after their team was done working for the night. "So what have you got for us?" Scotty quietly asked in a low voice while standing behind the trunk of the Cadillac.

"We brought along a couple of treats here for you, fellas," Teddy said with a wide grin on his face. He opened up the trunk of the Cadillac, and there was a bundled-up flannel shirt and shoebox underneath an unfolded sleeping bag. Teddy Pazzelli reached inside the trunk and unraveled the flannel shirt, which contained two sawed-off double-barreled shotguns. Randy Wyman nodded with his eyes wide, and Scotty McCormack audibly whistled. "And of course, we've also got these," Teddy said and then pulled open the shoebox, which contained two snub-nosed .357 Magnum revolvers. Down in the corner of the trunk, under the unfolded sleeping bag, there were a total of five boxes of ammunition for each of the shotguns and revolvers.

"We're plannin' on savin' the shoebox for all the spent cartridges, just so the cops don't end up findin' any of 'em after the workin' day's come to an end," Frank Moniarti said and then pulled one of the revolvers out from the shoebox. He held it up in the moonlight to examine it before passing it over to Randy Wyman. Randy nodded and then placed the weapon into the front side pocket of his worn-out varsity jacket. Moniarti then took out the other revolver and gently placed it inside the front pocket of his black overcoat. He then grabbed two boxes of ammunition from the trunk and placed one inside the other pocket of his overcoat before passing the other box over to Randy. He began walking back towards the front of the car and then stopped to look over at Scotty McCormack. "You and Scotty can take the shotguns, Teddy," Moniarti said, looking over at Teddy. "Buckshot has a tendency to get just a *tad* bit messier than revolver slugs do."

Teddy nodded. "I can certainly appreciate that," he said. "If we're goin' out huntin', we might as well act the role." Teddy and Scotty then began laughing as they both took their shotguns out from the trunk in one hand and gathered up a box of ammunition with their other hand. Teddy then passed the empty shoebox over to Scotty before he closed the trunk to the Cadillac.

Scotty and Randy both placed their weapons into the back seat of the Cadillac, alongside the empty shoebox. "Would you mind givin' us just a minute?" Scotty softly asked into the front seat, "We should probably find a better spot to park my car. Especially if the cops come lookin' through this area on a late-night patrol. Because just like we had agreed on at the club earlier, Randy and I were never here." Both Frank and Teddy started nodding. "I know of the perfect spot," Scotty said. "It's just around the corner from here. It's a heavily wooded area where the teenagers used to go to make out. Randy, if I push my car over there, would you mind steerin' it?"

Randy slowly shook his head and then said, "Wouldn't mind at all. At your service, boss."

Scotty quietly chuckled and then said, "That's what I like to hear." Scotty reached into the pocket of his yellow dress pants and passed his car keys over to Randy. They walked back over to the

BMW, and then Randy opened the door, placed the key into the ignition, and then put the car into neutral. Scotty came around the front of the car and then slowly began pushing it in reverse. Teddy rolled down the driver-side window of the Cadillac.

"You two kids have fun at summer camp, now! Don't forget to put on your bug repellent!" Teddy shouted.

Scotty McCormack grunted as he pushed the car with the weight of his body. "We're gonna have to save all the ghost stories for when we get back," Scotty said in a strained voice.

Teddy smiled as he looked back at him through the side mirror on the car door. Scotty then walked around to the back end of the BMW and slowly pushed the car out from sight behind the trees. A few minutes later, Scotty and Randy returned from behind the trees. The scent of the crisp evening air clung onto their clothes as they got into the back seat of the Cadillac, and they were both out of breath.

"That's one hell of a hill to climb up," Randy said as he panted. "I don't know how we're gonna get that car back up here after we're done."

Scotty just shrugged and then said, "Don't even worry about that right now. The point is that the car is completely hidden from view now. That's all that matters. Worst case is that I have to call the cops and report it stolen later on, and then they pull it back outta there for us."

Frank Moniarti shook his head and then sternly said, "No cops! I'll help pull it back outta there myself, if need be!"

Scotty raised his eyebrows in the back seat and then said, "All right, whatever you say goes right now. We're just here to help you out."

Moniarti sat quietly in the passenger seat of the Cadillac, loading the snub-nosed revolver. He spun the cylinder around before he closed the weapon and then placed the safety on before putting it inside of the glove compartment.

Teddy Pazzelli started up the engine to the Cadillac and then looked around at all the passengers inside of the car. "All righty. Here we go on our little field trip, class," he said. "Does anybody have to use the restroom before we leave?"

Frank Moniarti turned his head to face over towards the driver seat. "Come on, Teddy," he said. "Let's just get goin' already!"

Teddy looked over at Frank and then over into the back seat. "Okay, does everybody have their seat belts on?" Teddy asked.

Scotty McCormack's voice boomed up into the front seat, "If those things actually fit me comfortably, don't you think that I'd probably own a car like this?" Teddy Pazzelli began laughing as he threw the car into reverse and backed out of the parking lot at the drive-in movie theater.

As the Cadillac Coupe de Ville traveled down the expressway, Randy Wyman sat in the rear passenger seat of the car, loading hollow-pointed rounds into the snub-nosed .357 Magnum. After the pistol was loaded, he placed it inside of the shoebox that was on the back seat next to him and then solemnly looked out of the side window of the car.

"So how many of them do you think that there's gonna be?" Randy asked, as he looked over the front passenger seat at Frank Moniarti.

"Four or five of 'em, at the most. I can safely tell you that we've got the upper hand here. They won't be expectin' us. It should be just a simple matter of easy come, easy go," Moniarti said, and Teddy Pazzelli nodded in the driver seat as he turned the blinker on before switching lanes.

Scotty McCormack suddenly interjected from the back seat, "Good because I'm gettin' kinda hungry back here. I say that we stop and get somethin' to eat after this."

Randy quickly turned his head to the side and shot Scotty a piercing glance of irritation. "This is no time for jokes, Scotty!" Randy shouted, as he shook his head, "What happened at our club the other night had not only endangered Melanie but me, too! It also could've endangered you, if you had been in the wrong place at the wrong time! Don't you get that?!"

Scotty let out a soft chuckle. "Our club? Don't ya mean *my* club?" Scotty asked. "After all, I believe it was actually *you* who came to see *me* about a security job a couple of years back, now, wasn't it?"

Randy shook his head in frustration and then turned his head to look back out the side window. "Just shut up!" Randy shouted. "We can play around all you want to *after* we get this job done! But until then, we gotta remain focused on the task at hand!"

Moniarti looked over through the side mirror on the car door, and made eye contact with Randy, and then turned his head to look over into the back seat at Scotty. "Why don't the both of you just shut up? You're givin' me a headache," Moniarti said. "I'm startin' to think that maybe I mighta been further ahead doin' this job with those two spooks that came over here from Detroit. They probably wouldn't be arguin' *this* much."

Teddy Pazzelli began laughing behind the wheel and then shook his head. "That's true, Frankie! They wouldn't have been!" he said enthusiastically. "One of 'em very well might've been barfin' in the back seat by now, though! You should've seen 'em on the test-drive, Frankie! It was priceless!"

Frank Moniarti kept his head low as they drove on into the night. "I'm sure that it was," he said. "But we'll have all the time in the world to discuss that later. Right now, I need you guys to all stay focused and keep your eyes peeled for our targets *and* for the cops."

Teddy quickly nodded and then said, "Sure thing, Frankie! Sure thing!"

The Cadillac pulled off from the expressway, and all the men inside checked to make sure that their weapons were loaded and ready to be fired. "Teddy, do you still remember the directions that Charley gave us over to Rosebrook's Used Cars?" Frank Moniarti asked. "After all, we ended up chasin' Plemagoya all the way over to Scotty's club last weekend. So we never actually made it over to the garage."

Teddy Pazzelli quickly nodded. "Sure do!" he said over the rushing wind from his open window. "Hey! Speaking of Charley, is he still on bellboy duty for us tonight?"

Frank Moniarti reached into the glove compartment to retrieve his revolver. "I guess that we'll know soon enough," he said. "I told him that he needed to shape up and start carryin' more weight. We'll see what happens with him, though."

The Cadillac pulled around a corner, and there was a darkened sign that said "Rosebrook's Used Cars" about a quarter of a mile down the road.

"All right. Here we go," Teddy Pazzelli said. "Now, everybody just act natural." Teddy turned off the headlights on the car about fifteen feet away from pulling into the parking lot.

Across the parking lot and around the corner from the farthest garage door of the building, there was a silver 1954 Ford Crestline parked near a line of trees. Pedro Navilla was half awake in the driver seat, with the radio barely audible inside of the car. He hadn't been sleeping very much lately, and after losing all his money while sitting around the poker table tonight, his level of fatigue seemed to be taking its toll on him. The black Cadillac slowly pulled up alongside the silver Ford Crestline in the parking lot, and Teddy Pazzelli and Scotty McCormack casually looked out from the open windows on the driver's side of the car.

Scotty then leaned over the front seats, looking back and forth at Teddy Pazzelli and Frank Moniarti, and said, "Hey! Does anybody here know how to say, 'Hit the deck' in Spanish?"

Pedro Navilla's eyes suddenly snapped wide open as he saw all the occupants inside of the black Cadillac simultaneously raising their weapons from behind the doors.

CHAPTER 48

Odd Man Out

Charley Bennetti silently stood on the rooftop of Rosebrook's Used Cars and looked down at the hospital gurney that was positioned directly in front of him. He saw the silhouette of a human torso, which had been neatly wrapped up in a cream-colored vinyl shower curtain. Ronny Steiner had been the one who had supplied Charley with the hospital gurney; and thankfully, he had also been there to help hoist it up onto the rooftop. Ronny had always trusted Roger Bradshaw to operate the pool hall whenever he had a day off or needed to step out to run a few errands. Tonight was definitely one of those nights when Ronny had to step out to handle matters outside of the pool hall. A couple of weeks back, Vincent Plemagoya had pulled a switchblade knife on a customer outside of the pool hall after losing a game. Ronny had held a grudge against him ever since. He had barred him from ever returning to Lucky Nine's Pool Hall but had also refused to call the cops out of fear that the officers might have wanted to have a look at the lower level of the building. It still surprised Charley to have seen Ronny Steiner arrive in the parking lot shortly after Tony Tyler's murder last Tuesday night. But later on that night, he also remembered that it had been Frank Moniarti's anniversary, and all it had taken was a phone call from Teddy Pazzelli to send Ronny Steiner over on his day off to help clean up the mess. Charley had been very fortunate to have had Moniarti bail him out of jail yesterday, and he was grateful to be sleeping in his own bed once again. However, he was anything but thankful for the job that he was now being required to do in order to pay Frank Moniarti back for the fifteen grand that had ensured Charley's temporary freedom. He heard a dog barking off in the distance and looked off over to his right before returning his eyes back down towards the hospital gurney and then to the long extension cord that ran off from it and onto a thick tree branch that was only a few feet above his head. The hospital gurney was positioned about fifteen feet away from the edge of a long and rectangular fixed unit skylight, which looked down into the back room that was located behind Natty Rosebrook's office.

He walked over to the edge of the rooftop and saw the silhouette of a black car pulling into the parking lot. He then slowly and silently walked back across the rooftop and repositioned himself behind the hospital gurney. A short while later, he suddenly heard the echoing of repeated gunfire coming from down below. That was the sign that Frank Moniarti had instructed him to wait for in the envelope with the red geranium. Charley tightly closed his eyes, and his face winced up, as he began pushing against the hospital gurney with all the strength in his arms. He steadily sent the hospital gurney wheeling forward into motion, and it continued gaining momentum, until two of the wheels struck hard against the elevated edge of the fixed unit skylight. The body that was wrapped up in the cream-colored shower curtain slid effortlessly away from the rugged cloth surface of the hospital gurney and then went crashing straight through the glass surface on the rooftop.

* * *

Inside of Rosebrook's Used Cars, Vincent Plemagoya sat at a wooden table playing poker against Natty Rosebrook and two of Natty's auto mechanics. "Two hundred bucks?" Plemagoya asked one of the mechanics at the table. "I'll raise ya another fifty! You're gonna be cryin' for your momma after I get done with you tonight!"

There was then the sound of several explosions, which were muffled through the wooden paneling on the walls of the back room. "What the hell was that?!" Natty Rosebrook shouted as he rose up from his chair. "I know that we cleared Pedro out during that last game, but he'd better not be out there playin' with fireworks again! The last thing that I need to have right now is the cops showin' up here!"

Plemagoya folded his hand up and placed the cards into the front pocket of his shirt and then said, "I'll go check it out! But none of you'd better touch anything on this table while I'm away!"

There was suddenly a shattering sound above their heads, and broken shards of white sheet glass came raining down from the ceiling. One of the mechanics jumped behind a leather reclining chair, and the other mechanic ran straight for the door towards Natty's business office. Natty crawled underneath the wooden table, refusing to look up at the cause of the crash, and hunched his shoulders up in fear as he sat in a ball against the floor. The other mechanic then ran out from behind the leather reclining chair and made it out through the door.

Approximately three feet above the poker table hung the dead body of Tony Tyler. The extension cord was wrapped tightly against the white brace that was still attached to his neck. The extension cord was causing the neck brace to constrict under the weight of his body. The front of his white short-sleeve shirt was a dried-up, gory mess that clung onto his rib cage. Vincent looked down the length of Tony Tyler's body in horror. The ghastly tone of his skin had become a pale blue color, and his Converse shoes dangled loosely on his stiff feet, as his lifeless body swung back and forth over the wooden table. Plemagoya pushed his left shoulder into the poker table hard enough to knock it over for shelter. Natty Rosebrook quickly crawled out from underneath the table and ran over towards the door as the sound of gunfire began from outside of the broken skylight. Vincent Plemagoya could hear Natty Rosebrook screaming as bullets began ripping into his back from the rooftop assailant. Plemagoya refused to turn around to witness what had just happened.

"All right! Come on! Let's dance!" Plemagoya exclaimed, as he reached into his overcoat and pulled out his Colt .45 pistol. He switched the safety off and then pointed it up at the ceiling towards where the shattered glass had fallen. He saw the shadowy silhouette of the figure of a man standing on the roof. Bullets began to ricochet off from the edge of the overturned wooden poker table. Splinters began bouncing up off from it, obstructing Plemagoya's view of his attacker. He waited behind the table as the shots continued to fire, knowing that the gunman would eventually have to pause in order to reload. Just as that moment of opportunity appeared to arrive, Vincent sprang onto his feet and let off three shots towards the opening in the ceiling. He ducked back down behind the table in time to see a body fall down through the opening and then plummet hard against the surface of the floor.

Vincent Plemagoya looked over the edge of the table to see the body of Charley Bennetti lying motionless against the floor. The first shot that Plemagoya had let off had failed to be an accurate one. His aim had suffered from how quickly he had gotten onto his feet, causing the first bullet to hit the frame of the skylight, just below where Charley was standing. The second shot had struck Charley in the left shoulder, and the final bullet had struck him just below his right cheekbone. A thick red puddle was rapidly beginning to collect behind his shoulders and across the back of his neck. Plemagoya then turned around towards the door to the back room and saw Natty Rosebrook lying dead in the corner. He was positioned with his stomach against the floor, and his dark brown overcoat appeared wet as the blood from his wounds began soaking down into his plaid pants. Plemagoya reached down and closed Natty's eyes before reaching into the pocket of his overcoat for his car keys, and then he dragged Natty's body away from the doorway and over in front of the leather sofa. Vincent pulled open the door that led into Natty Rosebrook's office just in time to hear more gunfire.

* * *

Teddy Pazzelli drove the black Cadillac past the two open garage doors that were attached to Rosebrook's Used Cars, and Scotty McCormack fired a sawed-off double-barreled shotgun at one of the shadowy figures inside of the garage that hid behind a tool rack. One of the mechanics inside fired back with a revolver, and Scotty got down as the bullets ricocheted off from the side of the car. Teddy turned the car around to face the other direction as Frank Moniarti and Randy Wyman fired their snub-nosed .357 Magnum revolvers into the dark garage. One of the mechanics then came out into the open space of the garage to shoot at the Cadillac. Teddy Pazzelli kept his body crouched down low in the driver seat, as Frank Moniarti remained low behind the open passenger-side window. The bullet from inside of the garage struck the passenger-side car door between the open window and door handle and then ricocheted off from the body of the car.

"Damn!" the mechanic exclaimed, as his revolver began clicking. He then crept back into the dark garage in an attempt to reload his weapon.

Teddy momentarily stopped the car, and then Randy Wyman fired his newly reloaded revolver into the garage, hitting the dark silhouette of the mechanic two times in the body, before Frank Moniarti steadied his aim and shot the mechanic directly in the forehead. His body fell over backwards against the cement floor inside of the garage, and then the other mechanic began firing back at the Cadillac from behind the tool rack inside the garage.

The black Cadillac then turned hard towards the left, and Teddy Pazzelli began quickly driving back towards the driveway to the parking lot.

"What are you doing?!" Frank Moniarti shouted.

"Just trust me!" Teddy Pazzelli hollered back. "Everybody, roll your windows up!" As the Cadillac began pulling away from the garage, the other mechanic that had been hidden behind the tool rack inside of the garage merged out into the open. He fired four shots at the Cadillac, which all ricocheted off from the back window of the car.

"Damn! We almost had him!" Randy Wyman shouted.

"Patience, Randy! Patience!" Teddy Pazzelli shouted back from the driver seat. The black Cadillac then exited from the parking lot and took a sharp right turn out onto the paved road.

* * *

Inside of the garage, the mechanic reloaded his .38 Special revolver as he walked over towards Natty Rosebrook's office. "Hey, Vinnie!" he shouted across the garage. "Are you okay in there?"

Vincent Plemagoya crawled out from underneath the desk inside of the office and looked around as he made it onto his feet. "Yeah," he said, "I'm all right. I just wish that everybody else around here was."

The mechanic looked outside the open garage door. "I think that they're gone now," he said. "I just watched their car pull away." He turned his head to look over at Plemagoya. "Where's Natty?" the mechanic asked.

Vincent Plemagoya shook his head and then said, "He didn't make it."

The mechanic lowered his pistol and then solemnly looked down at the cement floor. "Neither did Pedro," the mechanic said.

Vincent Plemagoya stepped out through the doorway of the office and pushed his way past the mechanic, who stared at him blankly. He climbed over the other mechanic who lay motionless near the doorway to the garage and walked out the open door into the parking lot. He slowly approached the bullet-riddled body of the silver Crestline that was parked over towards the trees. He looked inside of the car to see what remained of Pedro Navilla.

"Oh no…This can't be happening," Plemagoya whispered. "Pedro…No…" He lowered his head for a moment and then began striking his fist hard against the roof of the car. "No! No! No!" Vincent Plemagoya repeatedly shouted.

"There's nothing that can be done about that now," the mechanic said, as he approached behind him. "I lost a friend here, too." The mechanic placed his hand on Plemagoya's shoulder, and Vincent just brushed it away before he walked past him and then stumbled in a daze back towards the office.

The mechanic followed Plemagoya back inside of the building and then closed the open garage door behind them. Keeping his head low and looking down at his dead partner on the floor, the mechanic asked, "So where do we begin?"

Vincent placed his hands over his face as he leaned up against Natty Rosebrook's desk. He looked out over the tips of his fingers as he began slowly pulling his hands away from his face. "What are you talkin' about?" he asked the mechanic.

"I say that we get Natty outta here first," the mechanic said somberly. "I mean, it's not like we can just call the cops after somethin' like this."

Vincent Plemagoya quickly shook his head and said, "No… We're *not* callin' the cops…"

The mechanic slowly walked into the office. "Do you happen to know where Natty's keys are?" he asked.

Plemagoya reached into his pocket and passed them over to the mechanic without making eye contact with him.

"Thanks," the mechanic said, "I'll go get the car unlocked and then come back in here to give ya a hand with him."

Vincent Plemagoya nodded and then sat in the chair in front of the desk. He didn't dare go into the back room alone.

The mechanic walked outside the front of the building and over towards the forest-green 1960 Pontiac Catalina four-door sedan that was parked a few feet away from the customer entry door. He opened the driver-side door and then pulled the pin up to unlock the rear door. He then left the doors to the car open to go back inside of the garage to look for a dark-colored plastic cover to tarp over the back seats of the car. He stumbled around inside of the dark garage and found a box full of oversize trash bags.

"You've got to be kiddin' me," the mechanic quietly said to himself. "Well, these will have to do." He took the box of oversize trash bags with him and placed a few of them over the departed mechanic that was still lying against the cold cement floor of the garage and then looked up through the closed garage doors to see a pair of approaching headlights. He quickly ran out the customer service door and made it back out to Natty Rosebrook's car. He then placed the box of oversize trash bags into the back seat, shortly before a light blue 1961 Chevrolet Impala Bubble Top pulled up about twenty feet behind him.

"Excuse me," Ronny Steiner said from the rolled-down driver-side window of the Impala. "Are you guys still open? My wife backed up into a shopping cart at the supermarket earlier on today, and I was wondering if you guys might be able to take a look at it for me?"

The mechanic got up out of the forest-green Catalina and looked into the windshield of the Impala. "What are you doin' here?!" the mechanic shouted. "Can't you see that we're closed?!"

Ronny looked up at the darkened red neon *Open* sign next to the garage door, and then he looked into the side mirror of the Impala and back at the bullet-riddled silver Crestline. "I *can* see that, in fact," Ronny said. "Is it all right if I just leave it here overnight? That sorta method seems to be workin' out all right for that other guy back there." Ronny Steiner pointed his thumb back over his shoulder towards the Crestline.

Suddenly, Vincent Plemagoya emerged from the customer service door. "What the hell's takin' ya so—" Plemagoya's voice momentarily came to a halt as his eyes grew wide with terror. "Hey! That's Tony's car!" Vincent shouted over to the mechanic.

The mechanic began reaching inside of his pocket for his revolver as Ronny Steiner threw the Impala into gear and hit the gas pedal. The mechanic was standing in between the two open doors of the four-door Catalina, as the Impala barreled forward and connected with the open doors with great force. Both driver-side doors of the Pontiac Catalina were violently torn off from their hinges, and the mechanic's body was crushed in between them. Ronny abruptly stopped the Impala upon colliding with the chain-link fence that was located straight ahead of the two cars. Vincent Plemagoya reached into his jacket for his pistol as Ronny Steiner threw the Impala in reverse to back the car away from the fence. Blood and shattered glass covered the front of the car, and one of the headlights on the Impala had gone out from the impact of the collision.

* * *

The black Cadillac momentarily sat parked down the street from Rosebrook's Used Cars as all four of the occupants inside the vehicle emptied their spent cartridges into the shoebox and reloaded their weapons. "Everybody ready to go back now?" Teddy Pazzelli asked as he looked over into the back seat.

"You bet I am!" Randy Wyman shouted.

Scotty McCormack nodded, and then Teddy turned his eyes over to Frank Moniarti in the passenger side of the car, who still remained low in his seat.

"Just get this thing movin' back where it belongs, Teddy," Frank said without making eye contact with the driver.

Teddy Pazzelli enthusiastically nodded as he put the Cadillac into gear. He threw his voice to sound like a sports announcer as he sped down the road, "Ladies and gentlemen, the following bout is scheduled for one fall!"

Frank Moniarti forcefully swatted his open hand against Teddy's arm. "Just shut up and drive, Teddy!" Frank shouted sternly as he rolled his window down.

"This time, he's not gettin' away from us," Randy said from the back seat, as the Cadillac turned back into the parking lot.

* * *

Vincent Plemagoya fired three shots into the windshield of the Impala as Ronny Steiner turned the car around to face the front of the building. He leaned down so that his right shoulder was over in the passenger seat as he continued to back the car up further from the garage. The gunfire continued, and Ronny heard and felt one of the bullets hit the driver-side tire of the Impala. As he backed the Impala up to the midpoint of the parking lot, he slammed his hands hard against the steering wheel in frustration. Ronny then suddenly saw a pair of headlights glaring in his mirrors as the black Cadillac sped back into the parking lot. It shot up a cloud of loose gravel as it drove past the light blue Impala Bubble Top.

Vincent Plemagoya continued firing his gun at both cars as he ran towards the four-door Catalina. Plemagoya kicked at the broken doors and the dead mechanic's body in order to gain entry into the car. He quickly started the engine and threw the car into reverse. As he forcefully turned the car to the right while backing up, the black Cadillac connected with his rear bumper, forcing the Catalina to come to an abrupt stop. The car lifted up and shook violently, as Vincent heard the rear taillights shattering. He put the car into drive and turned the steering wheel hard to the left, narrowly avoiding running into the closed doors of the garage. As he sped across the parking lot, bullets came into the car through the areas where the two doors had once been. Vincent Plemagoya cursed under his breath as one of the bullets came in between his body and the bottom of the steering wheel before embedding itself into the passenger-side door. The tires of the Catalina screeched against the pavement as the car reached the paved road. Vincent kept his head down low as the car continued gaining speed. He saw the glow of the headlights from the car that was trailing behind him. The wind from the open door blew his hat off from his head, and it landed over in the passenger seat. He made a hard right at the next intersection, and it was only five more blocks until he reached the expressway exit. *I can make it!* he thought to himself. *Once I'm on the expressway, I can go anywhere!*

* * *

Frank Moniarti squinted his eyes through the windshield from the passenger seat of the black Cadillac as they followed the forest-green Pontiac Catalina down the road. "Just keep givin' him some space, Teddy," he said. "And let's just watch what he does."

Teddy Pazzelli began to ease off from the acceleration pedal. "Ya know, this thing could catch him very easily," Teddy said.

Randy Wyman leaned up from the back seat. "So what if it could?" he asked. "Let's keep on toyin' with him! Just like he's been toyin' with us!"

Frank Moniarti slowly nodded. "That's what we're aimin' for. Givin' him a taste of his own medicine," Frank said in a low voice. "He wanted to use methods of fear and violence to get his point across to others, and that's exactly what we've got in store for him."

The men inside of the black Cadillac watched as the forest-green Catalina merged onto Route 40, and then Teddy Pazzelli hit the acceleration pedal to shorten the distance between the two cars. "I'll stay a little ways behind him, Frankie, just like you told me to," Pazzelli said. "But once he gets off the expressway, I'm gonna have a little fun with him."

Frank Moniarti held onto the dashboard of the Cadillac as they continued to gain speed. "Just don't get any of us killed in the process," Frank said sternly.

The Catalina began swerving back and forth as it continued to try accelerating down the expressway. One of the rims came off from a tire on the driver's side of the car, and the rear bumper was left dangling less than a foot above the road.

The forest-green Catalina was momentarily forced to slow down as it exited off from the Black Horse Pike, and then it quickly merged left onto Pacific Avenue. Once both cars were on a straightaway, Teddy Pazzelli hit the acceleration pedal, and the black Cadillac rammed into the back end of the Catalina. The rear bumper then fell further, creating a trail of sparks behind the car.

"What are you doin' now, Teddy?" Randy Wyman asked from the back seat.

"Just makin' sure that he don't go too much further," Teddy said and then shrugged. "His car looked itchy. So all I did was scratch it."

They watched as the Catalina began swerving even more, and then the car began spinning sideways enough for them to briefly glimpse at Vincent Plemagoya through an opening from the missing front door of the car. Plemagoya pulled the steering wheel hard to the right to correct the Catalina from spinning out. Then Teddy backed off to about the length of two car distances.

"That's it!" Moniarti said through gritted teeth. "I'm goin' after this little bastard's tires! Speed up, Teddy! Hit him again, if you have to! But we're gonna stop that car one way or another!" Frank Moniarti rolled his window down and began firing his revolver at the Catalina. One of the bullets hit the rear windshield of the car, and Plemagoya leaned down in his seat. Another bullet ended up hitting the rear fender of the car as both vehicles passed through the intersection at South New York Avenue. "Damn!" Moniarti shouted. "I can't seem to get a clear shot at him!" He tapped Teddy Pazzelli on the arm and yelled, "Hit him again!" Teddy sped up the Cadillac and rammed the back of the Catalina once more. The car swerved again before it began making a hard right down South Tennessee Avenue. Moniarti fired off three more shots at the Catalina as it turned, and then he smiled as one of the bullets hit the rear passenger-side tire. "Ha! I got the bastard!" Frank yelled enthusiastically. "He's not goin' much further now!"

Teddy Pazzelli slowed the Cadillac down as they made a sharp turn to continue following Plemagoya. The broken taillights of the Catalina lit up as the car reached the far end of the block, and it slowed down as it hopped over the curb and then turned left down the boardwalk.

"All righty," Teddy Pazzelli said out loud. "I already know this drill! Hold on tightly, guys! This is where the ride starts gettin' a little bumpy!"

The rumbling sound from the rear passenger-side tire of the Catalina became increasingly loud as the tire gradually ripped away from the car, and soon, it was riding along on the rim. He abruptly stopped the car just past the point where South Pennsylvania Avenue came to an end and then jumped out from the car through the open space where the door used to be. He put a new magazine into his Colt .45 and then began running as fast as he could down the boardwalk. He looked up as he ran and saw a sign that said "Steel Pier" above his head. The amusement park had just closed down for the winter months, and at this time of the night, there would be no workers around to prevent him from going inside to hide from the people who were pursuing him. He placed his pistol back into its holster and then climbed onto the railing outside of the front gate. He braced his arms against the thick wooden gate that said "Exit Only," which was located to the right side of the entrance. He hoisted his body around the gate onto the other railing before entering inside of the closed-down amusement park.

* * *

The occupants of the black Cadillac were able to follow the path of Vincent Plemagoya's whereabouts, as the glow of the headlights were able to trace his bright ivory-colored suit as he ran down the boardwalk. The Cadillac stopped next to the railing near the exit gate in front of Steel Pier.

"He must have gone in here," Frank Moniarti said. "Randy, you come with me! We're gonna try to flush this little bastard out! Teddy, Scotty, you guys stay here in the car, just in case he decides that he's gonna try to double back." He looked at the other occupants inside the car as he spoke. The two men on the driver's side of the vehicle nodded, and Frank and Randy emptied their spent cartridges into the shoebox before reloading their revolvers.

Vincent Plemagoya's footsteps echoed as he ran down the wooden deck on the right side of Steel Pier. He quickly ran past buildings and amusement park rides, looking for anywhere that he could safely hide from the people who were still sitting inside of the black Cadillac. They surely must have tracked him down here by now. He looked over to his right and saw the large hotels lighting up the skyline of the city as their ambience reflected on the surface of the water next to the pier. He then returned his eyes to look forward as he continued to run. He must have made it somewhere around fifty feet onto the pier, but for him, that distance was nowhere near enough to hide from his pursuers.

Frank Moniarti and Randy Wyman climbed around the wooden gate, crossing from railing to railing to gain access into the closed-down amusement park. Once their feet landed onto the deck on the right side of the pier, they both listened quietly for the sound of running feet against the wooden deck. There was only the sound of the tide rolling in from the Atlantic Ocean.

"Do you think that we should stay together? Or do you wanna split up?" Randy asked.

"I say that we stick together," Frank said. "If we spilt up, it's just gonna make it easier for him to try and hunt us down one at a time." Randy slowly nodded at Frank. "I say that we act as each other's eyes and ears," Frank said, and then the two men began slowly and cautiously walking down the length of the deck.

There had been a terrible storm last March that had pushed a barge into the pier, which had caused some considerable damage to the Marine Ballroom. Since then, it had been under construction throughout most of the summer and early fall. *The empty ballroom might be an ideal place for him to hide, if he's smart enough,* Frank Moniarti thought to himself. He and Randy continued to look up and down the length of the deck, waiting to hear or see some sort of a signal to give away Vincent Plemagoya's whereabouts. They saw restaurants and glamorous-looking buildings up and down the length of the pier. Randy Wyman looked over to his left and saw a poster that had advertised *Cavalcade of Stars* from 1960. The two men then continued slowly walking down the deck.

"He must be around here somewhere," Randy said quietly. Suddenly, there was the loud report of a gunshot, and then a bullet came ricocheting off from the metal railing that was located right next to Frank Moniarti.

The two men took shelter in the shadows of the buildings, and then there were several more shots fired in their general direction. Frank and Randy both had their revolvers out and crouched down until the sound of the gunfire had subsided.

"Stay close to the buildings and away from the water," Frank Moniarti whispered. "There's only so far that he can go down here before he reaches the end of the line."

The two men continued to cautiously walk down towards the end of the pier, seeking shelter in any momentary hiding spots that they could find. The sound of the waves had gradually begun to subside the further that they went out onto the pier.

There was a wooden staircase that led up to the furthest section of the pier where the circus acts were usually performed. Vincent Plemagoya turned and fired four more shots at the men who were following him, before he turned back around and changed his magazine. This was his last one. After this magazine ran out, he would be out of ammunition. He was breathing heavily, and his body was covered with sweat. He was running out of places to go and areas where he might be able to hide. He found a long wooden ramp that led about forty feet up into the air over a large diving pool. The sign at the top of the ramp said, "Steel Pier High-Diving Horses." He looked around for any sign of someone pursuing him and then began to ascend up the long ramp to try to get a better overhead view of the pier. He quickly made his way up to the top of the ramp and then remained crouched down and hidden from view. His enemies were going to be in for quite a surprise once they reached the end of the pier.

* * *

Frank Moniarti and Randy Wyman looked out towards the far end of the pier. "So where do you think that he went?" Randy asked.

"Keep lookin'. It's not like he could've vanished into thin air," Moniarti said, as both men kept looking around the area in circles with their revolvers pointed upwards.

Vincent Plemagoya sat with his back against the thick wooden side of the horse diving ramp and tried to subdue his heavy breathing. It had been quite a distance getting this far out onto the pier, and if he could just find a way to distract them, he might be able to double back around the other side of the pier.

"All right," Frank Moniarti said, "I'd say that now's the time that we split up to look for him. But not too far. Let's at least stay within each other's view."

Randy Wyman nodded and then said, "Okay, I'm gonna look over towards the end of the pier and make sure that he didn't jump over."

Randy Wyman began to walk towards the edge of the pier. The ocean looked serene as it gently lapped up against the side of the pier, and there were no signs of a disturbance on the surface of the water. He looked and saw a long ramp that went about forty feet above a diving pool. There was one section of the ramp that leveled out at about twenty feet before going further up into the air. Randy slowly and quietly began making his way up the lower portion of the ramp, as Moniarti stood as the lookout. He watched as Randy slowly ascending up the ramp and also looked around the ground level of the pier for any sort of movement in the darkness. Randy made it up to the first portion of the ramp where it leveled out and then looked all around the pier, before he turned to face Frank Moniarti.

Frank silently pointed up towards the top of the ramp, at the sign that said, "Steel Pier High-Diving Horses." Randy Wyman silently nodded to Moniarti before he began quietly ascending further up the ramp. Suddenly, Vincent Plemagoya appeared at the top of the ramp with his Colt .45 drawn and aimed it down the ramp.

"Randy! Look out!" Frank Moniarti shouted, as he began running over towards the horse diving ramp. Randy Wyman quickly crouched down as Vincent Plemagoya began firing his weapon. He got off three shots as Randy Wyman dropped down onto the ramp and began rolling back down it on his side. There were a series of sparks and splinters in the dark as Vincent Plemagoya continued to shoot down the ramp at Randy. Once Randy made it closer to the ground, he jumped over the side of the railing and dropped about five feet down onto the hard wooden surface of the pier. Frank Moniarti raised his .357 Magnum revolver and fired it up at the top of the horse diving ramp. He got off all six rounds and heard Vincent painfully grunting after the third shot. He had hit Vincent Plemagoya a total of three times and watched as his body spun around deliriously, before reaching the edge of the ramp. His body fell hard against the wooden release door, and then his body plummeted forty feet down into the deep diving pool with a loud and hard splash, before he disappeared underneath the surface of the water.

"Randy!" Frank Moniarti shouted, "Randy, are you hit?!"

Randy Wyman slowly made it up to his feet. "No, I'm all right," he said in a gruff-sounding voice. "That landing was a little bit rough, though."

The two men made it over the edge of the diving pool to watch Vincent Plemagoya's body floating up towards the surface of the water. "I'm glad that you're all right," Frank said, as he turned to his side to face Randy. "It looks like I've got a few phone calls to make yet tonight. We're gonna need quite a bit of help cleanin' all this shit up before we're all stuck answerin' a few too many questions underneath the interrogation lights. And I know that you've already been through somethin' like that over this past week."

Randy Wyman raised his eyebrows and then exhaled as he looked back at Moniarti. "That's true," Randy said. "As a matter of fact, I have."

Moniarti took his hat off to wipe the sweat away from his forehead with a handkerchief. "I'm just thankful that this whole thing is finally over with," he said and then placed his hat back on top of his head. "Now, it's time for the cleanup crew to get to work."

Both men then turned around and began walking away from the diving pool, and they eventually made their way back towards the entry gate where the black Cadillac was still parked.

CHAPTER 49

Sunday, October 21, 1962
Promises Kept

Randy Wyman drove hastily westbound on Route 30 in his white 1957 Ford F-100 custom pickup truck with the driver-side window down. The wind blew his hair down against his forehead just above his eyes, and he checked his side mirror before signaling to change lanes on the highway. Moving along at this rate, he hoped to be able to reach the New Jersey border and cross over into Philadelphia before nightfall. Melanie would undoubtedly welcome him with open arms once he arrived. There would be no more late nights in the interrogation rooms getting grilled by Morris and Farmers for information that they couldn't give them. There would be no more uneasy feelings of paranoia that forced them to constantly look over each other's shoulders whenever they were at The Golden Sandbox. They would no longer have to worry about any sort of an unexpected retaliation from an unpredictable force. Those days were behind them now. Now that business had been properly handled in Atlantic City, Conrad Hillsdale would hopefully grow to approve of Randy's involvement in his daughter's life. Having met each other for the first time at a police station after a thorough questioning regarding an unsolved murder had certainly caused Conrad to have a high level of unwelcomed concern toward any future predicaments that might consequently end up jeopardizing the safety of his daughter. However, Randy had vowed to him to ensure her safety after that, and that was probably to closest that he would ever get to seeing a smile appear on Conrad Hillsdale's face.

Scotty McCormack had even expressed a surprisingly high level of understanding towards the relationship between Randy and Melanie. Especially after they had done such a miraculous job of keeping their personal relationship outside of their professional careers such a well-guarded secret. Things between them had been kept pretty well under wraps until the night of their police interrogation. Upon calling Scotty from the police station, not only did Randy receive full approval of his relationship with Melanie, but he had also been granted the services of Scotty's legal counsel after McCormack had personally arrived to pick Randy up from the police station. Having refused to answer any questions from the press regarding the publicized murder of Tony Tyler had also won Randy and Melanie a few degrees of extra approval. After all, there was the future of a very lucrative business at stake, and there also happened to be a certain standard of professional integrity to maintain in Atlantic City.

He took a moment out to mentally reflect on watching Melanie depart at the crowded bus station last week. After helping her to board the coach with her luggage, he had kissed her face several times, while saying, *"This will all be over with very soon! And, once it is, I will come to find you! I promise! But, don't leave your father's house until I make it there!"* He recalled watching her head slowly nod, with her tearful eyes tightly closed as she turned around to get on the bus. Now the time had come. With Vincent Plemagoya and the rest of his gang no longer being a threat to the public safety, the cleanup work was now all in the hands of Frank Moniarti, along with the help of some of the political powers in that city. The days of dangerous living seemed to be passing Randy and Melanie by now, and once he would make it to Philadelphia, they would make a solid plan to disappear off to a safer place.

As Randy continued to drive along the expressway towards the setting sun, and rolled up the driver-side window of the truck.

He placed the folded-up road map into the glove compartment and then checked the rearview mirror for any police cars that might have secretly found their way behind his truck. The coast appeared to be clear, and then he looked forward just in time to see a road sign that welcomed him into Pennsylvania.

CHAPTER 50

Cleaning House

Mayor George Antill walked out from the front door of city hall that faced Atlantic Avenue and walked up to the podium that was set up in front of the building. There was a large crowd gathered in front of the building, and there were a series of flashes from the news reporter's cameras. He stood tall in a white suit with a dark blue dress shirt underneath it and reached inside the pocket of his sport coat to pull out the notes that he had prepared this morning for his speech, along with his reading glasses. He spent a short moment in front of the podium reviewing his notes as the cheering crowd and the flashes from the cameras began to settle down. He then looked up at the large crowd that had gathered up and down Atlantic Avenue. He quietly cleared his throat before he began speaking into the microphone. "After a long meeting with the city council this morning, I am standing here before you, the citizens of Atlantic City, to let you, the people of this community, know that we are not just going to sit back and let the bad guys get away! We have become tougher on crime in recent years, and our latest statistics have certainly proven that our methods have been very effective!" Mayor Antill said, before stopping to look back down at his notes. "I promise that, if I am reelected, I will ensure that Atlantic City continues to be a safe and vibrant community to live in! And the crimes that have happened in our city during some of our more recent days will become, and eventually remain, a problem of the past!" There was the loud sound of cheering and applause from the audience. Mayor George Antill smiled as he looked around at the crowd and then said, "Now is the time for all of us to begin working together as a team and start cleaning house!"

* * *

A giant waste barge slowly floated along in the darkness approximately ten miles south of Long Island. There were a series of men gathered on the deck of the barge wearing dark jumpsuits and tossing small fragments of dismantled weapons down into the ocean. The revolvers and sawed-off double-barreled shotguns that had been used by Frank Moniarti during his private war against Vincent Plemagoya were among the weapons that were being disposed of by the men. Towards the other side of the waste barge, there was a brand-new Coles Hydra Speedcrane that had the ability to help drag the black 1959 Cadillac Coupe de Ville, which had been discreetly covered over and sat approximately fifteen feet next to the crane, into the Atlantic Ocean. After the car had sunk down to the bottom of the ocean, neither the car, nor the bodies of Vincent Plemagoya, Natty Rosebrook, or Pedro Navilla would ever been seen by the outside world again. Ronny Steiner had been diligent enough to take care of Natty's two former auto mechanics, along with the late Tony Tyler and his light blue 1961 Chevrolet Impala Bubble Top, which were now neatly disposed of approximately twenty feet below the surface of the rear parking lot of a Brooklyn junkyard. Charley Bennetti had been cremated in accordance to his final wishes, although there had been no formal funeral service held for him. And his ashes were soon to be scattered off the coast of Camden, near Petty Island, where he used to go fishing during some of his more youthful days.

CHAPTER 51

Time Away

Behind a black wooden door on the far end of the lower level of the Lucky Nine's Pool Hall, Nicholas Malone was peacefully seated reading a newspaper behind a long cherrywood desk that was located on the left side of the room. He lit a cigarette and then tossed an extinguished match into the ashtray on his desk, before reaching down into one of the drawers to refill his glass of scotch. The phone on his desk began ringing as he hoisted the bottle of scotch up out from the desk drawer. He picked up the phone as he began twisting the cap off from the bottle.

"Yeah," he said into the phone receiver with a lit cigarette dangling out of his mouth.

"Nicky, it's Frankie," the voice on the other end of the phone said.

"Hello, Frank," Malone said. "I'm really glad to hear from you. Do I have another satisfied customer?" There was a short pause on the other end of the line.

"You bet you do!" Frank Moniarti said into the phone from inside the den of his home. "You've got a whole team of 'em, actually!"

Nicholas Malone placed his cigarette down into the ashtray on his desk as he refilled his glass and then smiled. "Good," Malone said, "That's what I aim for! Fast and friendly service, with customer satisfaction guaranteed."

Frank Moniarti had a sense of calmness in his voice as he spoke, "Listen, Nicky, I really appreciate your help with the situation that I was faced with a little while ago. I honestly don't think that I could've taken care of it without you." There was the sound of Moniarti exhaling in relief on the other end of the line before he continued, "I'm glad to know that I have a series of associates that I can depend on now. As you know, life isn't always easy, but it's good to know that you can always find a helping hand around here when you really need one."

Malone nodded as he reached back down to put the bottle of scotch back into the drawer of his desk. "Think nothing of it," Malone said. "Sometimes, that helping hand can come from some of the most unexpected of places."

"It sure can," Moniarti said. "Well, just know that I'm also here for you, if you should ever happen to need anything."

Nicholas Malone smiled into the phone receiver. "I really appreciate that, Frank," he said. "But now that you mention it, I'm goin' over to Las Vegas on vacation for a while. I'm just gonna be takin' some time away. Me and Angie are leavin' on a flight over there tomorrow, actually." There was a long pause on the other end of the phone.

"Good," Moniarti said. "I'm actually really relieved to hear that. Just know that if there's anything that you ever need while you're over there, I'm only a phone call away."

Nicholas Malone extinguished his cigarette into the ashtray on his desk. "I really appreciate that, Frank," Malone said. "But I could be over there for quite a while. See, I'm lookin' into startin' up a few new stores over on the West Coast. But you're always welcome to come out there to see me. Hell, maybe I'll even set ya up with a new suit."

Frank Moniarti began laughing on the other end of the phone. "I just might have to take you up on that!" Moniarti said with a growing level of excitement in his voice, "I know that I'm gonna need some new shoes after all this! I've been runnin' the soles right off of 'em!"

Nicholas Malone chuckled into the phone receiver. "I know ya have," he said. "But let's keep in touch, whatever happens with all this."

"Sounds like a plan to me," Moniarti said. "Thanks again, Nicky."

"Don't mention it," Malone said as he began reassembling the newspaper on his desk.

The two men then said goodbye to each other, and Nicholas Malone got up from his desk. He placed his hat on top of his head, stuck his folded-up newspaper underneath his right arm, grabbed his cane, and then began walking over towards the door to his office.

CHAPTER 52

Winner Takes All

Captain David Van Bulkem and Detective Stanley Morris pulled up into the gravel parking lot of the old metal factory in the docks of Hoboken in a sapphire-blue 1956 Oldsmobile Super 88. Van Bulkem looked over at Morris in the passenger seat of the car.

"Are you sure that this is place?" he asked.

Stanley Morris nodded, and then his eyes carefully scanned over the property. "Listen, why don't you just wait here," Morris said, and then he placed his sunglasses over his eyes. "This shouldn't take very long." David Van Bulkem nodded silently as Stanley Morris opened up the passenger-side door of the car. "Besides, I might need you out here just to keep an eye out for Farmers. He really shouldn't be any sort of a problem." Morris said, "But if he shows up here, we both know that he'll think nothing of creating one for us. So just be on the lookout. All right?"

Van Bulkem smiled as he turned off the engine to the car. "You got it," he said. "Take all the time that you need."

"Thanks," Morris said and then closed the car door and began walking around towards the back of the building.

Stanley Morris knocked hard against the hollow rusty metal door that was located next to the loading dock and then waited with his head down and his hands inside the pockets of his jacket. After a couple of moments, the door slowly opened, and Teddy Pazzelli stuck his head out through the opening.

"Hello, Detective Morris," he said. "How can we help you today? Are you interested in purchasing some office supplies?"

Morris lifted his head up and then pulled his hands out from the pockets of his jacket to remove his sunglasses. "No," he said. "Not exactly. I'm here to sell Mr. Moniarti some insurance, actually."

Teddy Pazzelli held the door open further to welcome Stanley Morris into the metal factory. "Very good," Teddy said. "He's been expecting you."

As the two men walked through the old and vacant factory, Stanley Morris could still detect the musty smell of warm metal lingering in the stuffy air. Teddy led him past a series of presses and conveyor belts. "You would usually be required to wear safety goggles whenever you entered this area," Teddy said with a smirk.

"Do you want me to put my sunglasses back on?" Morris asked sarcastically.

Teddy Pazzelli laughed and then said, "No, because you might end up tripping over somethin' in here, and we would much rather reserve any workers' compensation for some of the other potential catastrophes that could happen."

Morris nodded and then said, "That's perfectly understandable."

Teddy Pazzelli then led Morris up a long metal staircase that went up to a second-floor office that was located in the upper corner of the building.

Frank Moniarti sat quietly at a desk in the office, playing a game of solitaire. There was suddenly a knock against the old wooden door. "Come in, Teddy," Moniarti said without looking up. The door slowly opened, and then the two men entered into the office. Frank Moniarti looked up to see Stanley Morris step up in front of Teddy Pazzelli. "Oh, it's you," Frank said. "I was wondering if you were actually gonna make it here today or if you had somehow made some other sort of plans." Frank Moniarti quickly assembled the deck of playing cards and then placed them back inside of the box.

"No, I didn't make any other plans for today. I don't have any vacation time coming up just yet," Morris said.

"I see," Moniarti said as he placed the box of playing cards into the inside pocket of his overcoat. "And so that's why you're here right now? You're lookin' for some vacation time?"

Stanley Morris pulled up a chair in front of the desk and then said, "Yes, sir, that's exactly right."

"Good," Frank Moniarti said as he slowly nodded. "Because I'm about to offer you the sum of $1 million to help me and the rest of my crew straighten a few things up after certain recent events. I'm requesting your assistance just to help make that whole situation go away, *entirely*." Frank Moniarti's facial expression suddenly became very somber. "I *never* want to hear anything about any of it ever again," he said. "So consider yourself the newest member of my cleaning crew. I'm entrusting you to finish up the work that my men had started and to do a job that none of my other men are authorized to do." Moniarti folded his hands on the surface of the desk and studied the uncomfortable look on Morris's face, waiting for his response.

Stanley Morris repositioned himself in the chair and then leaned in closer to Moniarti. "That's why I'm here right now, sir, to help give you an update on things," Morris said. "After making such a generous offer, please be assured that the proper precautions are already being taken towards helping you realize your ideal goals."

Frank Moniarti raised his eyebrows from across the desk. "Such as?" he inquired.

Stanley Morris cleared his throat and then said, "Such as having the Crestline and that four-door Catalina neatly tucked away in a private storage garage, just like we had agreed upon, Mr. Moniarti. They're both waiting to be rebuilt. And once all the bullet holes have been removed from them, they are going to get stripped down and then sold off for parts."

There was a short moment of silence between the men, and then Teddy Pazzelli suddenly interjected. "That Catalina only qualified as a two-door the last time that I checked," he said and then began snickering.

Both Morris and Moniarti began laughing, and then Frank asked, "Does anybody else know about any of this besides you and David?"

Stanley Morris shook his head. "No, sir, I prefer to keep matters like this strictly off the record."

Moniarti slowly nodded and then said, "Good. I'll send Teddy over to meet you at the garage with the payment just as soon as those other cars have been taken care of. Nothing can be left to chance or to the imagination of any of your colleagues, in a situation like this one."

Stanley Morris said, "I can definitely agree with you there." And then he got up from his chair.

Frank Moniarti arose from his chair and shook hands with the detective. "And you can call me Frank from now on. You've earned it. You're considered to be a member of the team now."

Stanley Morris quickly nodded and then said, "Thank you. I can safely promise you that we won't let you down."

Frank Moniarti smiled and said, "You'd better not. I'm *really* countin' on you guys to make the grade on this one. Then you'll have earned some vacation time."

Stanley Morris smiled and nodded and then followed Teddy Pazzelli back out of the door to the office. He shook Teddy Pazzelli's hand before walking out the back door to the metal factory and then got back into the sapphire-blue Oldsmobile that was still waiting for him outside.

EPILOGUE

November 1962 to June 1964

Tuesday, November 6, 1962, Atlantic City, New Jersey

As construction workers continued to repair the storm damage that had been inflicted upon Steel Pier the previous spring, a group of men were taking a break from their day's work inside of the Marine Ballroom. For weeks, there had been banners and signs all around the city that had advertised "Reelect Mayor George Antill—A Better Future for You and Me." Today was the day of the election. Most of the working crew had spent the day waiting in line to cast their votes. Many of the crew members had been waiting several months for this day to arrive. Some of them were anxious to hear what the election results were, and others just wanted the day to be over with so that the commercials on the radio and the television would finally go away for a while.

It was getting to be break time for several members of the working crew. Some of men on the working crew went outside of the ballroom on their breaks to drink coffee, eat sandwiches, and smoke cigarettes or cigars. A small transistor radio was positioned near the center of the ballroom for the listening pleasure of the working crew. After break time had begun drawing to a close for several members of the current working shift, many of the men who had been out-side on their breaks yawned and stretched as they returned inside. Suddenly, a commercial on the radio had been interrupted by the voice of an announcer. *This just in from city hall… The election results are in from earlier today, after the all votes have been counted… George Antill has officially been reelected as the mayor of Atlantic City…* There was a brief moment of cheering from some of the men, as money was exchanged from the wagers that had been placed on the election. The announcer continued, *In other news, the General Assembly of the United Nations has reached a resolution condemning the racial apart-heid policies of South Africa. This new resolution calls for all members of the UN to halt all military and economic relations with that nation…* Just then, one of the workers reached down and turned off the radio as the other workers packed up their tools and lunchboxes to mark the end of the working day.

Wednesday, December 25, 1963, Paradise, Nevada

It was a warm and sunny Christmas Day all along Las Vegas Boulevard, and Nicholas and Angela Malone were cooling off inside of an air-conditioned hotel room at the newly built Castaways Casino. Nicholas Malone straightened his tie in the mirror as Angie continued to tidy herself up in the bathroom. There was suddenly the muffled sound of a knock at the door. Malone walked over and slowly pulled the door open to see Ronny Steiner standing on the other side, holding a bottle of champagne. He pulled the door open further to allow Ronny into the room.

"Merry Christmas, Nicky," he said, as he held up the bottle of champagne and then leaned in to give him a hug. "I was real sorry to hear about what had happened last month," Ronny said. "I know that he was your favorite president. And mine, too. But I wanted to come and see you and Angie for the holidays, just to see how you guys are likin' it out here."

Malone smiled and then said, "It's been really great. We've got a few new clothing store locations in the works and some new warehouses set up to handle all the imports and exports. Life's just been movin' right along."

Ronny Steiner nodded and then smiled. "I'm real glad to hear that, Nicky. The pool hall back home has been doin' better, too. And so has that little business that we started up in the basement awhile back," Ronny said. "And you know how Roger is. I have a hard time gettin' him to go home at the end of the night. He's constantly tellin' me about ways that we can make that little industry that you and I had started together even bigger and better. And we will someday. I'll have to find a way to fly you back over there so you can see it one of these days. Once we get some approval to expand the business, that is!"

Angela Malone walked out of the bathroom while she was still fixing one of her earrings. She wore a long, flowing white sequin dress, a pearl necklace, and a pair of pearl-colored high heels. Ronny Steiner looked up over Malone's shoulders with his eyes wide, causing Malone to quickly turn around.

"Well, how do I look, you guys?" Angie asked.

"Stunning," Ronny replied. "Absolutely stunning!"

"Yeah, what he said," Malone agreed.

Angie smiled and then asked, "Nicky, have you seen my purse?"

Malone nodded and then said, "Yeah, you left it over here next to the bed."

As he reached over to grab her purse from beside the bed, he bent down with most of his body weight on his right leg, holding onto the lower portion of his cane. Once he made it onto his feet, he handed it over to her.

"Merry Christmas, Angie," Ronny said with a smile.

"Merry Christmas to you, too," she replied.

Ronny looked down at the bottle of champagne that he was still holding and then said, "Well, it looks like we're steppin' out for a little while. Maybe I should consider puttin' this stuff on ice."

Angie nodded and then said, "I'll call down for room service."

After a bucket of ice had been delivered to the room, they began walking down the hallway towards the elevator to visit the hotel restaurant. Ronny Steiner pushed the button for the elevator; and after the elevator had arrived, they all got onto it. It was a relatively quiet ride down several floors in the elevator, and once they had reached the main floor to the casino, they made their way over to the restaurant.

As they entered into the darkly lit lounge, a host came up to greet them. "Hello," he said, "and how many of you will there be this evening?"

Suddenly, Nicholas Malone saw a distant hand waving from across the room. As he walked around the side of the host, he saw Frank and Megan Moniarti seated at a table towards the back.

"Five of us," Malone responded to the host. "We'll be joinin' those people back over there," he said, as he lifted his finger to point over towards Moniarti's table.

"Very well then," the host replied. "Follow me." The host grabbed three menus and then led the group across the lounge and over to the table.

Malone walked over to Frank Moniarti and said, "I'm really glad to see that you made it. Happy Holidays to you both."

Megan Moniarti smiled and nodded to Malone over her glass of red wine, and then she said, "Thank you. Same to all of you. Please, join us."

After everybody was seated at the table, Frank Moniarti leaned over towards Malone and said, "I'm *really* glad to have made it out here. I have *so* much to tell you."

Nicholas Malone nodded and then looked up from his menu. "Oh yeah?" he asked. "Like what?"

Frank Moniarti had a huge smile of excitement on his face. "Like my son got married last summer!" Moniarti said, "Even after all the problems that we had to deal with before their engagement, they're finally together in matrimony, and they're happy!"

Malone smiled at him and then said, "That's *really* great news, Frank."

Moniarti then went on. "And that's not all! They're expectin' their first baby next spring! Meg and I are gonna be grandparents! Can ya believe it?!"

Malone's eyes grew wide in surprise, and then he said, "Wow! No kiddin'? I'm really happy for you guys!"

After the waiter had returned with everyone's drinks, they all decided to order seafood entrées to celebrate the holiday together. Frank Moniarti dipped a piece of shrimp into some cocktail sauce and then stopped for a moment in reflection. "Ya know, Nicky," he said. "I got to thinkin' about that offer you made me last year about gettin' me a new suit. And I think that I might actually take you up on that."

Nicholas Malone nodded, as he wiped his mouth with his napkin. "Okay," he said, "I can bring ya over to one of my stores around here on Saturday. Some of the people who I got workin' for me should be back from their holiday vacations by then. That way, the return lines should be slowin' down right about then."

Frank Moniarti slowly nodded and then said, "Okay. We'll make somethin' happen. But I gotta get back home right after that. Because, like you've just heard, I got a *lot* of things goin' on back there."

Nicholas Malone smiled over at Moniarti and then said, "Yeah, I'd say that you've got a lot goin' on back home, too." Malone took a long drink off from his water glass and then said, "Listen, we're gonna go hit the game floor after we finish things up here. Do you and Meg wanna come along, just for fun?"

Frank Moniarti slowly shook his head and then said, "No, thanks. That's very kind of you to offer, Nicky. But it was a *very* long flight gettin' over here, and I think that we're gonna hit the sack after we get done here. All this food is probably gonna knock me right out!" Malone and Moniarti both began to laugh and then decided that they would meet up tomorrow morning for breakfast.

Once they had finished up at the restaurant, Ronny, Angie, and Malone said their goodbyes to Frank and Meg and began walking back down the hallway of the main floor towards the elevator. As Ronny Steiner walked ahead to push the button for the elevator, Malone and his wife walked side by side behind him.

"Hold on for a second, Nicky," Angie said, as she began reaching down towards her feet. "I have to fix my shoe." As Angie bent over to fix her high heel, Ronny Steiner pushed the button for the elevator to go back up to the hotel room. Suddenly, there were two men who were dressed in expensive suits that walked past them. They both looked strangely familiar to Malone, even from behind. He kept his eyes on them, even after he and his wife had gotten on the elevator. *Nah,* he thought to himself, *It can't be them.* However, his curiosity would not cease. And Nicholas Malone turned around in the elevator to watch the two men continue walking down the hallway, as they began disappearing between the closing elevator doors.

After they made it back to the hotel room, Nicky and Angie shared the chilled bottle of champagne with Ronny. They talked about old times and what each person had missed over the past year that they had been separated; and then they all decided to go down to the game floor of the casino together. The casino was crowded once they got down there, even for being a holiday. They all split up, with Angie going over to the slot machines, and Ronny heading over to the blackjack table. Malone continued to wander around the game room floor, looking for the two men who he had spotted walking past the elevator earlier on. Malone walked around the game room floor, until he came to the roulette table. As he looked across the table, he briefly thought of the painting that he had in his office back on the East Coast. Suddenly, as the people around the table began shifting, he caught a glimpse of David Van Bulkem standing right next to Stanley Morris. They were both looking down at the roulette wheel with their eyes wide, as the dealer rolled the ball and sent the wheel into motion.

Sunday, March 29, 1964, Hoboken, New Jersey

James Moniarti had just returned from a trip to the grocery store when his wife, Annabelle, had gone into labor. They quickly rushed off to the hospital, and several hours later, James Moniarti was holding onto his wife's hand in a third-floor hospital room as his parents waited outside. Teddy and Silvia Pazzelli had arrived with some flowers for the occasion and sat in the lobby across from Frank and Megan Moniarti.

"So how do you think they're doin' in there?" Teddy asked.

Megan shrugged and then said, "I know what I was like towards Frank during the births of our two children. That's part of the reason why we're waitin' out here. But I'm sure that everything'll be just fine."

Frank Moniarti began snickering and then said, "That's true! You were pretty ruthless towards me during this part of both the deliveries! In fact, I think that I still have the bite marks on my upper arm from when you were givin' birth to Jimmy!" Frank looked over at his wife and began rubbing the upper part of his right arm.

Teddy and Silvia both began laughing, and then Megan reached over and swatted at her husband's stomach. "You deserved that!" she said and then pointed at him with a playfully angry look on her face.

Inside of the delivery room, James Moniarti remained next to his wife's bedside. "Just a little bit further!" the doctor said, as he stood near the bottom side of the hospital bed.

"Come on, you can do this! You're doin' great!" James said encouragingly. Sweat poured down all their faces, and then Annabelle let out one final scream of exhaustion before the child was born. Nicholas James Moniarti came into the world just after eleven o'clock that night, and only a few days later, he left the hospital in perfect health with both his parents. The following summer, in a large cathedral on Willow Avenue, Nicholas James Moniarti was baptized with Theodore and Silvia Pazzelli serving as godparents to the young child.

Saturday, June 27, 1964, Chicago, Illinois

On a bright and clear summer afternoon, a long black limousine pulled up on North State Street right in front of a tall, brick gothic-style cathedral. Randy Wyman and Melanie Hillsdale walked out of the tall black double doors to the loud sound of applause, and there were handfuls of rice being thrown up into the air. Melanie Ann Hillsdale was now officially known as Melanie Ann Wyman. The newlywed couple stopped and kissed next to the limousine as a series of camera flashes went off and several people in the crowd loudly whistled. Once they got inside of the limousine, the chauffeur adjusted the air-conditioning before rolling down the dividing window between the front and back areas of the car. Randy and Melanie were engaged in a kiss, which was suddenly interrupted by the sound of Leroy Robinson's laughter.

He looked up at the newlywed couple from the rearview mirror, and said, "Hey, don't let me stop you. I'm just really glad to see somethin' happy goin' on. I had some angry truck driver cut me off on my way over here."

Melanie reached up into the front seat and swatted Leroy on his right arm. "Oh, stop!" she shouted playfully, and then she began laughing.

Leroy Robinson shrugged and then said, "Well, I'm guessin' that must be your way of tellin' me that it's time for us to get goin'!" He rolled the dividing window back up before he put the limousine into drive and then turned right down East Chicago Avenue.

After the limousine had reached the wedding reception destination at Lincoln Park, Doyle Reynolds pulled a tall five-layer wedding cake out from the back of a white catering truck and carefully walked it over to one of the picnic tables near the shores of Lake Michigan.

"Careful not to let that thing tip over!" Scotty McCormack said loudly while standing underneath the shade of a tree.

Doyle Reynolds gently set the cake down onto the picnic table and looked over as Scotty approached him with a full glass of champagne in each of his hands. Scotty extended one of the glasses over to Doyle, and then the two men clanked their glasses together. Scotty was taking a long pull off from his drink, as Doyle said, "Hey, I've been doin' this catering job for over a year now, and I never had one single accident with a cake spillin' over on me. Must've been all those years of practice I had handlin' milk bottles."

Scotty quickly doubled over in a fit of laughter, and he spit champagne out onto the lawn. "Yeah, I know that we can all trust you to keep an eye on everybody's car here," Scotty said. "But I'm really thankful that you found a new job that makes you happy, and it's a lot less risky."

Doyle Reynolds smiled. "I had a pretty good run doin' my old profession. But above all, I guess that I did that other job just to prove to myself that I could." Scotty nodded and then patted Doyle on the shoulder before walking away from the picnic table.

Scotty McCormack walked over to the main table where Randy and Melanie were seated. Scotty raised his glass of champagne to salute them and then said, "Congratulations again, you guys! That had to be one of the most beautiful ceremonies that I've ever been to, honestly!" He sat down in the chair next to Randy and placed his half-empty glass of champagne onto the table. He leaned in a little closer to Randy. "You know, if you guys ever get the chance, you really should come on out and see my new place, Diamond Jack's! We just got a new menu and some of the best cooks in the kitchen that money can buy!"

Melanie leaned over around Randy to face Scotty, and then she said, "We'll probably stop by to see you over there sometime after we make it back home from Europe. My father gave us a two-week honeymoon over there as part of our wedding present."

Scotty's eyes grew wide with excitement. "Great!" he said. "I've heard that some of the beaches over there are fantastic! But, don't forget to put on some sunscreen! I don't want you and Randy comin' to see me burned to a crisp after you guys come back from there!"

Melanie nodded and quietly snickered before turning her attention to some of the other guests who had gathered next to her. Randy began looking all around the park at the people who were still arriving to the reception. "I don't plan on heading towards any of the beaches around there until sundown," Randy said. "There are so many other things to see and do over in Europe, and I feel like the beaches can wait until I'm ready to sit still for a while."

Scotty nodded and then leaned in towards Randy a little bit further. "I can understand all that," he said. "But once Melanie finishes up her accounting degree at that college that she's been going to, I was gonna offer her a job as my personal accountant and also talk to you about a position as the head of security at my new place."

Randy Wyman began laughing and then said, "Now you're talking, Scotty! Now you're talking! Just remember that you're the best man here, which means that you've got a speech to make in front of everybody in just a little bit here. So just try not to drink too much before we get to that point. Okay?" Both men started laughing, and then Scotty began to blush before he finished off his glass of champagne.

"Hey, Randy, I'm at your service," Scotty said.

Both men stood up from the table, and then Randy gave Scotty a hug. "I knew that I could count on you!" Randy said.

After all the guests had arrived and had been seated, toasts and speeches were made, dinner and cake were served, and an old photo album now houses all of their memories from the occasion.

ABOUT THE AUTHOR

Thomas Koron was born in Grand Rapids, Michigan. Some of his previous literary projects have included writing essays, poetry, stage plays, and a series of short stories. This is his first novel. He currently lives in the Chicago Metropolitan Area.